OTHER LIVES

A novel

Jenn **Dashney**

Illustrations by Patrick Seeley,
Cover Art by Kamina Kapow

NEWMAN SPRINGS PUBLISHING
320 Broad Street
Red Bank, NJ 07701

First originally published by Newman Springs Publishing 2019

ISBN 978-1-64531-151-5 (Paperback)
ISBN 978-1-64531-152-2 (Digital)

Printed in the United States of America

To my Eric, for giving me possibility.
To Easton and Xander for sparking imagination.
To Freya for reigniting it.

Truths remain true, whether or not we believe in them.

Prologue

Ocean Park, Washington

On the front page of the *Chinook Observer* today, a smiling photograph of Nova Daniels blankly stared at its readers. Nova always hated this picture. Out of all the awkwardly staged shots the unimaginative photographer had coerced her into, this was by far the worst. So naturally, her mother had hand-delivered copies of it to half the peninsula. From graduation announcements to the full page of ad space she'd purchased in the Ilwaco High School yearbook, there was no escaping it. The classic fist under chin, elbow on thigh, unnaturally angled pose. This vapid expression was the one Jeanette Daniels had chosen to best represent her daughter yet again. Today, its purpose was to alert the locals to Nova's tragic disappearance. The picture reminded Jeanette of happier times...or at least of a time when she had successfully convinced her daughter to feign happiness as best she could for the purpose of memory preservation.

It was hard to say whether or not Nova had ever truly been happy. She wasn't one to talk about her feelings. She wasn't one to talk to her mother about anything for that matter. She had always been a self-proclaimed Daddy's girl. When she was little, Nova had been outgoing, imaginative, and even funny. She was enamored by her father's life as a musician and followed him like a shadow whenever she could. She idolized him. In her eyes, he had been famous and successful. He had it all—a great band, adoring fans, and a life on the road doing what he loved. He was practically perfect. Now that Nova was older, she understood why he never married her mother. The life of a rock icon is more conducive to the love 'em and leave 'em stereotype. Nova never blamed him for that. In fact, she had a hard time imagining her parents together at all. They were such polar opposites. Her mom just seemed so dreadfully small-town.

* * * * *

Shy wasn't really the word for it, Jeanette had told the detective the morning after Nova's disappearance.

"Age?" he asked gruffly.

"Seventeen."

"Can you describe her?"

"Of course. Um. Well, she has long, curly…wait, no…wavy blonde hair. Kind of brown. Sort of a dark blonde, actually. She has big brown eyes. She's average height and build, I guess, and shy. No, withdrawn. Reclusive?" She struggled to land on a fitting adjective.

The detective rolled his eyes. "Do you have a picture?" he asked condescendingly.

He recommended that she leave the description up to the reporter at the *Observer*.

"Introverted." That was all they wrote about Nova in the paper today. Just a brief physical description and that she was an "introverted young woman." No listed hobbies, personality traits, or clues as to where she may be now. Her mother couldn't think of a single thing that might help the police in locating her. No real friends to speak of that might help point them in the right direction. At least, none that she knew of.

Jeanette had not slept in forty-eight hours. A thousand scenarios had raced through her mind. Had Nova been swept away at sea? The surf seemed unseasonably agitated this morning. Had she fallen out of a climbing tree and injured herself? Perhaps she'd been kidnapped by one of the undesirables that frequented the area during peak season. Come to think of it, wasn't there a strange van parked down the road last week? Should she have been suspicious? What if it was a customer from the café? Was it her fault for insisting that Nova work there again this summer? Was it so wrong to want to keep her close by? Should she have been more lenient? If she had been a better mother, would she be able to prove more helpful in the search? Being a single mom and running her own restaurant was a lot to juggle. Did she neglect her daughter in favor of keeping the business afloat? Were her priorities out of whack, completely? Was this all her fault? Would her daughter ever forgive her for letting this happen?

Jeanette had never even once considered that Nova may have left of her own volition.

Part 1: Beginning

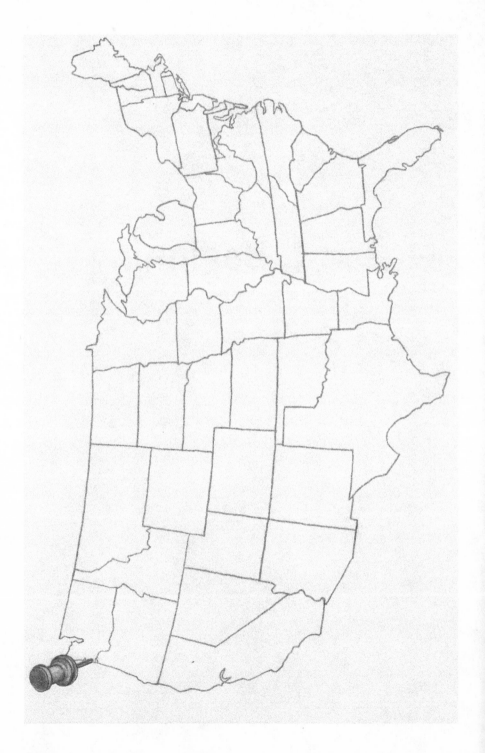

Nova

Ocean Park, Long Beach Peninsula, Washington.

The stars are out tonight in droves, reminding me how vast the sky is. I pause for a moment to quietly thank gravity for holding me to the earth in moments like these when I feel like I could so easily just float away into the aether. I feel so insignificant underneath this blanket of twinkling light. Insignificant, but not small. I always hear that expression of feeling so small, but I never feel small. Rather awkward and clumsy, overdrawn and cumbersome, even amid the endless obscurity of the night sky.

I take another deep breath in. The sea air grounds me. I close my eyes to let my other senses take over. The waves are gently crashing on the sand in a steady rhythm. I can hear them further off the shore toward the horizon line. The sound bounces off the rocks in varying volume. Loud echoes, faint whispers. Big waves. Faster. Angry almost. Reverberating along the sand. There isn't another sound. All of nature respectfully keeps quiet, submitting in reverence to the breaking of the waves.

The moon is so bright tonight that I can still see the perfectly rounded circle glimmering through my tightly closed eyelids. The air smells of salt and seaweed. The night is mild, but the frigid north wind feels like icy breath on my neck. I decide I'd better keep moving so I can stay warm.

I walk south along the beach from Bay Street like I have every other night. I'm not entirely sure why I always feel the need to wait for my mother to fall asleep before I sneak out. I guess it's a comfortable routine, just like every other solitary thing I do every single day of this dull life of mine. In a life set on autopilot, I take these midnight walks to think…just to remind myself that I'm capable of doing so. Some nights, I just walk a few miles and cut over to head home along the highway. Some nights, I go all the way to Loomis Lake State Park before turning back.

Tonight is different, though. I can't quite put my finger on it. Not a car in sight, even, though you can drive on the beaches here. Not another soul as far as I can see. The crashing of the waves seems more melodic than usual. The rocks more foreboding. I feel the gravitational pull of the full moon carrying me further and further like the tide. I reach the state park and rather than turning back toward home, I keep walking.

I'm lost in thoughts of the café. The smell of my mom's famous coffee cake wafting from the kitchen, the soft orange glow of the antique lamps she stubbornly insists on using exclusively, even, though the patrons often have trouble reading the menus in the dim light. The reclaimed driftwood table tops and mismatched thrift store dining chairs carelessly angled unevenly around them, giving the impression that there has just been a powerful gust of wind through the place. The chairs are each painted a different color from lavender to fire-engine red and back again. She calls it whimsy. I call it a mess.

The soundtrack is always the same. Laughter and conversation all muddled together in the crowded dining room. The clanking of pots and pans and the crackle of the grill in the kitchen. The faintest heartfelt jazz ballads being crooned by some of the greats of the era float from the ancient record player she keeps on the pastry case. It skips once or twice on almost every song, but she refuses to retire it. She says it reminds her of simpler times, though I can't even fathom why that would appeal to her.

My mother built the business from the ground up. A "self-made woman" she always says. "I want to be a positive role model for you," she said. Yeah, in case I ever need direction on being super boring. She wanted to create a life for us. A home for us. A future for me. I guess that's why I never had the heart to tell her how much I hate it here. This life she's built for us. I do my best to humor her, but I know she sees through me. Or she would, if she would let herself.

I'm not sure who is more afraid of shattering the illusion—her or me. Neither of us are much for confrontation.

The wind is harsh tonight. The ocean side of the peninsula always seems to know that the days are getting shorter before the bay side does as if it cannot bear the anticipation of the coming season a moment longer.

I stop to get my sweatshirt out of my backpack. I zip it all the way up to my chin and pull the hood up over my head. My reliable old royal blue hoodie has faded to a pale periwinkle over the years. It still suits me just fine, though. The left pocket has a hole in it, big enough for three of my fingers, but the right one is still intact. As the wind nips at my fingertips, I make a mental note to mend the pocket when I get home. I check my phone before tossing it back into the depths of my backpack and sling it over my shoulder. No one will try to call me at this hour. At any hour, I guess.

I figure that I'm about seven miles from Ocean Park at this point. I head down the beach and cut over at Cranberry Road. I can turn back toward home from here. "Just keep going, there's no rush to get home," I hear a faint voice urge. Sometimes, I feel like my subconscious has an agenda of its own.

I shrug in response. Rather than taking a left to head north, my feet just seem to carry me further south along the highway without my help. I'm moving fast now that I'm on solid ground. The predawn sky is just starting to fade from ebony to a deep blue as I pass through downtown Long Beach. Shops and restaurants usually packed with summer tourists look eerily vacant. I can still see the stars, but they are beginning to fade along the horizon. They look like tiny lightbulbs burning out, one by one. My stomach is growling, which momentarily distracts me from my aching feet. I decide to find a place to rest awhile.

Mercifully, there is a rustic looking little diner on the corner along Highway 101 as I walk numbly past the sign welcoming me to Seaview. The building front is almost completely camouflaged by a wall of English ivy that has been left to run rampant. I find it strange that I've never seen this place before. I could have sworn this corner was just an overgrown lot, but that doesn't keep me from making a beeline for the door.

A barely functioning vintage neon sign wedged in the corner of the front window switches from "_LOSED" to "_PEN" as I approach, almost as if they'd been expecting me. I love it when light-up signs have missing or burnt-out letters. I can't help but giggle, even in my exhaustion. My dad and I used to make a game of spotting them along the road in his tour bus when I was a little girl. He'd read me the word as is, and I'd have to try and guess the missing letters. He'd give me a point for each letter I could fill in. "_rug _ _ore" to Drug Store, three points. "_aundro_ _t" to Laundromat, four points. He gave me extra credit for harder words. *Two points*, I think to myself with a smile.

A tangled wad of jingle bells above the door jamb cheerily announces my arrival as I open the creaky door to the diner and tuck inside. I'm instantly overcome with the smell of smoke, like a bonfire on the beach that someone added herbs and flowers to. I cover my nose with my sleeve as I look around for the source of it. The place is just a hole in the wall. There are four small metallic silver tables in the front of the room and a small bar lined with red Naugahyde stools on wobbly chrome legs at the back. I don't see anyone else here. I cautiously let my arm fall and take a breath in. *Hmm. No smoke smell now. Did I imagine it?*

I'm still paused at the door, wondering if someone will come out to seat me but quickly put pleasantries aside at the urging of my throbbing feet. I take the table in the front window under the steady hum of the neon light.

I pull my phone out of my backpack. 6:28 a.m. My mother will have been up for over an hour by now and already have coffee cakes and raisin bread baking in the ovens at the café. Just the thought of it makes my stomach grumble loudly in longing. Right on cue, a round and grinning woman appears at my side with a basket of fresh baked bread and a coffee pot. She smells of orange marmalade and is wearing a pink quilted apron covered in a light dusting of what looks like ash but must be flour or powdered sugar. Her heap of curly silver hair is hard at work, trying to escape from its bun on the top of her head. A few rogue tendrils now frame her plump pink face. Her large red name tag says "Rosie" in white cursive letters. How fitting. Even with her olive complexion, she is in fact quite rosy. Rosie must be pushing seventy years old but moves with the grace of someone much younger. She has my coffee mug filled and is halfway back to the kitchen before I can even muster up a "hello."

I lift my head to see where she has scampered off to and am greeted warmly by a small tan-skinned man who now occupies the table next to mine. I didn't even hear him come in. "Early riser, I see," he says with a wink. He has a subtle accent that I can't quite place. *Eastern Europe, perhaps?*

"Good morning," I croak hoarsely. It's been hours since I have made a sound, and my vocal chords vehemently protest the sudden use.

He keeps his eyes locked on me as if expecting more information.

"I actually haven't made it to bed yet," I confess. Something about his dark focused eyes makes him seem familiar. His mouth is barely visible beneath a thick well-groomed mustache, black to match his wavy hair and unblinking eyes.

"Hmm." He eyes me thoughtfully. "You must be traveling," he states, no question in his voice.

I nod in agreement and divert my attention to the piping hot bread in front of me. Before it even occurs to me to notice that I haven't seen a menu, Rosie has appeared out of nowhere like an apparition. She places a plate heaped with impossible delights in front of me. *I must be daydreaming. Maybe the sleep-deprivation is finally catching up with me.* Slices of tropical fruits—some I know like starfruit, kiwi, and papaya, and a couple that I can't identify—are arranged in a colorful trim, like fine art around the rim of the oval platter. Slices of aged cheeses in several varieties, drizzled with what looks like marmalade and honey, line the inner ring. In the center, a small tasting dish with what must be candied almonds.

I'm speechless. I had this place pegged for a greasy spoon that would probably serve every dish with a heaping ladle full of artery-clogging gravy.

Rosie has materialized again as if by magic. This time, she comes bearing a soft-boiled egg in a delicate china egg cup that appears to be hand-painted. The details are breathtaking. Paisley blues and greens, interwoven with an intricate flurry of stars, swirling together in an abstract pattern. I'm so awestruck thinking how out of place such a treasure is in this odd little diner that I barely notice her add to my feast with a selection of crispy maple bacon and transparent thinly sliced prosciutto. I have never had as fine a meal in all my life.

The gentleman at the table next to mine strikes up a conversation that flows easily. Conversation never comes easily for me. When he asks me to join him, I only hesitate for a moment. If he has noticed my pause, he is too polite to comment. He introduces himself as Oliver and regales me with stories of his travels abroad. I can tell he is curious about me, but he doesn't ask any questions. By the time I have eaten as much as I physically can, we feel like old friends. Oliver must be thirty years my senior, but there is an ease to the way he carries himself. For a man who is barely over five feet tall, he is remarkably poised.

I find myself telling him the better part of my life story. "Sorry if I'm talking your ear off!" I say, a bit embarrassed. "There must be truth serum baked into the bread or something." I laugh awkwardly.

Oliver just smiles reassuringly.

I tell him about Dad and how hard it is to be without him. How much I hate my job and seeing the same faces every single day. How I have never felt like I fit in growing up. I manage to spill my guts to this perfect stranger without revealing too many details…like if I'm not already, I'll likely soon be reported as a missing person.

It doesn't occur to me that I have no intention of going home until I reach to collect my things and begin the hunt for my wallet in my cluttered backpack. It's 8:22 a.m. now. I've been here nearly two hours and I'm officially twenty-two minutes late for my shift at Jeanette's Café. So far, no missed calls. I'm sure she's watching the clock as we speak and giving me the benefit of the doubt. She always assumes the best from me, even though I've never done much to earn it. I can't help but wonder if she'd be better off without me. I see the way she looks at me. Day in and day out, wondering why I'm unhappy and blaming herself.

I take a quick inventory of my bag. I always bring a few things with me on my walks in case of emergency…but tonight, the nagging voice in my head urged me to bring along extra supplies. Now I'm glad I did. I have $179 dollars in tip money and a prepaid credit card with a few hundred dollars on it that Mom gave me—in case of emergency—my driver's license, (though I don't have a car), and a worn out paperback copy of Don Quixote that belonged to my father. A hairbrush, a toothbrush, and my cosmetics bag, my name tag from the café that says NOVA in all caps, a few seashells, and a rain poncho. I've seen enough crime dramas on cable to know that I can't use my credit card if I want to stay off the radar, so I make a mental note to hit the first ATM I find and take out cash.

Oliver is watching me quizzically. "I apologize. I did not ask your name. You must think me an old fool," he says, clearly fishing for a compliment.

"I'm Nova. Thank you for the company this morning." I smile warmly.

"May I ask where you're headed?" he says. "I couldn't help but notice that you arrived on foot."

I open my mouth to speak, but I am at a loss for words. I only know where I'm not going. I haven't left the peninsula in longer than I can remember and haven't even imagined where I might go. "I'm happy to give you a lift if you're heading my way," he says.

Without pause, I quickly accept his offer. "That would be great. Thank you."

I look around the diner for any sign of Rosie. "Will she bring us a bill?" I ask.

"No, no. It's not that kind of place," Oliver replies, chuckling like I've asked a ridiculous question. He stands up to put on his jacket. "I'm parked out this way," he says as he heads for the door.

"Nice! Dine and dash. I like this guy's style," chuffs the voice that seems to come from my own mind. I pause, confused. "Rosie?" I call toward the back. I walk back to the counter and call her name again. No reply. I cautiously step behind the counter and poke my head into the kitchen. It's deserted. "Hello?" I try, louder this time. No answer. I notice the smell of smoke again as I follow Oliver outside, a little bewildered. As we head to his truck, I turn back nervously to steal a last glance at the peculiar diner just in time to see the "_PEN" sign flicker back to "_LOSED." I shake my head. Maybe Oliver can explain all of this to me later.

With a bit of a running start, I manage to launch myself up into the cab of his oversized four-wheel drive pick-up. I'm still trying to unravel the mystery of how he got himself all the way up into the truck as the diesel engine roars to life. I know it's illogical. I can't explain how easily I trust him. I'm too tired to try. I slip into a dreamless sleep before we even hit the highway.

Eloise

Stonington, Connecticut

$\mathcal{E}$loise had been tired and chilled to the bone from her journey. She never seemed to be used to traveling through the frosty witch-fire. She awoke from her midday nap with a start, having just had another vision of Nova Daniels. She promptly hopped up from her bed, hurried down the stairs, and out into the gardens to tell the others. *They will be pleased,* she mused. In reality, though, it was Eloise that was rejoicing, for she already felt love in her heart for Nova and was ecstatic about what she had foreseen.

She reached Suzanne first and stopped for a moment to catch her breath. Though Eloise hadn't visibly aged in the almost sixty years since she and the other women of the circle had moved into the Borough house, she still felt the weight of time when she exerted herself.

"What is it?" Suzanne demanded impatiently. "You nearly made me drop these!" She had been in the gardens all morning and was proud of her harvest. It had been years since the crops produced such a bounty. This late in the season, she had begun to think it would be another barren year. She now held a large wicker basket, nearly overflowing with an array of colorful heirloom tomatoes. Rich gold, amber, and a spectrum of red shades caught the midday sunlight in a vibrant display. Everything else was ready to harvest too. Berries and melons, lettuces and broccoli, cucumbers and squashes, carrots and potatoes, and pots full of herbs and aromatics. She'd be out there into the evening at this rate. The sudden richness returning to the soil could only mean one thing.

"Oliver will take her as far as South Dakota. She will come to need our aid again in due time," Eloise said.

"Excellent. It was a good idea to take your brother with you," Suzanne replied. Eloise knew that Oliver was the only person who could get Nova safely on her way. He had the kind of presence that fostered trust effortlessly. That along with a little nudge from one of Carolyn's special recipes did the trick.

Eloise grinned at the memory. She'd loved meeting Nova and playing the part of Rosie. She and Suzanne stood in silence for a few moments, taking in the long forgotten sight of the gardens at harvest time.

As happy as Eloise was to have foreseen Nova's safe journey, her heart ached for the other woman in her vision—Nova's mother, Jeanette. Eloise went back to her room and sat down at her nineteenth century maple roll-top desk. It had belonged to her mother, and her mother before that. It still smelled faintly of her grandfather's cigar smoke. She treasured that smell.

Her desk sat next to the picture window overlooking the small apple orchard at the back of the property. It looks like they'll be picking apples this month as well. She smiled at the thought of Carolyn's apple cobbler and homemade apple butter. The women of the circle would not go hungry this winter, that was for certain.

Eloise was a powerful sibyl, but her passion had always been for poetry. Though she had written countless poems at her desk, this one was of unusual urgency.

A girl is lost and so she vies
To try on other lives for size
All you can do is hope she finds
Some semblance of peace of mind

The stars tell me that in the end
She will come back home again
It depends upon which path she'll choose
And just how much she'll dare to lose.

Trust that she'll return to you,
though not the same girl that you knew
a harvest moon when gold leaves fall
your little girl will come to call

Eloise didn't have to look up the address. It was one of her little gifts as a sibyl that had been passed down through the generations. Right before she sealed the envelope, she pulled the poem back out and scribbled on the back:

P.S. Consider readying the spare bedroom.

With that, she scurried back down the stairs and down the long drive, just in time to hand the letter to the mailman. "Hello, Dennis," she greeted him breathlessly. "Handle this one with extra care, if you please." She smiled sweetly and then happily skipped back toward the gardens to join the women of the circle in the harvest.

Nova

Headed East, August 26

The lonesome sound of a train whistle startles me awake. The landscape has changed from the familiar misty green wind-gnarled coastal forest to an almost alien looking scene. Dry cracked terra-cotta painted hills run along the riverbank. We're following the Columbia River Gorge on the Oregon side.

In the rearview mirror, I can see the fading green of the tree line in the distance along the gorge as it blends into the desert landscape. Worlds collide. It's as if the lines between two realities are blurred just enough to see through them. That is what I love the most about living in the Pacific Northwest. You can get to pretty much any ecosystem—from the beach, to the desert, a rainforest, to a snowy mountaintop in an hour or two.

It must be midday. The sun is high in the sky and beats down on me relentlessly through the windshield. I stretch my arms high to get the blood flowing and take off my hoodie, revealing my standard uniform of gray t-shirt and slim fit dark wash jeans.

"Well, good morning, Sunshine!" Oliver greets me merrily as I wipe the remnants of sleep from my eyes. "You're just in time to catch a glimpse of the river before the highway turns south. It's a beautiful day for a journey."

He's right. It is a perfect day. Despite my stiff legs, I feel better than I have in… I don't even know how long. I lean back, sigh, and take in the scenery. The cassette player in the truck plays Johnny Cash's greatest hits as we snake through the gorge.

"We'll push through to Pocatello tonight, if you don't mind a long day on the road," Oliver offers.

His large aviator sunglasses take up the whole top half of his face. He looks almost animated as he sings along to "Folsom Prison Blues" in a smooth baritone, all sunglasses and mustache. "With any luck, we'll pull into Sioux Falls just in time for lunch on Saturday."

Sioux Falls. Hm. I think that's North Dakota. Or is it South Dakota? I guess I'll find out.

After a quick stop in Pendleton for fuel and snacks, we're back in the truck. Oliver is educating me on the geography of this part of the country. "Did you know that you can follow Interstate 84 all the way to New York City?" he asks enthusiastically. "Well, I mean, technically the highway name changes and it all gets a little bit convoluted when you make your way around the Great Lakes, but it's essentially just one long stretch of road." He keeps talking, but he lost my attention at the mention of New York City.

My entire senior year at Ilwaco High was spent listening to other kids bragging to each other about their big plans after high school. Traveling to Europe to backpack for the summer, celebrating admittance to their dream schools, even joining the military didn't sound half bad compared to my prewritten destiny. Everyone knew that I would be working in the café until my mother died and then running the café until I died. End of story. All of my years on the planet would be measured in cups of coffee and biscuits and gravy. No one bothered to ask me what my plans were.

My lab partner, Bethany, got into some fancy art school in Manhattan. She was the closest thing to a friend I had. The thought of seeing her go made me a little bit sad. Some nights, I would dream that I went with her and became a great sculptor. The critics would say that I was the best they'd ever seen. My father would return from the grave to attend my big exhibits and write songs inspired by my work. I would be his muse. In all honesty, though, I never wanted to be an artist; but since I didn't have my own dream, Bethany's worked fine. I hadn't bothered to imagine a life other than the one I had for fear it would make my reality seem even more bleak.

Something about the idea of New York always appealed to me, though. Living in Ocean Park all my life, everyone knew everyone. Worse, everyone had an opinion about everyone. I hated the attention that I got. Being the daughter of bubbly, warm, outgoing Jeanette, I was expected to be a chip off the ol' block. I had gotten pretty good at donning a fake smile for the customers over the years, but it never came naturally. I imagine that it would be easy to fade into the background in a city as big as New York.

My focus shifts back to Oliver as he is wrapping up his diatribe on the history of Devil's Gulch. Some South Dakotan tall tale about the outlaw Jessie James jumping an impossibly wide ravine to avoid capture. "It's a shame how little faith most people have in the inconceivable, don't you think?"

I nod in agreement, though I'm not entirely sure what he means.

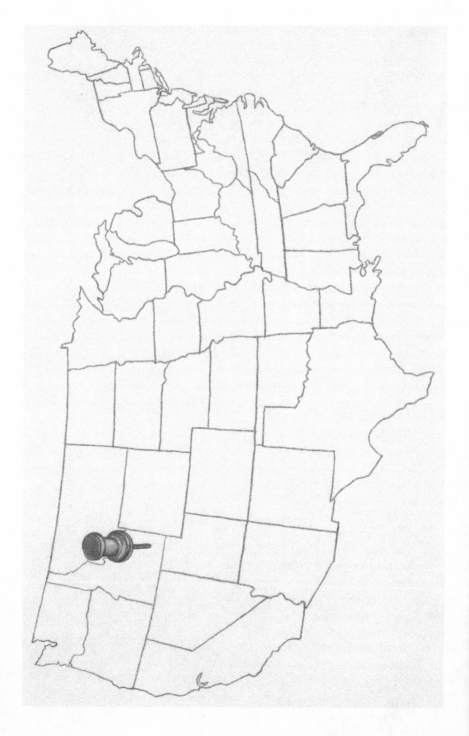

Nova

Pocatello, Idaho

By the time we reach Pocatello, I'm having a hard time keeping my eyes open. Oliver pulls in to the parking lot of a small motel and instructs me to wait in the truck. I watch as he hurries in through the door marked "Office" and greets the night manager. They must know one another. It occurs to me that I should be wary of this stranger…but I can't muster even an ounce of panic.

I sigh as I watch the two men through the window. They embrace and are laughing like old friends. *Oliver must come this way often.* As I survey the scene, I can't see why. This place looks a like a movie set from some low budget slasher film. If I believed in such things, I might wonder if it were haunted. The motel itself is a long single-level building with cedar siding and a bright blue roof. The roof looks freshly redone and seems very out of place atop the dingy mildewing building front. Yellow doors line the front of the motel. Each door has its own lamp above it at the right corner, illuminating the peeling and faded paint. There are no visible windows, save the one on the office door.

A small wooden sign atop a rusty post identifies the building as a motel, though not much else. There is no name, just a large owl depicted in shades of gray next to the word "MOTEL" in caps, painted in the same chipped yellow. I guess no one wants to put their name on such a dump. A neon placard dangles from two thin wires beneath the sign, just above eye level. It's obviously brand-new as I can see a stark white barcode sticker on the side.

"_acancy" it says. One point. Strange that a letter is already out. "They just don't make 'em like they used to," my father used to say…

about everything. I chuckle at the thought. No matter what it was—from toasters, to cars, to storm clouds—apparently every imaginable thing in life had been of a much higher quality at some unspecified time in his past. "The glory days," he'd call them. I hope for his sake that wherever we go after this lifetime, there are top-notch toasters.

Oliver is back at the truck, a toothy grin barely peeking through under his bushy mustache.

"Here's your key, m'dear," he announces proudly. "Victor is an old friend. He's covered our rooms for us. You're in room 6. I'll be right next door in 7 should you need anything."

"Thank you," I whisper.

Room 6 looks the scariest, of course. The light above the door is flickering like a cliché prop from a horror movie. "Don't go in the basement," I say sarcastically under my breath. I return Oliver's smile and slide down out of the truck. It's cold outside. I'm having trouble keeping up with the rapid climate changes today.

Oliver winks at me. "Nothing is open at this hour, but I'd love it if you'd join me for breakfast in the morning. Say, 9:00?"

Before I can respond, he's halfway across the parking lot. I can't get used to how speedy he is. I watch him in awe as I slowly will my stiff body toward my room.

The key he gave me looks like a relic. It's heavy in my hands and only has two teeth on it, a long one and short one. It's not rusty, but it looks corroded as if it has been sitting at the bottom of the salty sea for centuries. As I approach the door to room 6; the flickering bulb fizzles out completely. I'm starting to shiver while fumbling for the keyhole in the dark. "Perfect," I grumble. After a few tries, the lock clicks open and the heavy door silently swings away from me. The smell of crisp, under ripe citrus and sage fills my senses all at once. The air is warm and inviting. It's a far cry from what I'd expected based on the look of the place. I had been bracing myself for the stuffy smells of rancid air and mildew. I inhale deeply just to be sure I'm not imagining things.

I feel along the wall for a light switch with my right hand and am halfway through the room before I slam my thigh into the corner of the bureau. "C'mon!" I yell to no one in particular. My fingers

30

find a lamp and trace the rounded base upwards until they discover a hanging chain. With a tug, the room is alive with a warm orange glow, just like the lamplight my mother insists on at the café. My thoughts wander momentarily.

I've been gone now almost twenty-four hours. I wonder what she's thinking. I feel guilty. I feel even more guilty because I don't feel more guilty. *What kind of person am I?* I had let myself think that she'd realize I left on my own and just respect that I needed some space. *I'm practically an adult. I shouldn't need to ask permission anymore…right?* Now that I think about it, though, there is nothing to indicate that I left willingly. I didn't leave a note, because I didn't know I wasn't coming back when I snuck out my bedroom window to take a walk. I had packed a few things, but I always did in case I stayed out too late and had to head straight to the café. She wouldn't find anything missing. *Who knows, though? Maybe she's relieved to be rid of me…yeah, right. Well, it's too late to call now. I will call her in the morning and let her know I'm okay.*

As I look around the room, I'm overcome with a sense of relief. The decor is cozy and old-fashioned. It reminds me of the inside of a log cabin or something. The lamp itself is modeled after an old oil lamp and sits on a lovely oak chest of drawers. The queen-sized bed is welcomingly billowy beneath an overstuffed cream colored down comforter and a mountain of pillows. The two against the headboard are standard size. They are plump with feathers and covered in silky cream cases to match the comforter.

There must be eight pillows in total. Decorative throw pillows in various sized squares and rectangles have been tossed haphazardly at the head of the bed. One is embroidered with the American flag. Another a teddy bear in a rocking chair reading a book. The smallest just reads "Home is where the heart is" in red yarn. The "o" in home has been replaced by a pink heart. My gaze lingers on the heart-shaped "o" for some time. Something about this old cliché gives me a bit of solace.

I push the pile of pillows aside and pull back the covers. Under the comforter, the cushy mattress is topped with soft flannel sheets in a red, white, and blue plaid pattern. Without another thought, I climb into bed and pull the blankets up under my chin. I fall asleep in the soft golden lamplight.

* * * * *

My dreams are restless. Though my body lies as still as a corpse in the warmth of flannel and feathers, my mind races. I'm in the café. I'm working alone in the breakfast rush, and the daily dairy delivery is late. We're out of coffee creamer and the patrons are demanding it. They pound on tables with silverware and fists, angrily chanting, "Creamer! Creamer!" in unison. I apologize profusely as I hurry from table to table with a piping hot pot of regular coffee in one hand and a too full pot of decaf in the other. Two tables are still waiting to order.

A large woman in the corner booth glares at me while waving her menu, trying to catch my eye. The cook in the kitchen is ringing the bell impatiently, letting me know that there are orders ready. "Uuuuup!" he yells repeatedly, like an auctioneer that missed his true calling. The heat lamp is still broken, and the food is getting cold. It dawns on me that I left a quiche in the back oven to warm just as the smoke detector above the stove goes off.

The deafening cry of the alarm startles me and I lose my grip on the pot of decaf, just for a second. It goes crashing to the floor. Instinctively, I reach to catch it with the other hand, causing the pot of regular coffee to go flying. In slow motion, the glass shatters into a million pieces. Scalding hot coffee splashes onto the legs of the patrons on either side of me, one of which is wearing white trousers. "You'll pay for this dry cleaning!" she demands.

"Ouch!" cries man next to her. "The least you could do is get me some ice!"

A baby is screaming at the booth nearest the cash register. The unbearable volume of the alarm has her frantic. Her mother tries unsuccessfully to soothe her and looks at me pleadingly to do something about it.

Coffee has splashed into an electrical outlet and is sporadically sparking. Lamps flicker. Smoke begins to rise from the cluster of extension cords beneath the vintage 1950s gumball machine. I run to the kitchen to grab some towels. Clouds of smoke pour from the oven. I wave a towel at the smoke detector in vain.

I look around frantically for the cook and see a note stuck to the refrigerator with a Coca-Cola bottle-cap magnet that simply reads "I quit." His apron is crumpled in a heap on the floor. I hear a loud crash, like metal falling into glass from the front of the café. I'm hopping up and down, still fanning the smoke detector. "Creamer! Creamer! Creamer!" barely audible over the sounds of the screaming baby and the alarm. I hear the siren of a firetruck approaching just as the emergency sprinkler system engages and a heavy rain begins to fall throughout the café.

* * * * *

I startle myself awake and am relieved to find that I am still snuggled in the warmth of the bed. I take a few deep breaths to shake off the nightmare, but my heart is racing. It's still dark outside. I wonder what time it is. *How does this room not have a clock in it?* Reluctantly, I ease out of bed, in search of my backpack. It takes me a few moments to find my phone in the mess. 3:22 a.m. Seventeen missed calls. Voice mailbox is full. I turn off my phone and stuff it back into my backpack. Now wide awake, I decide to get dressed and head out for a walk to clear my head.

I step out into the parking lot and shut my door carefully so as not to wake anyone else sleeping in neighboring rooms. The whooshing of a street-sweeping truck up the road still doesn't mask the sound of nearby snoring. I realize it's coming from room 7. Oliver has a big snore for such a little man. I giggle to myself and head off into the night.

Not sure where I'm heading, I take the first right and find myself in a quaint middle-class neighborhood. *Anytown, USA,* says a voice in my head.

"Totally," I reply aloud. Street lamps cut through the darkness like fireflies illuminating the occasional front yard. All the houses look the same to me—double garage, L-shaped roof, and all beige... at least it looks that way at night. *Yuck.* That was one thing that

Ocean Park had going for it. The town was too small to have cookie-cutter housing tracts.

Ours looks like a gingerbread house straight out of a fairy tale. I remember thinking that it was the most beautiful house I'd ever seen when I was little. A sunny yellow with white shutters and detailed molding along the roofline, rosebushes lining the outside of the house. My mom had always managed to keep flowers planted along the front walkway, even in the wintertime. She said we deserved a nice homecoming at the end of the work day. Tulips were blooming the night I left—orange with bursts of red and yellow in the centers.

Seventeen missed calls. *Mom must be so worried. I should call her, but I don't know what to say. She'll ask why I left, but I don't have an answer. She'll ask me where I'm going, but I don't know that either. She'll ask me to come home, but I can't. I just can't go back there.*

"*Let it go, babe. You don't have to answer to her anymore,*" says a voice that seems to come from my head. Startled, I trip over a curb and land flat on my back.

I've now made my way around the block and am just down the street from the motel. I'm lying on my back in the parking lot of a steakhouse. As I look up at the big bright sign high above me, the lightbulb shining behind the "S" and "E" in "HOUSE" burns out with a flare of light and an audible pop.

"HOU__." Two points.

I slowly sit up, inspecting the damage. I definitely sprained my ankle. *Shoot. Ouch. I have to start paying attention to where I'm walking.* "Instant karma," my mom calls it. It serves me right. I hobble back to my room on one good ankle. As I try repeatedly to get the key into the lock in the dark, the lamp above my door that has been out all night decides to flicker back on. *Maybe there is hope for me yet,* I think to myself. I kick off my sneakers and crawl back into bed.

The minute my eyes close, I am transported to a familiar setting. It's a dream I've had hundreds of times. Thousands maybe. It's been a while, though. Months, maybe a year. In fact, this is the longest I've ever gone without dreaming of this place.

Rolling hills in dazzling shades of green sprawl out before me as far as I can see. It's near twilight, but the setting sun still illuminates the countryside. Tonight, the face of the shepherd boy brings me more comfort than usual. Something I can count on. Someone I can count on. I love that face—kind eyes, green and gray, the color of sea-foam during a storm. There is an understanding behind his eyes that conveys the many hardships he must have seen in his lifetime. He just seems like he could handle anything. Strong, yet gentle. He has the same nondescript hair color that I have, somewhere between brown and blonde. I think it looks much better on him.

Just like every night that I've dreamt of him, he is lackadaisically herding his sheep with no apparent direction in mind. They are some of the saddest looking animals you'd ever see, though. I always wonder why he doesn't take better care of them. In past dreams, I've asked him this, but he just shrugs and says, "They aren't mine to change." Some are thin and missing patches of fluff from their coats. One is blind and stumbles away from the flock, another is missing a leg. All seem perfectly contented somehow. Maybe they find camaraderie in their shared misfortune.

Something occurs to me as I sit cross-legged in the field nearest my shepherd. He's aged. He looks world weary and wise. I remember him looking like a child when last we met. He catches me staring. "You look older," I say.

"You do too," he replies.

Hmm. I guess he does look about my age. Now that I think about it, he always has. He's been aging with me my whole life. I remember seeing him for the first time, right after my father died. I was only seven or so. He was too. I remember thinking what a grown-up job he had. I didn't know any other shepherds my age. I'd only heard about them in Christmas stories. I didn't know anyone my age who had a job at all for that matter. He's been here all these years. My constant.

"Why do you stay?" I ask.

"It's just as good as anywhere," he says.

"That doesn't even make sense," I argue. "It's a field."

He looks at me thoughtfully for what feels like hours. Dream time is so hard to gauge. Not answering me, but not exactly ignoring the question either, he sits down in front of me, and the sheep wander away as if trying to give us our privacy. I can't help but notice how handsome he's become. His boyish face has transformed, chiseled jaw-line shaded by a shadow of facial hair. He's watching me watching him.

"I stay because I have found my place. You might want to think about doing the same," he says with not so subtle sarcasm. With that, he stands, turns, and walks westward toward the setting sun. *Rude*, I think. *Who does he think he is? How dare he judge me.*

"Fine. Stay in a field full of misfit sheep! See if I care!" I shout after him, but he's already too far off to hear me. I am trying my best not to be hurt, but I am hurt. His opinion is more important to me than I can explain. Just before he's out of sight between the hills, he pauses to look back at me. The look lingers. My face feels warm. My hands feel tingly.

* * * * *

Moments later, Oliver is knocking at my door. "Ready for breakfast, Miss?" he asks. "My treat!"

I wake up with a scowl, still trying to sort out my dream encounter. I limp over to the door, rubbing my eyes. "Good morning," I say with a half-smile.

"Oh, good heavens! What happened?" Oliver is gawking at my ankle. I look down and realize it's now swollen to twice it's normal size and is bruised pretty badly.

"Just twisted it. It looks worse than it is," I assure him.

"Nonsense!" he exclaims. "Let's get that looked at. Victor was a medic in the military, you know," he says as he scampers off across the parking lot.

"How could I possibly know that?" I say to myself grumpily.

I limp over to the sink, brush my teeth, and drag a comb through my hair before Oliver reappears with Victor in tow. Victor is carrying a First-Aid kit and a small cooler. I sit at the foot of the bed as they busily fuss over me. "Is it broken?" Oliver asks anxiously.

"No, I don't think so," says Victor. "It just looks like a bad sprain. You did a number on it," he tells me. "You'll want to stay off of it for a day or two, and no more midnight adventures for a while, eh?" he says with a smirk.

How did he know? Hm. Small town, I guess.

He hands me a small bottle of ibuprofen. "Take a couple of these every four hours. It'll help with the swelling." He opens the cooler and pulls out a bag of frozen baby peas.

I can't help but smile. Just like my mom would do. She never cooked frozen vegetables as a general rule but always kept them on hand for my bumps and bruises. He secures the peas to my ankle with a beige ace bandage. "Keep an eye on this one, Oli," he says to Oliver.

"Your patient is in good hands," he assures him.

"Thank you!" I yell after him as he trots back toward the office.

"I'll tell you what. Let's skip breakfast and get on the road. We'll drive through somewhere on the way out of town. I want to keep you off that ankle today," Oliver says.

I nod, relieved. I'm excited to put some distance between me and Pocatello…and my dreams last night. I pack up my cosmetics kit, pull on my hoodie, and Oliver helps me to the truck. It takes me three tries, but I manage to get up into the passenger seat. He helps me prop my bad ankle up onto the dashboard. "Vic said to elevate it."

He's in the driver's seat, all buckled up before I can even blink. I swear I will never get used to how fast he moves. "Sioux Falls, here we come!" he shouts cheerily.

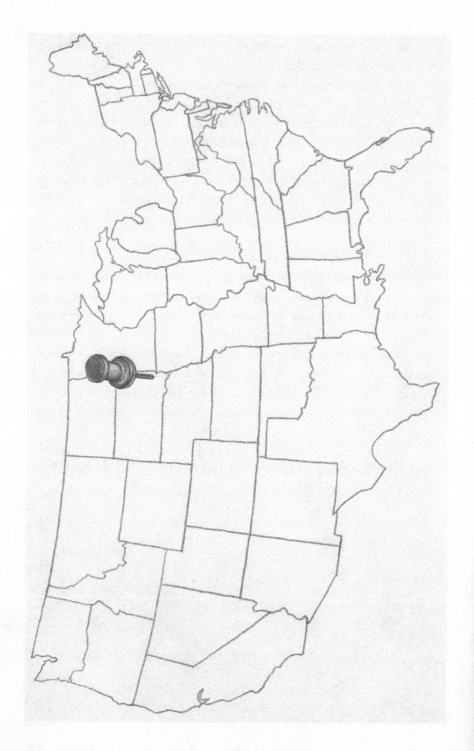

Nova

Sioux Falls, South Dakota, August 28

The highway sign says twenty-six miles to Sioux Falls. What a beautiful drive it's been, even after dark. My mother had always said that the Long Beach peninsula was the most beautiful place to live. Living in a world of greens and muted grays in the Pacific Northwest, it's easy to forget about the bright oranges of desert landscape and how a mountain really does look purple and majestic in the morning light. That combined with the literal amber waves of grain we passed in the farm country of Wyoming has me feeling a little bit patriotic. It's nice to get a dose of fresh perspective.

It's almost 3:00 a.m. now. We've been on the road just about eighteen hours, but the time has flown by. Throughout the day, Oliver has proven to be arguably the most competent tour guide on planet Earth. It's clear that he has made this drive more times than he can count over the years. He has a story to tell about every single "don't blink or you'll miss it" one-horse town between here and the Pacific Ocean. From local lore to political history, I feel like I've absorbed more valuable learning today than I retained my entire high school time in life. Fate was certainly smiling on me in the diner when I met this gem of a man.

Since the sun went down, Oliver and I have been swapping life stories. Mine obviously didn't take long. Only child. Successful musician dad, boring mom. Transplanted to a town that is hardly worth putting on a map and left to rot.

Oliver, on the other hand, has quite a story to tell. His parents migrated to the United States from Moldova in eastern Europe right before his thirteenth birthday. Oliver's father had found work on a farm in Kansas. The farmer had let he and his family stay in a small guest cottage on the property. His father worked for the farmer for many years and eventually inherited the farm. He taught Oliver all about farming and agriculture. They had a happy life full of love, but Oliver always longed to live near the ocean. When he was a grown man, he went into business as a broker selling farm machinery from coast to coast. He had fulfilled his childhood dream as well and had bought himself a quaint little Victorian-style house at Cannon Beach on the Oregon Coast.

Nowadays, Oliver was moonlighting as a realtor and specialized in historical and landmark properties. He was heading to South Dakota to take a client on a tour of several homes in the area that had been owned by early settlers and restored by the city's historical council. From there, he had planned an extended visit back to the farm in Kansas to stay with his parents. His mother's health was failing, he'd told me.

"My youngest sister is still in Kansas, but she has her hands full with her own family. My eldest lives in coastal Connecticut, but she's got her own concerns at the moment..." He trailed off before quickly changing the subject. "So, we'll have to go our separate ways in Sioux Falls, I'm afraid," Oliver had said with what seemed like authentic regret. "Will you be okay? Do you have a plan in place to get yourself to New York?"

I don't know why I told him I was going to New York. The truth is, I have no idea where I'm going. Normally, that kind of thing would terrify me. At this moment, though, I know it's the only thing keeping me calm. I'm enjoying every single unplanned minute. "Oh, um. Y-y-yes, of course," I lied.

"There is a truck stop just inside the city limits with a motel attached. I've stayed there many times. The rates can't be beat, and they provide a continental breakfast in the morning," Oliver tells me.

"That should be perfect," I smile doubtfully.

When we arrive at the truck stop, Oliver helps me to my room and sees me safely inside, going slow taking care to make sure my ankle will carry me.

"It's feeling much better already. Thank you for taking such good care of me," I say. It still hurts, but it looks like my ankle again rather than a lumpy purple balloon.

"Well, I'm not much for goodbyes," he says. "Take my business card. If you ever find yourself in need of a friend, please call. Thank you for the companionship. It has been my pleasure, Miss Nova." He slides his business card into the outside pocket of my backpack before handing it to me and then stands up on his tiptoes to give me a warm hug.

"Thank you so much…for everything," I say, choking up a bit. "I hope we meet again."

"I hope the same," he says with a tip of his hat, and turns to go.

My room is plain, but comfortable. A double bed with a 1970s looking gold duvet over crisp white linens. A round white laminate table and two bucket chairs sit in the corner. A chest of drawers with an outdated TV on top of it hugs the wall adjacent to my bed. I head straight for the bathroom and proceed to take the longest shower of my life. This might be the first time I've ever truly appreciated the value of really good water pressure.

I let the powerful streams of water massage the tension from my back and neck. When the water starts to turn cold, I reluctantly turn off the shower and towel off. I slip on the oversized bathrobe I find hanging on the back of the bathroom door and head to bed.

The moment I close my eyes, I'm standing face-to-face with an irritated shepherd. "You're late," he says crossly. "I need your help." The countryside looks as it always does in my dream, but it's raining tonight. It's never rained in this dream. "One of the sheep has run off," he says, a tone of panic in his voice.

This is the first time I've ever seen him upset about anything. It's unsettling. I scan the fields and see no sign of it. Something is a little bit off about the hills…like at the edges of my sight line, the colors are starting to run. It's as if this reality might wash away in the rain. My conscious mind rejects this idea and fights the image in my dream so that the lines flash from runny to solid in jerky sporadic intervals. My shepherd is annoyed by my lack of focus. "I'll see if I can find her," I say and take off toward the west. A melody I've never heard before is playing somewhere in the distance. It's sad, but hopeful somehow. *Beautiful.* As I scan the fields in search of its origin, I realize that it's him. My shepherd is humming his sorrowful song as he wanders gloomily in the rain. I spend the rest of the night searching with no sign of the lost sheep.

* * * * *

I wake in the morning, still exhausted. Maybe more exhausted. It's as if the sleep has drained what energy I had left rather than recovering any. Still, though, I can't ignore my empty stomach. The clock on the nightstand says 11:17 a.m. It's still breakfast time in some restaurants. Hopefully one nearby. *Must. Find. Food.*

Gingerly, I step out of bed onto my bad ankle. Miraculously, it already feels almost as good as new. *Awesome.* I pull my jeans on and make a note to self to procure another change of clothes soon. My stomach growls loudly. I don't think I've ever been this hungry in my life.

As soon as I walk out of my room, I see it right across the street like a bright beacon of hope. Pearl's Diner is bustling with people. Just underneath the name on the light-up sign are the words "Breakfast served all day." I do an awkward happy dance. Well, technically it says "_ _ _akfast served all day" as the bulb behind the "Bre" is burned out.

Three points, I think. *Four maybe, it's a tougher word.* "Dad?" I say, looking up at the sky as if giving him the chance to decide. No answer. *Okay, four points it is. Even "akfast" sounds pretty good right now.* I scan the parking lot for Oliver's truck, but he's probably long gone. The stoplight in the intersection turns green just as I approach the crosswalk. I take my chances and run across the street before the line of cars can stop me. I'm so focused on food that I don't notice the guitar player sitting on the curb in front of the café as he eyes me curiously.

I pull open the door, and the smell of freshly baked coffee cake overcomes me. It smells just like my mom's. I recoil at the thought of her. I meant to call her yesterday...or did I? I guess I had no intention of calling her. I see a display of postcards on a spinning rack near the cash register. *Maybe I'll send her one. I could let her know that I'm all right without having to call. Yeah. I'll get one when I leave. First things first, though.*

A sign by the door says "Seat Yourself," so I scan the café for a seat. Every table is occupied, but I see one empty stool at the bar by the kitchen. I sit down next to an elderly man in an unseasonably cozy snowy white sweater. He's hunched over the counter, leaning on his elbows. He has terrible posture. In his light colored shirt, he reminds me of the crescent moon hanging low over the peninsula. Even with his thick silver-rimmed glasses, I can see that he was handsome in his youth. He is engrossed in an article in the paper and doesn't seem to notice me.

This place is packed, yet I don't see a single person working. I can hear what sounds like bacon frying through the kitchen window in front of me, so there must at least be a cook on duty, but I don't see anyone working in the café.

As if on cue, the kitchen door bursts open and a frazzled girl in a burgundy waitress uniform comes rushing out. She has an oversized tray heaped with plates balanced on her right hand and a coffee pot in her left. She practically stumbles over to the large table in the middle of the café where a group of eight watch her nervously. The food staying balanced on the swaying tray all but defies the laws of physics. She hurries around the table, plunking plates down in front of each of the customers, and then turns to run back to the kitchen. "Coffee?" one woman calls after her. She turns back and sets her pot down on the table before fleeing. I watch them as they switch plates with one another until they all end up with the correct order.

Oh my gosh, I think. *I've been there.* Working alone on a day that is usually slow, and then an entire little league team along with their families, coaches, and fans fill the café. It reminds me of the nightmare I had in Pocatello. My heart goes out to the waitress.

She whizzes by again, in front of the bar to the other side of the dining room, then pauses to search for her discarded coffee pot. I survey the room and see that most of the tables haven't been served their food. Some haven't ordered and are holding menus impatiently.

"I hope you're not in a hurry," says the man next to me as if just realizing I'm here. He pushes me his menu. "I've been here a half hour and I haven't even gotten a cup of coffee. Luckily, I'm retired, so I don't have anywhere to be," he says with a long hearty laugh.

He thinks he's hilarious. I can't help but laugh with him. My dad used to crack himself up all the time. I find it endearing. "Is she the only one working?" I ask.

"Yes, ma'am. Her and old Hank in the kitchen. She's been on her own here since her parents' accident last winter. I'm not sure she knows where to start when it comes to hiring help," he says. "Sad, sad. The food is the best in town, though, if you've got the time." He shakes his head and goes back to reading his paper.

I watch her frantically rush around the restaurant for several more minutes. She can't be a day older than sixteen. Her burgundy uniform is a fifties-style dress tied with a wide cream colored sash. She has it paired with a pair of running shoes. Smart girl. Her dark brown hair is loosely pulled back into a lopsided ponytail, tendrils coming free and sticking out in all directions. Her milky pale skin leads me to believe she doesn't spend much time outside of these four walls. My heart aches with empathy for this girl.

Suddenly, I hear a crash of dishes in the kitchen and can't help myself. I hop up and push my way through the kitchen door to find the girl with who I'm assuming is Hank huddled together, trying to salvage what they can from the full tray she has just dropped. "I'm so sorry, Hank!" she pleads "I think I loaded this one too heavy."

I see an apron hanging on a hook next to the door and automatically reach for it. I toss my sweatshirt on the floor and tie the apron strings tightly at my back. I dig in the pocket of my jeans for a hair tie and am pulling my hair up into a quick bun when they notice me. "How can I help?" I ask.

They both look up at me, jaws dropped.

"I've been working in a café my whole life. Just tell me what you need me to do," I say.

The girl just stares at me with her huge piercing blue eyes in disbelief.

"Can you take orders?" Hank asks.

"No problem," I say quickly.

"There's an extra order pad and a menu by the register. Specials are on the board."

"Okay, I'm on it," I say and head out into the packed restaurant.

Just like Hank said, I find an order pad and a pen by the register. I tuck a menu under my arm in case I need a reference and grab a pot of coffee off the burner at the end of the counter. I start making rounds, and it's as comfortable for me as breathing. I'm actually enjoying myself.

Within fifteen minutes, everyone has been helped, coffee cups are full, and food is on its way. I send the waitress back to the grill to help Hank and I've got the café under control. I head down the bar with a pitcher of ice water to refill a few glasses and find the elderly gentleman peering up at me over his newspaper with a toothy grin.

"Looks like you saved the day," he says with a chuckle.

"I'm just trying to help, that's all," I say. I can feel a blush warming up my cheeks.

"I'm Martin," he offers, "and you are?"

Crap, I think. This is a point in the conversation when a decent liar would dole out a fake name and backstory. Me, on the other hand, I'm the worst liar that has ever lived in the history of mankind. When I even think about lying, I blush, stutter, giggle, or some embarrassing combination of the three. If I'm going to stay anonymous, though, it's imperative. *Think quick, brain. Crap. Maybe something that at least rhymes with my name so I can make a quick recovery in case I slip up. Nova...what rhymes with Nova? Nothing? Seriously. Worst name ever. Muldovah? Jehova? Oh, yeah, that's perfect. Hi, I'm Jehova.*

"Cat got your tongue, doll face?" Martin says with a wink.

Crap. "No. Ha-ha. Hi, I'm Nuh-nuh-no..." I stutter out with a giggle. *Dammit. I sound drunk and stupid. There is no way I can come up with a fake name let alone a story to go with it. No chance.*

He eyes me suspiciously.

"You can call me Nora," I say without a stutter. He can, so that isn't a lie at least. I silently vow to say as little as humanly possible for the rest of the day.

"Hi, Nora. I'm Kate," says the waitress. She must have snuck up behind me while I was in the middle of my inner monologue. "Thank you," she says.

"No problem." I smile at her. She looks like she hasn't slept in a week. Poor thing.

"Do you live around here?" she asks.

Double crap. "Um, I'm new in town," I say honestly. As long as I can find creative ways to tell the truth, I'll be fine.

"Need a job?" she asks hopefully. "I'm a little shorthanded at the moment as you can see." She giggles nervously.

Martin was right. She's in over her head here. "Well, I don't know how long I'm sticking around." I confess. "I could help out for a while, though, maybe train a replacement if that would help," I add.

She hugs me like an old friend. "Oh, thank you, Nora! You won't regret it!" she gushes.

"I just have one condition," I say. "Can I order some breakfast first?"

The three of us share a good laugh.

Kate and I have some time to chat; or rather, she does while I shovel down my belated breakfast of French toast and bacon. Martin was so right. The food here is awesome. Totally worth the wait.

Kate tells me that she owns this place. Her parents died in a car accident. They got caught in a snowstorm last winter, heading home from a trade show, and collided with an eighteen-wheeler hauling lumber.

I have to keep myself from telling her that I know what it's like to lose a parent. Too much information. I just nod sympathetically while chewing my hash browns. Keeping my mouth full turns out to be a welcome safeguard against my urge to tell Kate everything.

She has no siblings, so this place is all hers. The bank had taken the family home, so she is living in a makeshift apartment above the café. Kate convinced Hank to let her stay here on her own on her sixteenth birthday a few months back. He had been college buddies with her folks and was named her legal guardian after the accident. Hank tells Kate that he needs the job, but she knows better. She doesn't mind, though. He is a great cook, and it's nice to know she's not alone.

After breakfast, Kate offers me a wage of $10 an hour plus tips. She hands me a uniform. "It's my extra one," she says. "I can wear my mom's. I'll give you this one too once I wash it."

"That would be great," I say. The clock above the bar says 2:45 p.m. We're alone in the café.

"The dinner rush starts around six. See you then?" she asks, hopefully.

"I'll be here in uniform," I tell her. I smile and turn to leave.

"Nora?" she calls.

I keep walking.

"Hey, Nora?"

I'm almost to the door.

"Nora, wait!"

Oh, right! That's me! I turn back.

Kate hands me a wad of cash from her pocket. "Your tips from today. You did pretty good!" she tells me.

"Thanks. See ya later," I say and head out the door. I can't believe I didn't answer to my own fake name. *Ugh. I am literally the worst liar ever. So frustrating. This is good, though. She needs me, and this place will give me something to keep my mind off of my mother until I figure out what I'm going to do. Shoot, I forgot to get a postcard. Well, I can grab one later. Or tomorrow. Anyway, the job is a good start. I'll have to figure out someplace to stay before long, but at $49 a night, I can wait it out at the motel another day or two.*

I'm lost in thought as I walk out of the diner and almost trip over a man with a guitar, sitting on the curb. His guitar case lays open in front of him with a surprising amount of crumpled up bills in it. Not just dollars either. I see several tens and twenties.

"Watch it!" he says.

"Sorry, I didn't see you," I say apologetically.

"No kidding," he snaps. He turns to look at me and we lock eyes for a moment.

"Hey, don't I know—" I start.

"Don't you know what?" he asks.

47

"N-n-never mind. Sorry again," I stammer and hurry away across the street to the truck stop. He looks so familiar. I know him from somewhere. That's impossible, though. I don't know anyone, let alone anyone in South Dakota. Still, though, those eyes. It's like he's looking straight through me, yet holding something back. I know those eyes… I'm sure of it.

* * * * *

The large truck stop is laid out like the world's most disorganized department store. There is an automotive department in the back left corner that takes up a good 25 percent of the space. In front of the displays of auto parts are tidy rows of grocery items. Just a moderate selection with a little bit of everything. They obviously didn't want to take precious square-footage away from the 900 different kinds of wiper blades.

In the center of the store, way at the back, is a little makeshift laundromat. There are two ancient looking washing machines, then two video poker machines, and two dryers all in a row. In the back right-hand corner, a sign hangs from the ceiling that says "Grooming." There is an old-fashioned shoeshine stand and a small barber's station where the barber is carefully shaving a burly looking man with a straight razor. A door to the locker room and showers is to their right.

At the front of the store, just to my right, is a small deli counter and two cash registers. I peek in the deli case and see hotdogs spinning on a rotisserie rack underneath a heat lamp. They look old and wrinkly. *No wonder the café was packed this morning. Slim pickings over here.*

I see a few racks of clothes tucked back behind an aisle of housewares and cleaning products and make my way over. Most of the clothes are rugged looking menswear, but I can see that there are a few selections closer to my size as I approach. There are three different t-shirts to choose from on the rack marked "Gals." Blue, pink, and gray. All three say Sioux Falls. The blue one has a silhouette of an Indian Chief in full headdress. The pink one has a screen-printed outline of a waterfall. The gray shirt makes me laugh out loud. It has a picture of the head of a wolf looking straight at you. He's drawn in thin black strokes and has deep golden eyes. To the left of his head is the same image in profile view, sort of faded into the background. It looks like one of the cheesy school pictures my mom had done of me in grade school. "Must be a big seller," I say out loud, sarcastically.

A shelf next to me has a few stacks of folded pants. One type of jeans, certainly not my style. Light blue wash, loose fit. *Yuck. Maybe they are Nora's style, though. Hm.* I wonder what a waitress from South Dakota would wear. *Maybe coming up with a backstory for Nora isn't such a bad idea after all. It might make things easier. I don't want people to ask too many questions, so I'll have to keep it simple. I'll give it some thought before my shift later.*

In the meantime, I'm thinking that Nora might really like wolves. It's the cheesiest shirt ever, but that makes it even better. I may be worthless when it comes to telling lies, but I was always a pretty good actor in school. I sort of liked the feeling of pretending to be someone else. It's not exactly lying. Acting.

I pick up the wolf shirt in a small and grab a pair of black leggings in my size as well. At least it will be something to wear while I'm doing laundry. I grab a blue, green, and white plaid flannel shirt from the "Kiddos" rack in a boys' medium. It fits great. *This will be fine for now.*

As I start to head for the cash register, I catch a glimpse of my reflection in the full-length mirror against the wall and stop. All I see is Nova—long wavy dishwater blonde hair, brown eyes that sort of fade away without makeup on, and my trademark gray t-shirt and jeans. *What would Nora look like?* I wonder. I tuck the clothes under my arm and head back to the "Grooming" department.

The barber is a gruff looking man with liver-spotted leathery skin and a square jaw. He's sweeping up around his barber chair. "How much for a haircut?" I ask timidly.

He sizes me up and doesn't answer for what feels like an eternity. "I ain't no fancy hairdresser," he says and goes back to his sweeping.

"I just need a basic cut, that's all. My hair is too long. Nothing fancy," I assure him.

49

He thinks about it a moment and is still looking at my hair when he asks, "Ten bucks sound fair?"

"Yes, sir," I say, thinking that sounds like something Nora would say. *I bet she'd be polite like that.*

No wash, dry, or style…five minutes later, just eight inches cut off of my hair in a straight blunt bob. My hair barely grazes my shoulders now and hangs almost stick straight. *I guess the waves were in the length*, I think as I look down at the veritable mountain of hair beneath me on the floor. I look up into the mirror and take in my reflection. "This is good," I tell him.

"Thank you."

It's good, but not good enough. I still look too much like Nova. I pay him in cash and collect my pile of clothes to purchase.

In the center of the store, I see a few rows of shelves that I haven't yet explored. I head over and find that my hunch was right— personal care items, including a limited selection of cosmetics. I grab an eye-liner pencil in brown, a tube of mascara, and a warm coral colored lipstick. Usually, my makeup routine includes some foundation, a little blush, and Chapstick. *Time to mix it up. Still, though, that isn't enough.*

Out of the corner of my eye, I notice a few boxes of at-home hair dye. I grab the one that says "Color in under 10 minutes" and head for the register. The gal behind the cash register has been watching me carefully since I left the barber's station. As I approach, she greets me.

"Hi, there. Find everything you need, Hun?"

"I did. Thank you," I say.

"I saw you this morning at the café. How long you been workin' there?" she asks.

"Today was my first day," I tell her.

"Oh, good. I know Kate has been needin' to hire someone for a while now. So what's your story? You new around here?"

I know she is just trying to be polite, but I'm instantly annoyed by the question. I need a back story, pronto.

"Yep. Just getting settled," I say, hoping that will suffice. I hand her my credit card and anxiously drum my fingers on the counter top.

"Well, I'm Crissy. If you need anything, you just let me know," she says. She hands me my card and my items and I practically run for the door.

"Hey!" she calls after me. I stop and turn. "I didn't get your name, Hun," she says.

"Nov...um, Nora. Thanks again!" I say and scoot out the door before she can ask any more questions.

* * * * *

Back in my room, I dump the contents of my shopping bag onto the bed and grab the hair dye. *My shift starts in ninety minutes. That should be plenty of time.* I open it up and read the instructions on the box. "Chocolate Brown" it says. All I have to do is pour the little bottle into the big bottle, shake, and then shampoo it in. Easy enough.

While I'm waiting, I put on my new makeup. The eyeliner makes me look a bit like Cleopatra. I wipe it off and try again. After ten minutes, I rinse out the color and blow dry my hair. It feels so short. *This will take some getting used to.* I slip into my uniform dress and tie the sash in a neat bow at my back and stop at the mirror to see the finished product. *Wow. Now I don't look like me. This should do nicely.*

"Hello, Nora," I say to my reflection with a smile before heading out the door to work. I practically float across the street to the diner. I feel so free all of a sudden. Being Nora is such a wonderful rush. Nora isn't a runaway; she's home. Nora didn't abandon her mother without a word. In fact, she doesn't even have parents. Yeah, Nora is an orphan, just like Kate. No one is depending on her or waiting for her call. I feel like a thousand-pound weight has been lifted off my shoulders. Once again, I nearly walk right into the guy with the guitar, sitting on the curb by the front door.

"Oh, I'm sorry. I didn't see you there," I say. I had been sort of rude to him earlier, but I feel like Nora would be more sociable.

"Clearly," he says sarcastically.

"Nora," I say, offering him a handshake. "It's nice to meet you," I continue.

"Evan," he says, not returning the gesture. He looks down and starts humming a familiar melody while strumming his guitar.

Rude.

I head into the café where Kate greets me with a wide grin. "Nora!" she exclaims. "Wow! I like your hair! Going dark for fall, huh?"

"Oh, right. Yeah, I guess so. Thanks," I say. Funny, I had already forgotten that I look different than I did this morning. Being Nova is just too complicated right now.

"Hey, come into the back office real quick so we can do your paperwork," Kate instructs.

Another complication. I follow her reluctantly into the kitchen. There is a small windowless room tucked into a corner behind the large walk-in fridge. A desktop is propped up on two slim filing cabinets. Kate sits down in a rolling chair and spins herself around twice before flashing me her bright smile. This is the first time I've really seen her act like a kid. She's had to grow up far too fast.

In front of her is a manila folder. The tab on the top of it says "New Hires" in sloppy faded cursive. She pulls out a form that says "Payroll" at the top in bold lettering. She reaches for her pen and starts filling in the name section.

"Nora with an H?" she asks.

"No, but—"

"What's your last name?" she asks.

"Oh, it's Dan...bert." *Crap,* I think. *I forgot to give Nora a last name. Danbert. Too close to Daniels. Dumb. Questions are a bad idea.*

"Age?" she asks, sounding extra professional.

I bite my tongue, literally, to keep from telling her. I can't say seventeen. I don't even know if I'm old enough to get a job without a work permit. She looks up from the paperwork expectantly.

"Eh-eh-eighteen," I stutter like an idiot. "Actually," I begin, "is there any way we can sort of skip this part?"

Kate thinks about my request for a moment. "You mean, like, pay you under the table?" she asks.

"Yes, exactly. See, I don't have a bank account or anything right now, so cash would be easier until I can get settled in and all." That was true. Nora does not have a bank account. Nora doesn't have much of anything for that matter.

"Sure, Nora, if it's easier for you."

"Thank you." I smile with relief. "So, where do you want me this evening, boss?" I ask.

Kate giggles at the thought of being a boss. "Well, why don't you take the tables in the back and cover the bar, and I'll take the front dining room. Sound good?"

"Works for me," I say.

Hank peeks his head around the corner. "Show's on, ladies," he tells us.

It's just after 6:00 p.m. We head out into the café as the tables begin to fill up, just like clockwork. I can't help but smile. This new routine already feels natural, yet without the burdens of Nova's life. I roll my shoulders back and stand a little taller, settling in to Nora's easier posture.

Sioux Falls, August 30

*I*t's Monday, and Pearl's Diner is closed just like it has been every Monday since 1962 when Kate's grandmother opened the place. Her grandfather had purchased the land with the intention of opening up an auto repair shop, but with the Vietnam war came a new plan. Pearl was left to her own devices, and like a good American woman, she had no intention of letting the proverbial home fires burn out. Kate felt the same way about the café. She said it gave her purpose when her parents passed away to know that she had a responsibility to this place.

Kate has invited me to meet her at the café for breakfast. The closed sign suction-cupped to the inside of the front window is just a simple black text on white. It seems more efficient than a light-up sign to me. No bulbs to replace. As I near the front door, I can see that there are several occupied tables in the dining room. For a moment, I freeze in panic. It is Monday, right? I could have sworn she said we were closed on Monday. *I need to get a calendar. Oh wait, I can see Kate now.* She's in jeans and a T-shirt. I pull the door open and stop in the entryway.

"Say hello to Nora, everyone!" Kate says.

"Hello, Nora," say the patrons with varied enthusiasm.

I feel my cheeks heat up as a blush rises from somewhere deep within the pit of my stomach. "Um, hi," is all I can muster. Real eloquent.

"Have a seat," Kate says, motioning to a stool at the end of the bar.

There is a guy sitting at the stool next to mine with his back turned. He's tall and muscular and immediately has every bit of my attention. Something about him feels instantly familiar, like the hum of the particular charge of electricity that runs through the lamp you've had on your bedside table for years. The sound you can't hear until one day, the light burns out and the absence of it seems deafening. I feel compelled to reach out and touch him, but I fear that the energy might cause me to spontaneously combust. I regain enough control over my thoughts to wonder whether or not he can feel it too. He starts to turn toward me.

"Nora." Somewhere in the distance, someone is saying my name. "Nora?" Kate grabs my hand and snaps me out of my trance prematurely. I grimace.

"Geez, Louise! Someone hasn't had her coffee yet!" Kate jokes

"Sorry," I say.

"Oh gosh, I was just giving you a hard time!" she says. "Have you met Evan?"

"We met yesterday," says the guy next to me.

I turn my head toward him slowly, letting my eyes follow last. *Evan. The guy from the curb, right? Grifter, street musician, hobo? Right. Evan with the eyes.*

As our eyes meet, I'm swept away at sea. His eyes are a storm cloud threatening to capsize my vessel, and I'm helpless against its power. The waves beneath me rise suddenly, fighting to be heard beneath the thundering sky. His eyes. The flecks of green reflecting the sea, the glints of gold are the rays of the sun itself sent from the heavens to absolve the storm. I am but a meek observer in this violent battle between nature's great forces.

"Nora? Nora! Can you hear me?"

Why is Kate yelling at me? I'm flat on my back and disoriented.

"Oh my gosh, I think she fainted! Nora! Are you okay?"

"I think so," I say. My ankle hurts again. I must have twisted it in the fall. I try to get up and collapse again as soon as I try to put weight on it. Evan and Kate each grab an arm and help raise me back on to my stool. I am mortified.

"You took quite a spill there," Evan observes.

I can't bring myself to look at him. "I'm f-f-fine. I think I just need to eat something," I lie.

"Well, you're in luck!" Kate chirps. "It's a Monday tradition. I cook...sort of badly and invite Evan and his houseguests to come and keep me company. No charge, of course. I couldn't charge for dry eggs and burnt toast," she says, blushing. "I guess the cooking gene skipped a generation." She shrugs.

I look around the café, curious about what she meant by Evan's houseguests, still doing everything in my power to avoid his gaze. Aside from the three of us, there are six adults and one child seated in the room. All eyes are on me. I guess I really made a spectacle of myself.

I nod a greeting to the two men seated at the table nearest me. Both smile. One has absolutely no visible teeth. I flinch. I hope that my visceral reaction wasn't offensive. Both men are wearing stocking caps and ill-fitting clothing in various stages of disarray. The table to their left is occupied by three men that I could describe similarly, all with unkempt hair and wrinkled clothing, but three warm smiles just the same.

At the third table, an elderly man sits staring blankly. From this angle, it looks as though his focus is fixed on something in the distance, just inches above the head of the little girl who sits in front of him. She is staring at him in wonder. There is something else in her expression but I can't tell if it's layered with fear or empathy. Either would make her wise beyond her years, though, to be sure. She can't be a day over eight.

The elderly man is wearing denim overalls that are about four inches too short on his spindly legs. He is missing a sock. The little girl's gaze is now fixed on me. She has long wavy dishwater blonde hair with straight bluntly cut bangs that almost reach her eyelids. Big almond shaped eyes the color of rich milk chocolate peer up at me, suspiciously making her look cartoonlike. Her right cheek is smudged with three streaks of strawberry jam to match the three sticky fingers she is now using to nervously twirl the ends of her hair. I wave at her and she quickly looks down at her plate. I can't help but feel drawn to her. Maybe it's narcissism, considering she looks like a carbon copy of me…well, of Nova at that age. Regardless, she seems like she is looking for the courage to ask for help.

I walk over to her and kneel down. "Hello. I'm Nora. What's your name?"

She sizes me up from head to toe before answering. "Hi, I'm Annabelle. Pleased to meet you," she says and offers me a sticky handshake. I oblige.

"Would you care to join us?" she asks.

Her speech is eerily perfect. It's startling to hear such advanced social graces from the lips of a child. She sounds more like an English professor on helium than a kindergartener.

I sit down between Annabelle and the old man. He hasn't even blinked during our interaction.

"Are you here alone?" I ask.

"Of course not!" She giggles, shaking her head at me. "I'm here with Grandpa."

She points to the spacey old man to my right. *Yikes.*

"Oh, I didn't realize," I start. "Will your parents be joining us as well?"

"My parents are in heaven now," says Annabelle sadly.

"I'm so sorry," I say.

"It's okay," she says. "They will show Kate's parents around. Plus, Evan's parents are there too!" Her face lights up at the thought of it. "I miss them, but I'm happy that I could stay here with my grandpa. He'd be so lonely without me," she explains and looks at him lovingly.

Wow. Sioux Falls, the city of orphans. My heart aches as I watch Annabelle.

She reaches her fork across the table and feeds her grandfather a bite of cold eggs. He chews slowly with his mouth open, eyes still glazed over and blank.

"Grandpa can't stay in the care center anymore, but we get to live at Evan's house," she tells me.

I turn to follow her gaze and see Evan sitting and laughing with the toothless man at the front table. "Do you all live with Evan?" I ask.

"Sometimes," she says, with no further explanation. "Do you like wolves?" she says, giggling at my new t-shirt.

I can't help but laugh.

Kate trots up beside me and sets down a steaming plate of scrambled eggs and toast. It looks like she tried to hide the burnt surface of the toast by smothering it in strawberry preserves. "Breakfast is served!" she says cheerily. She fills my coffee cup and makes a lap around the café to give refills.

Annabelle and I chat through breakfast. She tells me how she loves to draw and that she can't wait to go back to school. She tells me how Evan has helped her enroll in the local elementary school and promised to take her shopping for some new crayons before her first day. She left school the day of her parents' accident and didn't return. "Grandpa needed me," she explains.

Kate filled me in on the rest. For the first few weeks, she had stayed in her grandfather's room at the assisted living center. I'm guessing that her parents had been paying the bill. Once the money ran out, the center had no choice but to release both he and Annabelle. Within a few days, they had found their way to the truck stop. It was a place they could shower and find shelter to sleep under where they wouldn't be noticed. She had met Evan late in the spring when her curiosity had gotten the best of her and she'd ventured across the street to watch him play his guitar.

"I have to help Evan with the chores. He needs me," she says proudly.

"So you both live with him now?" I ask.

"Yep!" she says happily. "We take care of everyone."

Such an old little soul. I want to be like Annabelle when I grow up, I think to myself. I hear a horn honk outside and turn my attention to the window. A white utility van is parked in the lot with the engine running.

Annabelle bounces out of her chair and around the table to help her grandfather navigate his way to the door. The rest of the men in the café follow suit. Kate has stationed herself next to the door to give hugs to each of the men as they leave. Though a couple of them look uncomfortable doing so, no one would dare turn her down. What she lacks in age and stature, she makes up for in gumption and in heart.

I stand next to Kate, offering a smile and a wave as each "houseguest" says farewell and heads to the van. Once everyone is loaded, Evan hops out of the driver's seat and comes in to say his goodbyes, with Annabelle in tow.

"We're at capacity," Evan explains to Kate. "Would you mind dropping her by the house? We weren't expecting to see Jerry today."

"Not at all," Kate says.

Annabelle looks disappointed.

"I could use another set of hands around here to help pack up the day-olds," Kate adds.

Annabelle perks up immediately at the notion of being useful. "Okay!" she chirps.

Kate stands on her tiptoes and leans in to give Evan a hug. When she releases him, he looks at me hesitantly. I am at a loss. I start to offer him an awkward high-five. Just before our hands meet, it occurs to me that physical contact might not be the best idea after what had happened earlier. Too late. Before the thought can even fully register, I feel a jolt of electricity travel through my fingers, up my arm, and straight to my heart. The impact of the charge knocks me off my feet and I'm once again flat on my back.

In an instant, Evan is with me. He caught my head just before I hit the ground and is kneeling beside me, cradling my face in his strong hands. I'm blinking tears back from my eyes as I stare into his. He locks my gaze, unblinking. Unwavering. No one has ever looked at me so...searchingly. All my life, I have felt like people look past me, even right through me as though I'm invisible. Right here, in this moment, it's like I'm being seen for the first time.

"Nora!" Kate demands. "What is with you today? You're going to give me a heart attack!"

Reluctantly, I look at her, breaking the spell that Evan has cast on me. "I'm fine," I say. "Just a klutz, I guess." I look back up at Evan, my head still resting on his arm. "Thank you," I say.

We lock eyes for another moment. He's still searching for something. I can feel it. I roll over quickly onto my knees and stand up, hanging onto the doorframe for support. Annabelle is at my side.

"I'll take care of her," she says, pushing Evan toward the door.

He smiles at her warmly. "Looks like everything is under control then," he says with a nod at Kate and heads to the idling van.

* * * * *

Kate, Annabelle, and I make quick work of tidying up the café. The three of us take comfort in the silent bond we've forged. Three souls cut from the same cloth. In many ways, I feel more a part of a family in the company of these near-strangers than I have in all my life. Both girls, though chronologically younger than I am, have been through more than most will in a long lifetime. Both so strong; both cloaking their heartbreak behind a wall of unabashed optimism and hope, ever forward facing. The potential for heartache is too likely in the rearview. Their hope is the tie that binds. Kate, so proud and self-sufficient. Annabelle, such loyalty to put family above all else, absolutely.

I flinch when I think about it, literally as though I'm dodging a swift backhand from some unseen disciplinarian. Don't get me wrong. I don't mean that metaphorically. When Annabelle talks about the things she's done to ensure that she and her grandfather aren't separated, my thoughts wander to my mother. The last time I thought of her, Annabelle had said, "He may not know me now, but that doesn't change how much I love him. I know he would take care of me if he could, but he can't right now."

I felt a weight in the pit of my stomach and crouched over at the sensation. The air had changed around me in that moment. Colder, more alive somehow. In my peripheral vision, I could have sworn I saw an arm…a hand aiming to slap me like the spoiled child I seemed in comparison to Annabelle's selfless example. Had I not been hunched over, I knew with certainty that I would have been left with the puffy red finger marks of a hearty and much deserved backhanding. I saw no one, but that didn't change the truth of it.

Thank God for Nora. Being Nova would have made it impossible to look either Annabelle or Kate in the eyes. Nova was unworthy of such honorable company. So, I stay busy and try not to think about it too much. I'm cleaning the table tops a second time, just in case I missed a spot. Kate gathers the day-old baked goods and wraps them up to take to Evan.

"Well, I'm going to run Annabelle home," Kate says. "Go enjoy your day off!"

"I can take her for you," I say with more than a little bit of desperation in my voice. I have no car, but I'm not ready to be alone with my thoughts. Problematically, I'm not sure I would be alone, entirely…a thought I *really* don't want to be left with.

Kate is watching me with empathy in her eyes. She can see that I need her to keep me occupied. Puzzled, she says, "Okay," and hands me her keys. "Annabelle can show you the way."

"I know how! C'mon!" says Annabelle as she slings the plastic bag of day-olds over her shoulder like it's weightless. She's a sturdy little thing. She leads the way as we head out to Kate's royal blue 1980-something Pontiac Firebird. I'm guessing it had belonged to her father as I note the "Gone Fishin'" bumper sticker. The back end of the car is coated in a thick layer of mud. I wonder sadly if he left it that way and Kate hadn't had the heart to wash it. Still, I take great satisfaction in the powerful rumble of the engine as I turn the key in the ignition and shift it into gear. I've never driven a car with this much muscle under the hood.

As I peel out of the parking lot, Annabelle reaches to click her seatbelt and gives me a nervous sideways glance.

"Hang on tight!" I call to her over the surge of power I just fed through the heavy gas pedal beneath my foot.

To my utter delight, the drive to Evan's house takes us a good twenty minutes. By the time we turn on to Cliff Avenue, a white knuckled Annabelle looks as though she's aged about ten years. I reluctantly slow down as we enter the neighborhood and can't help but marvel at the enormous houses that line the beautifully land-scaped street.

"It's that one on the right," she says, pointing to the largest home on the block. Ever so faintly, I hear someone whistle, obviously impressed. Perhaps just over my right shoulder. Perhaps inside my own head. I look around us in the car, startled.

"Did you hear that?"

"Hear what?" Annabelle asks.

"Never mind."

I pull into the sloping driveway next to Evan's van. I can see three stories of windows stretching out above us. The house is white and expansive, a mansion in the traditional sense. It's classic American architecture and looks simultaneously intimidating and inviting.

The minute I turn off the engine, Annabelle has hopped out of the car in obvious relief. She laboriously lugs the bag of baked goods out behind her without even thinking of asking for my help. I bet it wouldn't even cross her mind. Once again, I am in awe of this little girl. As I follow her up the limestone staircase to the front door, I reach for the bag and take it from her shoulder. She turns around with a scowl.

"Hey!" she scolds. "I can do it!"

"I know you can," I say simply and wait for her to let go.

She looks at me for a few seconds and then I see her make the decision to let me in. To trust me. To trust Nora, rather. To say I feel vulnerable under her inquisitive gaze would be a crude understatement. I find myself afraid that she can read my thoughts…learn my secrets. What's more, I find that I care very deeply what this little girl thinks of me.

"Are you going to keep your guest out there all day?" Evan asks. He had been watching our exchange from the front door with interest.

"No!" Annabelle snorts a laugh at the absurd thought of it.

Ah, the literal mind of a child. I love every minute of it.

She runs up the last few stairs and into the house in a blur, still giggling under her breath. I follow, trying to avoid eye contact with Evan until the last possible second. He holds the door open wide.

"After you," he says, taking the bag of food from me. His fingers brush mine for just a fraction of an instant and my stomach flutters. I can't tell if the butterflies are caused by the physical contact or the dual acts of chivalry. Both maybe.

I step into the marble entryway and lose my breath at the beauty of the sitting room before me. It looks like something out of a magazine. It's as though every last detail has been planned, edited, revised, and made to look picture perfect. A large plush cream colored sofa sits against the wall beneath a stunning realistic painting of a forest scene in autumn. An ornately designed cherry wood coffee table sits on an oriental rug in front of it. The rug itself must be worth more than all of the furniture in our house in Ocean Park combined. *Who is this guy?* I'm baffled, and I'm sure he can tell. I glance at Evan and catch him shyly looking down at his shoes.

"I'm just going to put this down in the kitchen," he says and quickly retreats.

I'm left alone to explore. Normally, I would have waited politely in the entryway for him to return, just on ceremony. In this case, though, I don't even think twice about whether or not to snoop. My curiosity gets the better of me. There are two ways out of the room other than the front door. To the left, after Evan, or straight ahead down the long hallway. I head forward. The hall is lined with doors. I stop at the first one I come to on the right, expecting more of the highbrow decor I'd seen in the formal sitting room.

To my surprise, I find a modest bedroom, maybe a small den. A twin bed sits alone to my right. The mattress is bare and worn. Not a single other piece of furniture. *Peculiar.* I close the door and move on to the next.

The second door only opens a foot or so before it stops on something. I peek my head around it and see that there is an occupied sleeping bag on the floor. I can't tell who is inside, but I am relieved at the sound of light snoring that my intrusion did not wake him. The room is dark. It looks like a blanket has been tacked up over the window, but I hear the muffled sounds of another sleeping body somewhere near the back of the room. As quietly as I can, I pull the door shut and move down the hallway.

There is an opening to my left. I can hear Evan and Annabelle discussing what to make for dinner later. I hurry past, unnoticed. The next door is on my left. I open it more carefully this time. Bathroom.

I'm not sure if I'm hearing a TV in the background or if it's my own subconscious playing tricks on me, but I keep hearing music. Fearing that my snooping time may be running short, I head to the last door on the right. The door is open a few inches, so I peek in. Unoccupied. I push the door open and start humming the *Mission Impossible* theme song out loud along with…well, wherever I'm hearing it.

Bunk beds, a set on each side of the room. A double bed on the bottom with a ladder up to a twin bed on top. Both bottoms and one top look slept in. The top bunk on the left just has a set of white sheets on it. No pillow. There are several piles of what look like personal belongings around the room. It smells like feet and cheese in here. Cheesy feet. *Gross!* Impulsively, I run to the back of the room and open the window a few inches before swiftly exiting. I'm careful to leave the door open just as I found it.

At the end of the hallway is a staircase leading to the upper floors. I tiptoe up the first short flight which veers off to a landing on the left at a single door. I open it quickly, tuck inside, and close it behind me. This room is enormous! It must be the size of the other rooms I've seen put together. Again, it's modestly furnished. A king-sized bed is centered on the main wall with a door on each side of it. One door leads to an elaborate master bathroom. The other, a walk-in closet large enough to fit another couple of sets of bunk beds. In the corner at the front of the room, there is a single collapsible cot in army green. It has a worn looking brown comforter on it and an equally raggedy pillow. I recognize Evan's sweatshirt laying at the end of the cot.

The sound of a groan startles me. I stifle a yell just in time. My heart is beating like the wings of a hummingbird. Someone is in the bed…awake. I back out of the room as quietly as anyone has ever moved in the history of the world. No joke. When I am out of the room, I turn and head down the stairs in a dead sprint. I pass the bathroom and am planning to slow down before the opening to the dining room, but instead, the toe of my shoe catches on the rug and I land hard on my face.

As I look up, I see a well-worn pair of men's running shoes looking back at me.

"We have to stop meeting this way," Evan says.

Before I can protest, he has me by the hand and is helping me to my feet. I feel my body temperature rise on contact. I find it utterly impossible to keep my center of gravity when he is touching me. I find it impossible to want to. I realize that I have been hoping for this, rather than dreading it. Something in me has shifted. When he is near me, I lose all reason. I feel as though the rotation of the earth might be enough to spin me off into another dimension. I'm trying to collect my thoughts when I realize I'm on my feet, if only because of his steadying hold on me.

He's watching me now, just patiently waiting for me to collect myself. I dare to look him in the eyes. I decide to indulge in a good long gaze into these mysterious green windows into his soul. I'm tired of fighting the urge. So close to him with his arms around me, I feel somehow complete. He smells like fresh cut grass and clean linen. I sigh audibly and feel myself relax into his hold. As he leans in closer, I close my eyes in anticipation of the inevitable first kiss. My body is aching for it. He must feel the same. He reaches his right hand along the side of my face, gently tucking my hair behind my ear.

"Looks like you took out part of the rug," he says with a chuckle as he pulls a tuft of carpet fibers from the side of my face and lets me go.

Annabelle is beside him with the giggles. *Crap. I must look ridiculous.* I shiver involuntarily at the abrupt lack of Evan's warmth. I try to laugh with them in a fruitless attempt to hide my humiliation.

"Well, I'd better get back. I guess I'll see you guys around," I say, fleeing the scene.

* * * * *

Back in the car and on the road, I try to sort out what just happened.

"Did I imagine it?" I ask aloud.

"*No way, honey,*" says the voice that I've been ignoring.

Note to self: silence is bad. I turn up the classic rock station on the radio and sing at the top of my lungs along with Tom Petty as I push the speed limit down the I90 on-ramp. "And I'm *freeeeeeeeeee! Free fallin'!*"

Jeanette

Ocean Park, Washington, August 31

*J*eanette Daniels hadn't slept in days. She'd prayed to every God she could think of that her daughter was somewhere safe and that this was all just some big misunderstanding. Still, though, when the mail arrived, she almost couldn't believe her eyes. Special priority delivery. A letter, no return label, postmarked from Connecticut, addressed to her. A poem, written almost in riddles, had somehow brought her immense comfort. Maybe it was that she was so desperate for hope she would have believed anything. Maybe on some level, she had been expecting this very letter.

She didn't show the letter to anyone. She went back to work. She stopped her frequent phone calls to the local authorities and fell back into her routine. Though she avoided any questions about the whereabouts of Nova, she managed to make cheerful conversation with her regulars. After work, she made up the bed in the spare bedroom.

Los Angeles, California, 2000 / Ocean Park, Washington, 2004

*J*eanette never had the heart to tell her daughter the harsh truth about her father. As much as he loved Nova, the control that his drug addiction had over him was stronger. To this day, it still amazed Jeanette just how quickly he had changed from the charming and magnetic band front-man that swept her off her feet with promises of a fairy-tale life. She wasn't sure if it was her cynicism from growing up as a child of divorced parents herself or her intuition that kept her from accepting his repeated marriage proposals. "What's the rush?" she'd ask him with a wink. That kept the conversation at bay for a month or so; but without fail, he'd ask again.

Each time he proposed to Jeanette, he'd concoct a romantic gesture, somehow more grand and over-the-top than the last. The first proposal was always her favorite. The most honest. He had spent the entire day in the kitchen, trying his best to make all of her favorite foods—Capresé salad, butternut squash ravioli, and key lime pie. The unfortunate outcome certainly did not do justice to the effort he put in.

He had been trembling as he fumbled with the ring box over the candlelit table. His sweaty palms fought him every step of the way. He clumsily got down on one knee, taking the table cloth and the inedible meal with him. With red wine dripping from his collar, he stuttered the words "M-m-marry me." More of a statement than a question. Maybe if he'd asked, things would have turned out differently. Maybe not.

When she gracefully deflected, it only piqued his interest in her further. To prove how serious he was, he took a job in sales and traded in his guitar for suits and ties. As a compromise, she agreed to move in with him. He bought them a ranch-style stucco-sided house in the valley. "Perfect for a family," he'd said, idealistically.

In the beginning, life together was wonderful. Easy. She really did love him. Occasionally, Jeanette would delicately broach the subject of his "recreational" drug use. He assured her he had it under control. "Just with the guys from the office," he'd say.

She knew better. She had been finding his little hiding places all over the house for months. She opened up a savings account and started to tuck away money.

After Nova was born, he began to use extreme tactics for his proposals to her. At first, it was a game to him. A sky writer, on stage at the Viper Room during a performance by her favorite band, the Jumbo Tron at an LA Lakers game, two plane tickets to Paris—each attempt more extravagant than the last, and all with the same presumptuous demand: "Marry me." Those words had progressed from sweet sentiment to desperation…to rage.

Even now, the sound of those words could make her cringe. He no longer just wanted to marry her. It was more than that. The need to own her, to possess her, had consumed him.

Shortly after he lost his job, the bank foreclosed on their home. Afraid for her safety and that of her daughter, she made quiet preparations and waited until the timing was right. One night in the spring, she waited for him to come to bed and then turned out the light. Without daring to move, she held her breath until he fell into a deep sleep. Jeanette quickly packed what belongings she could fit into her small Datsun, noiselessly carried her drowsy toddler to the car, shifted into neutral, and let the car roll silently down the road away from him.

She cashed out all of her savings and applied for a small business loan. Knowing of Jeanette's passion for baking, a family friend had suggested the old café. Though she had never been to the Pacific Northwest before, the idea of some sea air and a fresh start sounded perfect. The Long Beach peninsula looked so picturesque in her research, and she longed to raise her daughter in a small town without all the complications that life in Los Angeles brought with it. She found a small cottage for rent just three blocks west of the café and settled in. It took the better part of six months and every dollar she could scrape up to finish the renovations. The day Jeanette's Café celebrated its grand opening was the first day of the rest of her life.

* * * * *

After Jeanette left him, Nova's father pooled together what resources he had and bought an old tour bus. Now claiming to be a Christian, he reasoned that it had been God's plan for him all along. He never had the courage to follow his dream of playing music, and now the decision had been made for him. He had nothing left to lose. He reached out to his old bandmates and took the show on the road. Unfortunately, they never found their audience.

After a few years, the guys in the band headed home to their families and left Nova's father to his own devices. He died that autumn alone. His body was discovered some time later, guitar still clutched in hand. "An accidental overdose," they'd said when they called Jeanette to inform his next of kin.

She hung up without a word. As a mother, one loses the luxury of indulging in the emotional instant gratification that a nonparent takes for granted. You don't get to fall apart. Nova had been coloring at her little table in the kitchen when the call came in. Jeanette was afraid to breathe for fear she would break down. She called a babysitter and sat coloring with her daughter while she waited an unbearable twenty minutes.

Jeanette gave Nova a kiss and got in the Datsun. Dry eyed, she drove as fast as she could to Ledbetter State Park at the northernmost tip of the peninsula. Normally, she took this drive leisurely to marvel at the beauty of it all—the trees that line the road reach across to one another, treetops touching to create a sort of green tunnel. There was magic in these woods.

She abandoned her car in the parking lot, driver's door left ajar, headlights on, creating eerie tunnels of white light that cut into the lush forest. She ran down the path and across the rickety wooden bridge, straight into the water. Ankle deep in the icy sea, she fell to her knees and sobbed. She cried for the man that he could have been, the man that she had pictured a future with—sharp-dressed and charismatic with the world at his fingertips, the man that seemed too good to be true.

She cried for the life they never had together. She cried because she felt relief, but the guilt over being relieved overwhelmed her. If she'd been holding her breath in worry that he would show up and disturb their daughter's simple life, she let it out. Then she cried for a world that no longer contained the great love of her life. She cried for the hole in her heart left behind as any future hope of reuniting their family disappeared. Last, she cried for Nova. She decided in that moment never to tell her daughter the truth. The world was cruel. Jeanette knew that better than most. Nova didn't need to know. Not yet.

Nova was only seven when Jeanette told her that her father had died in a car accident.

Nova

Sioux Falls, August 31

*L*ying awake, listening to the sounds of the big rigs starting up and navigating their way out of the narrow motel parking lot, I can't stop thinking about Evan. My mind is racing. *Who is he? Why can't I stay on my feet when he's around?* My alarm is set to go off any minute. I have to open the diner this morning and I can't imagine I'll be lucky enough to avoid him completely. He'll be sitting outside in the sun, singing like a friggin' angel, while do-gooding members of the community who happen to be "in the know" come by to give him copious amounts of money thinly veiled as a tip. All of which he'll use to give back to those in need. *Ugh. Why does he have to be so perfect? So annoying!*

My alarm goes off and I'm about to fall out of my bed. This whole double-life thing really has me on edge. *I have to get Evan out of my head. I can't actually have a relationship with him. The minute he asks me a question about my life, I would totally spill every single detail to him. I just know it.* I head to the sink and take a long look at my… well, Nora's face in the mirror, medium brown hair and all. "Stay as far away from him as possible," I tell myself aloud.

I take a quick shower, dress in my uniform, and am out the door just a few minutes before 6:00 a.m. I see Hank's car in the parking lot already. *Hmm. That's odd. I thought I was opening up this morning on my own.* I can see lights on upstairs in Kate's apartment too. I swear that girl never sleeps.

I approach the door and pause to stare just a little bit too long at the spot on the curb where Evan usually sits. I let out a long sigh. As I reach for the front door, I see Kate's curious eyes peering at me through the glass. She opens the door abruptly.

"Good morning, Nora. I'm glad you're here," she says. "We need to talk."

Hank is leaning against the end of the bar with his arms folded, regarding me with a stern expression.

Oh crap! He knows. They know, don't they? How can they know? I've been so careful! I haven't told anyone the truth. I haven't even used my credit card…oh wait. Oh my God! I did use it! What was I thinking? I used it at the truck stop to buy hair dye and supplies. Classic rookie mistake! How could I be so careless? By now, the cops will have traced my card and found out what I bought. They'll know I have a new hair color and exactly where to find me. How could I be so stupid?

I am panicking. I can feel my cheeks flushing and I'm starting to sweat. *Oh, poor Kate. What must she think of me?*

"Do you mind sitting down?" she asks. "Hank'll pour you some coffee."

Right on cue, Hank brings over a fresh pot of coffee as I sit down at the four-seater in the front window. My heart is pounding in my ears. I feel like I might faint.

"Why didn't you tell me, Nora?" Kate asks as she sits down in front of me. "Don't you know by now that you can trust me?"

She sounds rueful. "I didn't know how to tell you," I say weakly.

"Well, Hank saw you," she says.

"I didn't mean to rat you out," Hank offered.

"Saw me? I don't know what to s-s-say," I stammer.

"Just say you'll move in with me. At least for a while," says Kate.

"Wait, what?"

"Seriously, Nora. You can't live in the truck stop! And don't try to deny it. Hank saw you going to your room last night. We know you're staying there. I just don't know why you wouldn't tell me that. After all you've done for me!"

She sounds genuinely hurt. "Honestly? I haven't really thought about it much," I say truthfully. "I haven't been in town long and have been so focused on the diner. I guess I haven't gotten around to finding a place—"

"Well you're staying here with me and that's the end of it," she says with authority.

"I couldn't—"

"You can and you will!"

"Better listen to her. She's stubborn just like her mother. No sense in arguin'," Hank advises.

"He's right," she says with a wink. "I have an extra room anyway. It's small, but it has a bed and I can make it up for you."

I sit silently, looking back and forth between them. They are both looking at me in anticipation. They both care. I feel so unworthy. This charade isn't just about me anymore. Not only is my mother most likely inconsolable by now thinking the worst…now Kate and Hank are involved. They trust me. I don't know what to say. I feel the urge to come clean and tell them everything. That I'm a runaway. That I'm selfish. That I'm a coward. That I don't deserve their trust or their generosity. I want to tell them why I lied…but I can't. I'm not even sure I know why myself.

"Nora? You okay?" Kate asks.

Nora. That's right, this is Nora we're talking about. Nora didn't lie. Nora doesn't have a past. Nora doesn't have a family.

"Sorry," I say, "I don't know what to say."

"Say you'll stay," she says.

"I'll stay. Thank you."

"Yay!" Kate shouts. "Okay, then, it's settled. I'll help you move your things over after lunch." She starts heading toward the kitchen. "I'm gonna go get your room ready!" she yells behind her.

Hank and I sit in silence, listening to her hurried footsteps up the stairs. I can tell that he's about to ask me something, but the oven timer beeps loudly in the nick of time. *Saved by the bell!*

"That'll be the biscuits," he says and turns away. He stops in the doorway and looks back at me thoughtfully.

I have a feeling that this conversation isn't over. I grab a clean towel and start wiping down the tables. Our early bird customers will start arriving any minute. With a sold out motel across the street, it'll be another busy morning. As I look out the window, it starts to rain. First a drizzle, then hard and steady as the sky turns from a pale gray to the color of fresh asphalt. This is certainly not good weather for a street musician. I smile to myself and get back to work.

Nova

Sioux Falls, September 6th

More than a week has passed since I moved out of the truck stop. Living with Kate is easy. We've settled into a routine that it feels like we've been in forever. We stay up late, talking like I imagine sisters would. We take comfort in the companionship of one another, both grateful not to be alone. We have an unspoken agreement not to talk about things in the past, and that suits us both just fine.

Working in the diner has been a welcome distraction. We've been so busy that there isn't time for much else. It's been raining all week, and the truck stop across the street has been packed every night. The "No Vacancy" sign above the motel casts an amber glow into my bedroom window. I lay in my twin bed, waiting for sleep to come. I can hear Kate snoring ever so softly in the next room.

Just like every night, my thoughts wander to Evan. I haven't seen him all week. In the beginning, I was relieved. I've had enough embarrassing moments in his presence to last me a lifetime. After the first couple of days, though, I found myself eagerly looking toward the door every time it opened, hoping to see him.

By yesterday, I had started to worry. I know I could ask Kate about him, but I don't want her to know that I want to know. She would see right through me. She'd immediately start to ask questions, and then I wouldn't be able to keep myself from telling her everything. That there is something about him that I can't explain. Like I have known him forever or like he's my soul mate or something. I'd tell her that, even though I barely know him, I miss him. I might love him. That would make it all too real...not to mention it would make me sound completely bonkers.

Besides, it doesn't matter anyway. Nora doesn't have a past, so how can she build a future with Evan? A future built on barely believable lies will never work.

My thoughts are interrupted by the song in my head. I've been hearing it every night lately—the song my father used to sing to me at bedtime when I was a little girl. He didn't know any lullabies, so he just sang me his favorite song—"Every Breath You Take" by The Police. He idolized Sting, so he wanted to make sure I grew up with what he called "a healthy appreciation" for his music. He almost always got the words mixed up and would eventually just make up his own. Last night, as I was prepping the coffee cake for the morning, I heard his voice in the back of my mind singing:

> *Every mess you make*
> *Every cake you bake*
> *I'll be watching you*

Tonight, he is just humming the melody, albeit slightly off-key. If I didn't know any better, I would think he was sitting at my bedside. As he starts to add in some made-up words, I can hear him on my left side as clearly as if he were here in the flesh.

> *Oh can't you see*
> *You belong to me*
> *My proud heart swells*
> *With every lie you tell*

If this is a memory, it's weirdly vivid, and I swear I don't remember this particular version of the lyrics.

> *In your truck stop room*
> *In the diner too*
> *I'm watching over you*

"Wait, what?" I say aloud.

The singing stops. I have goosebumps all over. I lay perfectly still, holding my breath, listening. The room is silent, save for the faint rise and fall of Kate's snores. I close my eyes and listen carefully. I start to giggle to myself at the ridiculousness of it all. I haven't been sleeping well all week. Obviously, the exhaustion is starting to take its toll. That or I've finally lost my mind completely. I drift off to sleep, contemplating my probable mental breakdown.

* * * * *

In an instant, I'm blinded by light. It takes a few moments for my eyes to adjust. Slowly, the familiar rolling hills of my shepherd boy's pasture comes into focus. I'm so relieved. He'll know what to do. He is always brutally honest and certainly isn't afraid of hurting my feelings. My heart rate doubles in the anticipation of seeing him. I haven't dreamt of him since I left Nova behind.

As I scan the horizon, there is no sign of him. I turn around slowly in search of him, but he is nowhere to be found. I've never noticed it before, but this pasture is a small valley floor. I spin around again and see hills all around me in an almost perfect circle. No sign of the shepherd or his flock. Not a single motley sheep in sight. In all the years I've been dreaming of this place, I've never been here alone. And I am very alone. It's dead quiet. No birds. No breeze. Just profound silence in this empty field.

The sun is rising in the sky now. I decide I'll climb the closest hill to find a better vantage point. As I begin to approach the hill straight ahead of me, I realize how deceptively large it is. I climb for what feels like hours before I reach the summit. From here, I can see the circular valley far below me. Beyond it, only more hills as far as I can see. Behind me, another valley that seems infinitely expansive. I can't see where it ends. Not a tree, not another living creature, not a shepherd, not a sound. The world is still.

It occurs to me that I don't have a care in the world. I can't remember what I was looking for or why I'm up here. I turn slowly again around and around. I start to spin faster as I close my eyes and lean my head back to feel the warmth of the sun on my face, spinning more of my cares away with every rotation, faster and faster until it feels like I can fly. I start to laugh. I haven't felt this free in a long time, laughing and spinning with my arms open wide.

"Oh, grow up," a voice says right next to me.

I stop and open my eyes. My shepherd.

"Where did you come from?" I say as dizziness gets the best of me and I fall into him.

"I should ask you the same thing," he says. He holds me steady in his arms. He smells of fresh cut grass and clean linen. I look up to meet his gaze, the face I've seen a thousand times. Those eyes. Like the sea at dusk with the winter wind at its back. Those eyes I've seen somewhere else. I can't put my finger on it.

"Why don't I know your name?" I ask, still trying to place where I've seen these eyes.

"You never asked," he says, pulling me closer. "It seems like you don't even know your own name these days." He strokes my hair tenderly and cradles my face in his sun-warmed hands. He's never touched me like this. That much I know for sure.

"What's that supposed to mean?" I ask. I'm right on the verge of remembering. I can't quite remember who I am or where I'm from. I can't remember anything but him. My mind is in a fog. "What's your name?" I ask him.

It all starts coming back to me. Losing my father. Ocean Park. My beach. My mother. The café.

"Evan," he replies.

Evan. Evan. Where do I know that name?

I'm searching my mind. Slowly, the pieces are coming together. Oliver. Leaving the peninsula behind. Twisting my ankle in Pocatello. Dreaming of my shepherd boy there. The night he sang the most heartbreakingly beautiful melody I've ever heard. Sioux Falls. The truck stop. The diner. Annabelle. Kate and Hank. Evan. Sitting on the curb…singing the same song…the most heartbreakingly beautiful melody I've ever heard.

I look up at him in disbelief. "Is it you?" I ask.

He opens his mouth to answer me, but all I hear is a loud beeping sound. Louder and louder as the feel of him fades away and sunlight dissolves to the darkness of my little bedroom above the diner.

I slap my alarm to silence it and close my eyes tightly, trying to go back to the top of the hill...back to my shepherd...back to Evan. I still have so many questions for him. I squeeze my eyelids shut and pull my pillow on top of my face to block out the dim neon light bleeding in from the window. No luck.

My alarm starts to sound again. I hear footsteps coming closer.

"Nora?" Kate says quietly.

"Hi," I say reluctantly.

"Why is your alarm set so early? It's Monday, remember? We're closed! Evan and the others won't be here for at least a couple of hours. Go back to sleep," she orders and heads back to her bedroom.

Monday. The day Kate makes a horrible yet extremely well intended breakfast for Evan and his houseguests. No other customers because the diner is closed. I'm not working, so there is no excuse for me to be busy; and I live here, so there is no excuse for me to leave. I feel like the walls are closing in on me, lying here in the gray predawn light, trying to make sense of it all. My dream was just a dream; it didn't mean anything, right? There must be some logical explanation as to why I've been dreaming of Evan all of my life. Some simple reason why a figment of my imagination has turned out to be an actual real human person. An easy answer as to why he's here living in Sioux Falls, South Dakota. In the flesh.

I feel like the illusion of everything I know to be true about the way the world works has shattered around me like glass. *Does he know me? Is he dreaming of me? Have we been meeting in these dreams all our lives? How is that possible? I mean, this is not possible, obviously...right?*

Maybe he's been toying with me somehow this whole time? Or is it some cruel joke? Maybe I'm overreacting and this is just a wild coincidence. Maybe Evan and my shepherd boy just happen to have the same name. Yeah. Evan is a pretty common name I guess, right? Maybe I'm just dreaming about him and my mind is playing tricks on me, placing his face onto the shepherd. That could be it, I lie to myself.

I plunge into a dreamless sleep, contemplating the possibilities.

I awake to the smell of coffee and burnt toast wafting through the vents from the kitchen below. I hear voices and laughter in the diner. *Kate must have let me sleep in. I know she's been worried about me not sleeping, though she hasn't said anything.*

As I start to sit up, I notice a very curious little girl sitting at the end of my bed with a tray of food next to her. She giggles and grins at me. "Your hair looks funny!" she says, delighted.

"Good morning, Annabelle." I smile.

"Hi, Nora! Kate sent me up with breakfast. She told me to leave it on your bedside table if you weren't awake yet, but I thought you were. You were talking in your sleep. What's a shepherd?" She eyes me expectantly with her head cocked to the side like a curious puppy.

"Someone who herds sheep for a living. Not too common these days, I suppose." I try to breeze over the question as best I can, hoping that is all she heard me say. "How are you this fine morning?" I ask, reaching for the tray. Sure enough, two slices of burnt toast made soggy by coffee that I'm sure sloshed out on the way up the stairs, and a runny pile of scrambled eggs. My stomach turns at the sight of it. I set the tray aside and grab the coffee mug. Even Kate can't screw up a pot of coffee. "How's your grandpa?" I change the subject.

She looks down at her lap without a word. Her long dishwater blonde bangs cover her eyelids almost completely, but I can tell she is trying to fight back tears. She's wearing a blue and cream floral patterned dress with an apron sewed into the front. It looks like something out of a spaghetti western, so out of place on this little girl. I'm certain it was something Evan found at the thrift shop for her.

"Annabelle?" I tried.

"I'm okay. Grandpa is sick. He's staying at the hospital right now. They won't let me see him until he's done being in the No See You part."

"The ICU?" I ask.

"Yup," she concedes sadly, looking back down at her lap.

He's all the family she has in the world, and I have a sneaking suspicion that she doesn't know the implications of the "No See You."

We sit in silence for several minutes. Me sipping my coffee and contemplating the fate of this sweet little girl. Her twirling her hair and humming to herself, humming a familiar song. I'm trying to place it. It comes to me suddenly, like lightning in a black sky. I gasp.

"What's that song you're humming?" I ask, much louder than I intended.

She is visibly startled at my sense of urgency. "I don't know," she says, worried.

"Where did you hear that?" I ask, though I think I already know the answer and I really don't want to hear her say it.

"In my room. At night," she explains.

"On the radio?" I whisper, overreaching now.

"I don't have a radio in my room," she informs me.

"Then tell me where." I'm holding my breath.

She opens her mouth and then shuts it again. I can tell that she's trying to decide whether or not to trust me, how much to tell me. I don't dare make a sound.

"My guardian angel sings it to me at bedtime," she confesses. "At least, he has lately. Since you got here," she adds.

I'm stunned silent. I literally have no words.

Annabelle looks uncomfortable under my wide-eyed stare. She's fidgeting with her apron. "I'm gonna see if Kate needs my help," she says and disappears out of my room as fast as her little Mary Janes can carry her.

I lay back down without a sound. I feel a chill up my left side and pull my blankets up under my chin. I know he's here and I can't keep pretending I don't notice. Whether or not I believe in these things doesn't change what's true.

"Why are you doing this?" I say, fighting back tears. No response. "Why are you tormenting me?" The tears are coming now, streaming down the sides of my face and pooling on my pillow.

Still nothing.

"And now Annabelle? You're singing our song to Annabelle? Why?" I'm shouting now. Sobbing. I have lost control.

No answer.

I sit up and look around. I don't know what I'm expecting to see, but nothing is here. My sobs start to wane, first relegating to whimpers, then to nothing. Just silent tears. I wait for them to stop and wipe my face with the back of my hand.

"Coward," I say loudly to the room. I kick off my covers and head to the shower to get ready to face the day.

* * * * *

By the time I'm dressed and done trying to figure out what to do with my hair at this awkward length, I look out the window of the apartment just in time to see Evan's van pulling away from the diner. My heart sinks. I'm terrified to see him after my dream last night, but I'm equally terrified not to see him. I had borrowed a black jersey tank dress from Kate's closet and dressed it up with a pair of her sandals. They are a little tight, but I want to look my best today.

After seeing the van pull away, I kick off the sandals in favor of my new ultra-tacky fluffy leopard print slippers. I picked them up at the truck stop the other day. They look like exotic roadkill but with little spots of glittery silver fuzz mixed in. They're hilarious.

I slip on my faded purplish hoodie, zip it up, and pull up the hood before taking one last look in the mirror. Yep. Just as I suspected. I look like an overgrown toddler. Kate will get a laugh out of it.

I shuffle down the stairs and into the kitchen. To add to the look, I decide to reach in to the flour bin and give my face a nice powdery dusting. I'm already giggling in anticipation of Kate's reaction. Things have been so serious around here. I'm looking forward to getting that girl to laugh a little.

I hear the kitchen door open behind me and turn around just in time to run face first into Evan's chest. I jump back in horror while he surveys the damage. He has a perfect me-shaped floury face print on the front of his black dress shirt and tie. *Oh my God, he's all dressed up!*

"But I saw you leave," is all I manage to get out.

"I sent the guys home with the van," he says slowly.

I can tell there is more to the story. He's searching for the right words and looking down at his shoes. His beautiful black dress shoes. Italian leather? I've never seen any as nice. We don't exactly have designer stores on the Long Beach Peninsula. His black belt matches perfectly. He looks like he stepped right out of a magazine. Well, with the exception of the mess on his shirt.

"I want to take Annabelle on my own," he explains, brushing off his shirt with care.

Take Annabelle? His expression is apologetic, almost sullen even. It dawns on me that he's dressed head to toe in black.

"Oh, no. Please don't tell me—" I cover my mouth with my hands to keep from saying more in case she is within earshot.

"He passed in the night. I got the call this morning," Evan says sadly. "The hospital is letting us hold a quick service in the chapel. I wanted her to have closure. She needs to say goodbye. He's all the family she had left in the world." His voice cracks as he says the words. It's all he can do to hold back his tears.

"Where is she?"

"With Kate." He points to the dining room.

"I'm coming with you," I say and turn back up the stairs to trade in my slippers for Kate's sandals. I quickly rummage through her closet, looking for something appropriate to bring down for her. I settle on a long black raincoat. The girl only wears pastels. There isn't much to choose from.

I run back down the stairs, frantically wiping flour off of my face as I go. I push the door open into the dining room. Annabelle spots me right away and comes running in my direction. I don't know how to react. I'm caught off-guard as she throws herself toward me and flings her arms around my waist, sobbing. I've never heard anyone cry like this. I've heard cries of frustration, of exhaustion, of selfish disappointments. Never the cries of a truly broken heart.

I drop to my knees and gather her into my arms. I realize I'm crying as well. We stay like this, just holding onto each other and crying. She's crying for him. I'm crying for her. How could life be so cruel? There is no reason that would make it right for such a bright little soul to be crushed like this. She's crying for her parents too. I'm crying because I feel so ill-equipped to comfort her.

Soon, Kate is kneeling beside us, telling us it's time to go. She reaches to pick Annabelle up, but she resists.

"No. I want Nora," she says between unsteady breaths. Kate looks at me for a sign.

"I've got her," I assure her. I get up and haul Annabelle up with me. She clings to me. I motion to the raincoat, and Kate nods in gratitude. The four of us walk toward Kate's metallic blue Firebird in a somber procession.

The hospital isn't far. We're pulling in the visitors parking lot in a matter of minutes. Evan opens the door and I pass Annabelle to him.

"I can walk," she tells him. She hops down from his arms and takes his hand. She looks back for me. I quickly catch up to them and take her other hand. Kate leads the way. She knows better than anyone how to find the chapel in this hospital.

If she's thinking of her parents, it doesn't show. She's being strong for Annabelle. Maybe she's being strong for all of us.

Evan's eyes are red and puffy. The light catches the tracks of his tears ever so subtly as we make our way to the tall entry doors. Right away, Annabelle is looking around the chapel frantically.

"Where is he? Where is Grandpa?" she demands, looking back and forth from Kate to Evan to me.

"He's not here, I'm afraid," the chaplain says gently from behind her.

"What do you mean? Evan said I could come and say goodbye!" Tears pour from her eyes as she looks up at the chaplain pleadingly.

Evan drops to his knees and spins her around to face him.

"He has already gone off to heaven." He pauses to give her time to consider this.

"Is he with my parents?" she asks.

"Yes," he says matter-of-factly.

Her tears stop. She is twisting her long hair around her index finger, deep in thought. "Well, why are we here then if I can't say goodbye?"

Now Evan is the one deep in thought.

Annabelle begins to cry again.

"Does he know I love him?" she asks Evan. The chaplain answers.

"We're here because this is God's house here on Earth. Even though your grandpa has already left to go to heaven, he can hear you here. Anything you need to tell him, you go right ahead," he tells her.

She considers this briefly and decides to believe him.

"If it's all right with you, Annabelle, I'd like to talk with you," says the chaplain. He offers her his arm and escorts her to the front of the aisle. They sit side by side in the front pew while he tells her all about heaven.

"Streets of gold?" I hear her say. "He will like that. He likes shiny things the most." She smiles at him as he continues.

I sit two rows behind them. Kate is at the back of the chapel in her knee-length raincoat, lighting a candle. Evan sits down next to me. We watch Annabelle slide off of her pew, onto her knees at the altar. The chaplain shows her how to fold her hands in prayer.

"Grandpa?" She waits for a response, but none comes.

"It's okay, my dear," the chaplain assures her, "he can hear you, even if you might not be able to hear him just now."

"Okay," she says. "Grandpa? Well, I guess you're in heaven now. I don't know why you had to go, but I hope it wasn't because of me. I've been trying to be a good girl."

Evan is crying now, reserved and stoic at my side. I reach over and take his hand in mine. Our eyes meet as electricity runs through me. I can feel his heartache as though it is my own. He has so much empathy for this little girl. And guilt. He's not sure where his concern for her ends and where the loss of his own parents begins. He feels guilt over feeling his own sadness. I can feel it with him. I don't know how, but I can.

"Even though you haven't been able to talk in a long time, I still know you love me. Do you know I love you?" Annabelle asks, looking up at the stained glass skylight. "Because I do. A whole lot. And I miss you." She pauses to look behind her at the chaplain. "Am I doing it right?" she asks him.

"Perfectly." He nods in encouragement.

She turns to continue. "Well, I don't want to keep you here all day. I'm sure you're really excited to get to talk to my mom and dad. Will you tell them hi for me? And that I miss them too? And that I've been trying real hard to be a good girl?" She pauses and turns to look at us. "If you see Evan's parents, will you tell them he misses them too?" She looks back at Evan and smiles, just for a moment through her tears. "Anyway. I just wanted to tell you goodbye. You were a super good grandpa. I love you very much. I hope I get to see you when I go to heaven someday. Will you wait for me?"

She looks up at the skylight for a long time, I'm sure imagining her grandpa flying up to heaven and being impressed by the golden streets. Then she stands up, smooths out the front of her dress, and walks to the back of the chapel where Kate stands. Kate lifts Annabelle up, just high enough to light her own candle as Evan quietly composes himself. After lighting her candle, Annabelle hops down and runs back to the altar. She kneels down one last time and looks up to the ceiling. "Bye-bye," she says finally.

It takes us half an hour to get to Evan's house. Evan and Kate are in the front seat talking about his current houseguests while Annabelle sleeps with her head in my lap. We pull into the driveway, and Evan reaches in and carefully scoops up the sleeping girl. She doesn't even stir. I climb out to join Kate up front and stop to steal a glance at Evan. He pauses in the doorway to turn back and look at me.

"Thank you," he mouths to me, careful not to disturb Annabelle in his arms, and then closes the door behind him.

* * * * *

I decide that Kate and I need to get out and suggest we go out to an early dinner. She has hardly said a word all day, and I'm sure she needs to talk. We tuck into an authentic looking Mexican restaurant not far from Evan's house. It smells amazing. The place is packed.

A four-piece Mariachi band is crammed in on a small corner stage in the back of the room. The singer is wearing an oversized woven Baja shirt and a black bejeweled sombrero. He's shaking two maracas as though his life depends on it. The other three band members are in traditional Charro suits, full black with contrasting silver buttons and stark white sombreros with flames embroidered along the brims. They are doing their best to keep the choreographed foot-work going in the small space. From what I can hear, they sound wonderful, though I'm only catching every other measure. The voices, laughter, and clanking of glasses in the crowded restaurant nearly drown them out altogether.

"Hola!" says the hostess

"Hola, Maria!" Kate greets her.

"I see you brought a new friend with you. Oh wait, I know you!" Maria says, pointing a finger at me, eyes narrowing.

"Um, I don't think so," I say defensively.

"Hmm… I never forget a face," she says certainly. "It'll come to me. Well, let's get you seated. Right this way!"

We follow her through the dining room, weaving between tables, and turning sideways to squeeze between chairs. They are defi-nitely getting the most of their space. She leads us past the kitchen, down a narrow hallway. It opens up to a long narrow sunroom lined with floor to ceiling windows. It's quiet back here, just a few two-seater tables line the windowed wall. The room is illuminated with the warm glow of candlelight; the reflections in the glass are an eerie contrast against the stark black night. Red glass candle jars adorn each table.

"Romantic," I say sarcastically.

Kate laughs. "This is great, Maria. Thanks," she says.

Maria places our napkins in our laps as we sit down and hands us menus. She's staring at me. It makes me uncomfortable.

"You sure we haven't met?" she asks. "Maybe you were here before?"

"No. You must be thinking of someone else," I say nervously. "It gets dark so early" I say awkwardly, attempting to change the subject.

"Oooh!" Kate chirps, ignoring me. "Maybe you have a twin or something! I was reading an article online that says we all have a twin, just statistically, you know? 'Cause of the number of people on the planet. There are only so many ways a face can look or something."

"That must be it." I smile at Maria.

She looks, unconvinced. "Your waiter will be right over" she says, eyeing me as she walks away.

I look at Kate, worried. She clearly hasn't given it another thought. She grabs her menu and starts to contemplate the choices. We decide to share something. Neither of us has much of an appetite. When we're ready to order, I start looking around for our waiter. Maria is standing in the doorway to the sunroom. My skin tingles in the way it only does when I know someone is talking about me. Talking quietly with who I'm assuming is our waiter and pointing in our direction. I feel sick. *Why can't she just let it go? She doesn't know me. I've never been here.* She's freaking me out.

The waiter starts to walk toward our table with a serious look on his face. I'm bracing myself for the worst. My mom knows all kinds of people in the restaurant industry. Who knows how many people she's shown my stupid senior picture to? Or worse! How many people have seen it on social media! I look down at the table as he approaches, to hide my face from view.

"Hola, ladies." He greets us in a thick accent. "Como estas?"

"Bien, gracias!" Kate responds with a giggle.

"Ladies, I am so sorry to keep you waiting. Maria just showed me that you were back here. Please forgive me. I didn't see you come in," he says humbly.

"Oh, it's fine!" Kate assures him.

I let out an audible breath. I didn't even realize I'd been holding it in. I look up at him and smile warmly, now feeling guilty for not doing so sooner. *I have got to stop being paranoid. I'm worried for nothing...imaging things.* He returns my smile with one even larger that fades as quickly as it came. As he gets a good look at me, his expression changes to one of shock. I tense up immediately. Kate is blissfully unaware of our exchange.

"Okay, um, we're gonna share the chicken fajitas please. I'll have a diet Coke too. Nora, you want anything to drink?"

The waiter is still fixed on me. I'm staring at my lap. I may barf in it.

"Nora?" Kate says impatiently.

"No, thanks, I'm good with water," I say to my napkin.

The waiter hesitates. I can still feel his eyes on the top of my head.

"Gracias. I will get that going for you," he says curtly and heads toward the kitchen.

"Geez, Nora. Rude much?" Kate says in one of the rare moments when she actually sounds like a teenager.

"Sorry. I just have a lot on my mind."

"I know. Me too. I get it," she says.

"You live such an adult life," I tell her.

"Well, it's not like I'm a kid! I'm sixteen," she says. "Not for long, though!"

"Oh, really? When's your birthday?"

"Let's see…" She looks at her watch. "In about six hours."

"Six hours?" I repeat, surprised. "Why didn't you tell me? We should have a party! Oh, let's do it!"

"No, no, no," she says sternly. "No party for me."

I'm disappointed. Kate of all people deserves to kick up her heels and be celebrated a little bit.

"But we can throw one for Annabelle! Her birthday is on Friday!" she says excitedly. "Really? Oh we have to!" I decide.

We spend the rest of the evening talking about the party. We decide to have it at the café on Friday afternoon. We are always slow then anyway, so we decide to close after lunch so that we'll have the place all to ourselves. We talk about Annabelle and how courageous she is. An old soul in a soon-to-be eight-year-old body.

"Yeah, eight going on twenty-eight," Kate jokes.

We work on the guest list and start to plan the menu. Before we know it, it's almost ten and the restaurant is closing up. I realize that we've been here for hours and have managed not to talk at all about the funeral or about Kate's parents. We also didn't talk about mine, so maybe it is for the best.

I tell Kate that I need to run to the restroom so I can sneak off to pay the bill. Mercifully, the nosey hostess is gone for the night, and the pimply-faced guy at the cash register doesn't give me a second look. Kate walks up behind me just as I'm getting my change. "Nora! What are you doing? The least I can do is buy you dinner after all you've done for Annabelle today."

"Nonsense!" I say instinctively. I've never said that before. My mother says it all the time. I feel a pang of sadness. I miss her today. "I refuse to let you buy your own birthday dinner!" I tell her. "That's that." Without thinking, I lean in to give her a hug. I realize in that moment how important she is becoming to me.

"Thank you," she says.

When we get back to the diner, we both shift right back into autopilot and get to work cleaning up the morning's abandoned dishes. Kate heads upstairs to take a shower. I change for bed and then quietly sneak back downstairs to see what's in the bakery case. Half an apple pie, some blueberry bran muffins, and a few of Hank's famous giant cinnamon rolls. I decide on the pie and put a slice onto a dessert plate.

A few moments of rummaging through drawers behind the counter and I've found a small pink birthday candle and a book of matches adorned with the truck stop's logo. The big white clock in the dining room says it's just a few minutes before midnight. I tiptoe back up the stairs to our apartment. Kate is already in bed but reading in the dim light of her tiny bedside lamp. I stop just outside to poke the candle into the middle of the slice of pie and light it. I start singing "Happy Birthday" as I slowly walk toward her, careful not to let the candle blow out. When I finish, she's crying.

"Am I that bad?" I ask playfully.

"Oh, Nora." She cries and wraps her arms around my neck, pulling me into a bear hug. I narrowly save the plate from falling.

"You're an old lady now!" I try a joke to hide my awkwardness.

"I always wanted a sister," she whispers.

"Me too. Happy birthday," I whisper back.

Tonight, for the first time in a long time, I have no trouble falling asleep.

Sioux Falls, September 10

*T*oday is Friday, the day of Annabelle's super-secret surprise birthday party. I haven't seen Evan all week. He's been spending extra time with Annabelle. I have called him a few times, though to get his advice on colors, cake flavors, and other frivolous details. Every time I call him, we end up talking for an hour or more.

On the phone, I don't feel charges of electricity. I don't faint or trip and fall on my face. I don't get lost in his eyes and start thinking all kinds of crazy thoughts about impossible things. It's just a boy and a girl having an easy conversation. Friends even. Last night, we stayed on the phone even longer than usual. I called him to make sure that Annabelle wasn't suspicious. She's been poking around the diner all week. I can tell she knows we're up to something, but I don't think in a million years she would guess that it has to do with her. Bless her sweet little heart.

Evan had me cracking up laughing, telling me stories of how he's met some of his ragtag crew of houseguests. The first one he ever took in came about six months after his parents' accident. Evan had been unable to sleep and was taking a walk through the city after dark. He saw police lights up ahead. As he got closer, he had seen two young officers handcuffing a homeless man. They were being unnecessarily hostile as the man seemed to be cooperating without resistance. Evan thought he was probably looking forward to spending the night in jail with a roof over his head. As he approached, he recognized one of the cops as an old acquaintance from high school.

"Hey, Williams," he'd said, "what's wrong? Have a fight with your girlfriend or something? Now you gotta take it out on this poor guy for doing nothing?"

"Mind your own damn business," he snorted. "Besides, I picked him up for indecent exposure and urinating in a public place."

"He's homeless, you asshole. Where do you expect him to piss?" Evan was getting angry.

"That's not my problem," Williams shot back.

He had seemed so smug. So proud of himself. Evan told me he just couldn't help but "poke the bear."

The cops went back to yelling a slur of insults at the homeless man. The man didn't say a word; just closed his eyes and braced himself for the worst. He hoped they wouldn't decide to hurt him, but he didn't much care at that point.

Evan watched the exchange, exasperated for a moment, feeling determined to intervene. It was the first real emotion he'd allowed himself to feel since his parents' passing had left him numb. Without thinking it through, he did the first thing that came to mind. He'd walked over to the open driver's side door of the cop car, unzipped the fly of his Levi's, and proceeded to take a good long pee right into Officer Williams's driver's seat.

"Well, it worked!" Evan said defensively after I had yelled "Gross!" through uncontrollable laughter.

In the end, the cops had let the homeless man go in favor of arresting Evan. They tried to charge him with assaulting an officer, but he had a great family lawyer and got off with a warning after his arraignment two days later.

After his release, he had driven back down that street in search of the homeless man. He had almost missed him camouflaged beneath a green tarp, fast asleep. That's how he met Jerry who has lived with him ever since. He took him back home with him right then and there. "The rest is history," he'd said.

Jerry had been instrumental in helping take care of the other guests that came and went, helping to secure resources and assisting in finding longer term housing and employment for them, helping them navigate through the government paperwork to get medical care—whatever they needed. Evan paid him a modest salary to stay, but Jerry would have happily done it for nothing. He was happier than he'd ever been, and Evan was too.

I'm still giggling about the story he told me this morning as I am taking care of the last customers of the breakfast rush.

"More coffee, Martin?"

Martin was sitting in his usual seat at the end of the counter with his newspaper. He was the first person I'd met in Sioux Falls and had quickly become one of my favorite customers.

"Depends. You're not trying to pawn the old stuff off on me, are ya?" He faked a grumpy disposition and then laughed at himself. *Always cracking up at his own jokes. I love it.*

"Only the freshest for you." I winked at him and refilled his cup. "Staying for the party?" I asked hopefully.

"Wouldn't miss it."

We are expecting quite a crowd this afternoon. Little miss Annabelle is quite popular as it turns out. Martin, Hank, Kate, Evan, Jerry, all the houseguests…even Crissy from the truck stop. Evan had called Annabelle's teacher and invited a few of her new friends from school along with their parents.

Hank taped a messily written sign on the front door that read "Closed for private party" and is now busily decorating the strawberry sheet cake he baked last night. Kate and I say goodbye to the last few breakfast customers and lock the door. We have just about an hour to go before guests will be arriving.

"Let the fun begin!" says Kate happily as she pulls out the bag of decorations she picked out from the party supply store. Rolls of streamers in shades of pink and cream. A dozen or so silver plastic tiaras and some gaudy pink boas for the girls to dress up in. Cups, plates, you name it—all pink.

"I've never even seen her in pink. Are you sure this isn't over-kill?" I ask.

"Don't be crazy, Nora. She's a little girl!" Kate dismisses the notion with a wave of her hand and stands on her tiptoes to turn on the TV above the bakery case. "Background noise," she explains.

I wait until she's distracted and sneak back into the kitchen to conspire with Hank. What Kate doesn't know is that he baked a cake just for her too, even more pink and girly than the one he'd made for Annabelle. She'll love it! Hank and I had pitched in together to buy her a countertop CD player made to look like a jukebox for the diner. She's been complaining that we needed music in here since my first day on the job. I can hardly wait to see the look on her face when she opens it!

I head upstairs to change out of my uniform and get dressed for the party. I have a gift for Annabelle too. I see it on the dresser and walk over to pick it up. I so hope she likes it. It's a little silver locket on a delicate chain. Inside, I put a picture of she and I that Kate took one day in the diner. We're looking at each other with matched ear-to-ear grins. I want her to have it as a symbol of what she means to me. I haven't admitted it to myself, but I also want her to have something to remember me by when I…in case I…well…just to have it.

"*You're kidding yourself,*" I hear a familiar voice in the back of my mind…or maybe in my ear. "*You're going to break that girl's heart, you know.*"

"No one asked you!" I quip, annoyed.

"No one asked me what?" Kate asks as she comes up the stairway.

"Oh, n-n-nothing," I stutter.

"Okay, well, hurry up! You aren't even dressed yet? C'mon, slow poke!" she says, pushing me toward the closet. "Want me to wrap that for you?" she offers.

"Oh, that would be great," I say. "The box is on the dresser."

"She's gonna love it," Kate assures me.

I'm about halfway dressed in one of Kate's denim skirts and a pink t-shirt I found in her room when I hear the sirens. I run over to the window in time to see three police cars pulling into the truck stop parking lot, lights flashing. One cop gets out and walks into the store. He's holding something about the size of a postcard. A picture maybe? I'm frozen in place.

A few moments later, he comes back outside and says something to the other cops. Then he and another officer walk across the street toward me, to the parking lot of the diner. Evan's van pulls in just ahead of them. He hops down out of the driver's seat as they approach. I open the window to try and hear what's going on.

"What do you want, Williams?" I hear Evan say with chagrin. I get a mental image of Evan peeing in the cop car and can't help but chuckle. I can't hear what Williams is saying, but he shows Evan whatever it is that he's holding. All the color seems to drain from his face. Evan asks him something quietly and then looks up toward my window. I step back, but I know he saw me.

"Nope. Can't help you," I hear him say.

The policemen walk back to their cars. Evan glances back up at me. He looks like he might be sick.

"*What did I tell you?*" says the voice in my head. I ignore it. I turn on the little TV on the table in the living room to distract myself. A news anchor is announcing a special report. I'm only half listening and barely notice when she says, "Nova Daniels." I gasp in horror and run over to the TV. I must be imagining things.

"If you have any information on the location of this missing person, please call the number on your screen right away."

I stare wide-eyed at the screen. Staring back at me is my horrific senior picture. There I am, elbow on knee, fist under chin. Vacant smile. I realize now how stupid I was to think that dying my hair would make a difference. My hair even looks darker on TV. I look exactly the same.

I'm frozen in panic. So many things are flashing through my mind all at once. Using my credit card in the truck stop that first day. Crissy asking my name, Maria, and the waiter from the Mexican restaurant. How long have these cops been flashing my picture around town? Kate is downstairs wrapping my gift for Annabelle. Evan and Annabelle are most likely walking in right now. Annabelle is probably just realizing that we've planned a surprise party for her.

The TV blares my name again as the anchor repeats her story, this time even more dramatically. "There is a reward for any information leading to the safe return of this young woman," she says with an overly contrived pleading in her voice. An image of Kate turning on the TV in the diner flashes into my mind. We only get one channel with decent reception. Is it still on? Is she watching this? Is everyone watching this right now?

Without another thought, I wiggle out of Kate's skirt and grab my old jeans out of the hamper. I fish my gray T-shirt and hoodie out of the dresser drawer. I push over the little trashcan next to the TV stand and dump the contents onto the floor, taking the empty bag. I practically fly into the bathroom, tossing my meager belongings into it as fast as I can. I grab my backpack off of the hook on the back of my bedroom door.

Money. Right. I reach under my bed and grab the coffee can I've been using as a bank and head toward the stairs. I hear someone coming up the first few steps and freeze. I remember the fire escape and run back into the bathroom. I see my name tag on the back of the sink that says "NORA" in all caps. I grab it.

"Nora?"

It's Evan, calling from the stairwell. I open the window and pop out the screen. It clanks loudly down the side of the building. "*Smooth criminal,*" says a sarcastic voice that I absolutely cannot think about right now.

"Nora?" Evan's voice is louder this time. I hear more footsteps coming up the stairs.

I toss my backpack out the window, onto the landing below, step onto the toilet, and fling myself out headfirst. I reach desperately for the ladder and push it hard. It makes a loud creaking sound as it reluctantly extends down toward the ground. I swing my backpack onto my shoulder and slide down the handrail on the side of the ladder. No time to climb down. I land on my bad ankle, re-injuring it.

I hear my name being shouted from upstairs. Nora's name. It will only be a matter of seconds before they realize where I've gone. I take off in a dead run toward the wooded area behind the diner parking lot, trying my best to ignore the excruciating pain in my ankle. As soon as I'm in the trees, I stop and collapse, holding my ankle in agony.

I hear voices and quickly scoot myself behind the large tree trunk nearest me. I carefully peek around and see Hank and Jerry walking around the parking lot, looking for me. And Evan. Evan is standing outside the bathroom window where I climbed out on the fire escape landing. He bends over to pick something up. My bracelet. I can see it gleaming in the sunlight and look down at my now empty wrist to confirm. My father had given it to me. It was way too big at the time, but I've been wearing it since I was fourteen or so.

Evan examined the bracelet slowly and then looked up right at me. *Wait. That's not possible,* I think as I tuck my head back behind the tree. I peek around again and he's still looking in this direction. Hank and Jerry are moving this direction now too.

It's as if he can sense where I've gone. If he can, he doesn't say anything. In fact, I hear him say, "She must have headed for the highway." The others follow his hunch and turn their focus away from me. Kate has joined them.

I watch the three of them disappear behind the building. Evan stays where he is, looking into the trees. I stand up without thinking and step out of the shadows. He sees me but doesn't look surprised. We lock eyes for a brief moment. Even from here, I feel a charge of energy wash over me. My heart aches at the notion that this may be the last we ever see of each other.

"Thank you," I mouth to him, and turn into the woods.

* * * * *

My adrenaline is pumping as I run as fast as my ankle will carry me. In a matter of seconds, I come through the wooded lot to the street on the other side and stop to catch my breath. I feel the primal instinct to get as far away from here as I can. I see a gas station across from me. I can call a cab. They must have a pay phone. *Wait, no. I'm sure they'll be looking for me there. I need to think this through. I can't take a flight. I'll have to use photo ID to get a plane ticket, not to mention all the security cameras. Train station security is pretty tight these days too. After my credit card blunder at the truck stop, I have to be extra careful with my next move.*

There is no room for error. I see flashing lights out of the corner of my eye and hit the ground just before the first police car pulls in to the gas station. The second car stops right in front of me along the curb. I'm mostly hidden in the tall weeds, but I'm afraid my faded blue sweatshirt will give me away. I unzip it and slide it off ever so slowly as not to make a sound, then toss it in to the bushes. I toss my backpack the other way into the trees.

I can see the cop in the passenger seat right in front of me, just a few feet away. He's looking the other way, waiting for direction from his counterparts at the gas station. Wait, now he's looking this way. His door starts to open, and I instinctively start rolling to my left until I bump up against a tree. Stupid! He must have seen me.

His head jerks in my direction. He's looking right at me. Wait, no. Right over me.

"Hey, Williams? I'm going to check this wooded lot out. The perp might have climbed a tree or something," he says.

He takes a couple of steps toward me. I'm holding my breath. I see the sleeve of my sweatshirt sticking out from the bush just to his right. Another couple of steps and he'll be able to see it.

Now Williams is out of the driver's seat and looking this way. "Climbed a tree? Don't be a dumb-ass, McGraw. It's a teenage girl, not a damn monkey, you idiot! Look low."

"I know she's not a monkey. Pshht. Whatever..." McGraw mutters under his breath, ego bruised.

"Besides. She's probably half way out of town by now. I doubt she's dumb enough to stay around here."

Oh no, I'm dumb enough trust me.

Williams turns his attention back to the gas station. The other cop is yelling something at him, but I can't make it out. Something about splitting up it sounds like.

McGraw clearly still thinks he's onto something with the whole tree-climbing theory. He's scanning the tree tops now, totally oblivious that he's standing on the sleeve of my sweatshirt. This guy is a real asset to the force...not. I stifle a giggle.

"C'mon, monkey boy," Williams yells, "Sutton and Davis are heading to the airport to make a sweep. We're gonna hit the train station, maybe swing by the bus depot over on Maple on the way back through."

McGraw obediently trots back over to the car and hops in. Williams flips on the siren and speeds out of sight, tires squealing. The smell of burnt rubber hangs in the air. I roll back over and reach for my hoodie. I fling my backpack over my shoulders and start heading back through the woods to the other side of the lot toward Maple Street. I had forgotten about the bus station until the cops reminded me. "Thanks, dummies," I whisper.

It can't be more than a block or two from here, and I'm pretty sure it's the safest bet at this point. It will take those morons at least a half an hour to get over to the train station and back. I'm running again. Even with a limp, I'm making good time. I stop when I come to the clearing to get my bearings and see the blue neon sign just down the street. "BUS" in electric blue light beckons me. As I near the sign, a sound like a down power-line buzzing and crackling on the ground startles me. I look up just in time to see the "B" in BUS fade to black. "_US" it says.

"One point," I say to no one in particular.

Once inside, I see a line for the ticket window. There are TVs in every corner of the room, and I'm suddenly very aware of every person in the station. No one looks up at me as I make my way through the crowd. There are two lines forming near the doors. Two buses must be loading now. I need to move fast, but I'm afraid to go to the ticket window for fear they will know my face. I stand frozen, thinking about my options. I could try to sneak on to a bus. Maybe I could mug someone and take their ticket. People in movies get mugged all the time, right? How hard can it be? I'm not exactly sure how to mug, though. Note-to-self: Google that.

Luckily, I spot a machine the size of an ATM near the doors that says "Tickets" in small red letters just above it. I hurry over and push the button that says "Buy." Too many choices. I choose to search by schedule. There are four buses leaving in the next hour. Two now within five minutes of each other. The next isn't for thirty-five minutes. I don't have that kind of time.

The next bus leaves in two minutes for Seattle. *Nope. That's out. Too close to home.* So it looks like I'm bound for Boston. I select the Boston ticket and the option to pay cash. I feed a couple of bills into the machine and it spits my change out at me. Now, where's my ticket? Crap. It wants me to enter my name for the boarding pass.

I stare at the screen.

"C'mon already!" demands the irritated woman behind me.

I stare at the screen again. My hand is hovering over the keyboard, just waiting for my brain to instruct it. I stare at my dirty sweatshirt sleeve. I'm drawing a blank. The name I chose in Sioux Falls didn't work out so well. It's too close to my real name. I nearly said Nova at least a dozen times. If I'm going to believably start another life, I need to get more creative.

"What's the hold up?", someone shouts from behind me.

I'm still lost in thought, staring at my fraying sleeve cuff. This sweatshirt used to be such a nice blue. Now it's almost lavender. Bluish lavender. Or more of a …oh, hey! That'll work! I snap back to the task at hand, enter my new name, and print my ticket. I grab it from the machine and run through the door closest to me out to the bus that says "Boston" on the destination sign. There are a lot of empty seats. Apparently, buses are not the preferred method of transport these days. I head all the way to the back row and plop my backpack down on the seat next to me.

"Tickets!" A station agent got on behind me and is checking tickets. He makes his way down the narrow aisle, smiling and greeting each passenger. He takes my ticket, gives it a quick glance, and then scribbles his initials in the corner of it in bright orange highlighter pen.

"Enjoy the ride, Miss Shepherd." He gives me a wink and turns to go.

"It's V-v-violet," I say to his back. Practice makes perfect.

He hops off the bus and the driver pulls the big doors shut. As we ease out of the bus station, I look from side to side, expecting to see the flashing red and blue lights of the Sioux Falls police. Nothing. I breathe a sigh of relief.

As we round the corner and head on to the eastbound onramp, I catch a glimpse of the truck stop and Pearl's Diner. Before I can stop it, a single tear escapes my eye. What must Kate be thinking? She'll never forgive this betrayal. My betrayal. And Annabelle. Oh, sweet Annabelle. She believed in me. Her birthday party, ruined. And…Evan.

I pull my thoughts together and tuck my emotions back down into the deep dark canyons that have formed in my heart.

"Goodbye, Nora," I say to no one in particular.

"*Who's the coward now?*" no one in particular replies from somewhere over my shoulder.

* * * * *

Kate was sitting in the diner at a table in the window watching Annabelle twirl her hair while staring down at her enormous pink cake. Hank had cut her a slice, even though they hadn't sung the "Happy Birthday" song yet to try and cheer her up. She hadn't touched it. Most everyone else was still out looking for Nora, but Kate knew in her gut that they wouldn't find her.

Evan must have known that too, she thought. He was sitting at the counter writing something. He'd been there for a few minutes now. Kate would have wondered what he was writing if her mind wasn't completely overwhelmed with the events of the day. Nora was a runaway? That didn't even make sense. Why would she do that? Obviously, someone back home was worried enough to call the police. Someone, somewhere loved her. Kate couldn't understand how the Nora she knew could do that to anyone. If she had parents that were alive, why would she leave?

The TV in the corner was still tuned to the news. They hadn't had a story this big in South Dakota since who knew when and were milking it for everything they could. More reporters were out interviewing witnesses. A bottled blonde journalist that Kate had never seen was interviewing Crissy from the truck stop now. Kate wasn't really listening to the interview, but Crissy looked like she was loving the attention. Kate focused her attention on Annabelle.

"You haven't even touched your cake," Kate said.

"I'm waiting for Nora," Annabelle replied sadly. "The lady on TV says that isn't even her name, though. Why would she tell us that it was if it wasn't?" Her eyes welled up with tears. If she blinked, they would fall.

"I don't know," Kate answered, stroking Annabelle's hair.

A news van pulled up into the parking lot of the diner, and the way too blonde reporter hopped out followed by a camera man. He scrambled to keep up with her as she jogged up to the front door and barged in. She looked right at Kate.

"Is the owner of this place here?" asked the reporter, looking around the room with a look of distaste.

"You're looking at her," Kate replied.

"Roll it!" the reporter ordered the camera man while adjusting her obviously fake boobs. She then attacked Kate with a slew of questions.

"Did you know you were harboring a runaway?" she asked dramatically. Without leaving Kate time to answer, she continued, "Did you notice anything odd about her? Did she steal from you?"

Kate could feel her cheeks heating up in frustration. Nora was—well, whatever her name is—she may have been a lot of things, but she wasn't a thief. Kate trusted that there must have been a good reason why Nora... Nova, rather...had kept this from her. "Do you feel angry now that you know she lied to you?" the reporter asked, trying to get a rise out of Kate.

"She didn't lie to me," Kate said instinctively, protecting her friend, and then realized it was true. Nova had never said why she came to town. She'd never said anything about her past. "Not about anything other than her name...and her age, I guess," she added. "I thought she was eighteen."

While the reporter continued asking questions, trying to twist Kate's responses to make the story sound more sensational than it was, Evan snuck out undetected. Three letters sat on the counter top. One addressed to Kate, one to Jerry, and one to Annabelle. Evan walked across the street to the truck stop and bought a map of the United States. News vans and nosey locals jammed the parking lot. He weaved his way back through the congestion to the diner and got in his car. He was twenty miles west before Kate found the letters. She opened the one addressed to her.

Dear Kate,

Please forgive me for running out without saying goodbye. It seems to be the theme of the day. I know. The news says she's from Washington state along the southern coast. I'm headed there. I'm not sure what I'll find, but I know there must be something she hasn't told us. She came here for a reason, and I'm going to find out what it is. I'll call when I get there. Please keep Annabelle with you.

Evan

Next, she opened Annabelle's.

Annabelle,

    I had to go away for a few days to see if I can help Nora. Kate is really going to need your help around here. It would really make her happy if you stay here so she doesn't get lonely. I'll be back soon and we'll have a real party.

                                        love ya, kid.

                                             Evan

Kate knew there was something between Evan and Nora. It had been brewing ever since Nora showed up in Sioux Falls. She knew what love looked like. She also knew how hard it was to walk away from. She smiled in spite of herself.

Eloise

Stonington, Connecticut, September 11

*E*loise awoke from her afternoon nap giggling. She popped out of bed, landing on both feet with barely a sound. She felt light as air. Nova was on her way! Preparations would have to be made! She hurried over to her desk to make a list. She dipped her grandfather's quill into her little ceramic pot of ink made mostly of crushed berries from the garden. This was a much slower way to write, but she loved the sweet smell of the thick ink on aged parchment. As much as Eloise loved living in the modern era, there were just some things that didn't need updating.

- ☐ *Put clean linens on the guest bed*
- ☐ *Cut fresh flowers for the vase on the vanity*
- ☐ *Fetch some new clothes from town, her dress size is medium*
- ☐ *Start a pot of stew. She'll be half starved!*
- ☐ *Don't call her Nova. She has not yet chosen a name for herself and we wouldn't want to scare her off.*

Before Eloise herself left the house, she pulled a stack of parchment paper from her desk and brought it into Nova's room along with a pen, a pencil, a quill, and a pot of her blackberry ink. She displayed them out artfully on the ornate white desk in the corner. She then laced up her boots and pulled on her traveling cloak before scurrying down the stairs. She nearly ran head-on into Elaina.

"Eloise, for crying out loud! What has you half out of your mind?" Elaina demanded.

"She's coming! Here, I made a list!"

Elaina smiled and took the sheet of paper from Eloise's shaky hand. All the women of the circle were anticipating Nova's arrival, but none of them were as excited as Eloise. As if it were possible to be. Elaina eyed Eloise curiously.

"Do we have enough time to make it to town to shop?" she asked.

"Oh yes! She won't arrive until tomorrow evening," Eloise answered.

"I see," said Elaina calmly. "So why the traveling cloak?"

"I'm going to Mystic to wait for her. There is something I can't quite understand in my visions. I want to make sure I'm there should she need me."

"Very well," Elaina replied. "Trust that we will have everything ready for her arrival. I will consult the stars tonight to see if they have anything to tell me."

Eloise was headed for the door when a flash of Nova hit her.

"And shoes!" she called back to Elaina. "It looks like she'll need shoes. Size 7!"

Violet

I must have been asleep for hours, though it feels as if I just closed my eyes for a moment. I wake up to the bitter smell of diesel fuel and look out the window. It's dark out. I'm guessing it's the middle of the night. We've stopped in the short-term parking lot of a truck stop in Who Knows Where, USA, and I'm alone on the bus. A lucid wave of guilt washes over me. What am I doing? I'm running, but from what? My mother who loves me in her own way? A little girl who needs me? The sister I never had?

"What am I doing?" I say aloud.

"*You're finally living, Babe! My little Super Nova!*" says the voice I'm trying to ignore. "*It's about damn time too,*" the voice adds.

Not wanting to be alone with my thoughts, I grab my backpack and head into the truck stop. This place looks eerily similar to the one in Sioux Falls. I guess if you've seen one, you've seen them all. No barber station, but this place has a restaurant in the back. I head there first, following the hearty smell of beef stew in the air. I order a cup of stew and a sandwich to go.

Passengers are starting to meander back to the bus, so I move fast. I grab a plastic shopping basket and work my way through the aisles. A tacky display full of kitschy souvenirs catches my eye. Shot glasses, key chains, magnets all printed with a big white state building and "Welcome to Madison" in large red letters. Wisconsin? Wow, we're making good time.

I grab a travel bottle of ibuprofen for my ankle, a book of crossword puzzles, a can of almonds, and a blank notebook. I feel like journaling. I used to write in a journal all the time when I was younger.

I guess there came a point when I didn't have anything interesting to write about anymore, so I gave it up. It's time to start again if for no other reason than to start keeping track of all the lies I'm telling.

As I pass a full-length mirror along the wall, I physically recoil at the sight of myself. These past few weeks have made Nova feel like a distant memory; yet, there she is, staring back at me. My cheap boxed-dye job has all but faded away. Nova with her same old boring hair, same old boring clothes, same old bored look on her face. I spin the rack of women's clothes next to me and find nothing of interest. I move to the next one. Jackets. *Perfect.* I slip out of my sweatshirt, letting it fall into a heap on the ground at my feet and grab a black lightweight jacket from the rack. It zips up easily and fits well. I walk away, leaving Nova's sweatshirt behind. Violet isn't a sweatshirt kind of girl.

After paying cash for my things, I head back to the bus, just as the bus driver starts the engine, and make my way to the back row. As we pull away, I open my notebook to the front page. In big inky black letters, I write:

Property of Violet Shepherd

On the next page, I decide to make a list:

Facts about Violet

From: Madison, Wisconsin

Family: Deceased. Lives in Wisconsin.

~~A sister named Kate~~

No siblings

~~Job: Artist, Writer, Does not wait tables~~

Now I'm drawing a total blank. Hobbies? Friends? Backstory? Nothing. I close my eyes and try to picture what Violet's life might be like, what she might look like. She needs to look completely different from Nova and Nora. No more amateur mistakes. I've come too far to go back now. It's time to take this seriously. If I can just visualize it...

I picture my reflection in the mirror of the truck stop motel. First Nova, then Nora. Both plain. Both forgettable. I picture Nora's muted brown hair and shake my head. Violet isn't plain. Besides, plain isn't a good enough disguise. Maybe the best place to go unnoticed isn't in the background after all. Maybe it's in living color.

I picture my reflection and watch as my hair turns from brown to black. *Nope. Still Nova. Still Nora.* I refocus and watch it turn back to brown, then blonde. Platinum blonde. Then to gray and into shades of blue. I giggle aloud as it turns to violet. Too literal. Funny, but no. The color fades again to brown, transitioning to a rusty copper. Close, but not quite. As if someone is adjusting the contrast on a TV screen, my hair color comes alive in shades of red. It moves like dancing fire in waves around my suddenly not so plain face. It's perfect. Perfectly Violet Shepherd.

I smile, satisfied with my choice. Eyes still closed, I am lulled back to sleep by the baritone hum of the bus engine. My dreams are chaotic. They keep switching from scene to scene. At one point, I find myself on a hilltop high above Evan's valley. I'm looking for him, but all I see are sheep. I could swear I hear him calling my name, but then the dreamscape changes and I'm flying a kite with Annabelle on the beach by my house in Ocean Park. Dreams are fickle that way.

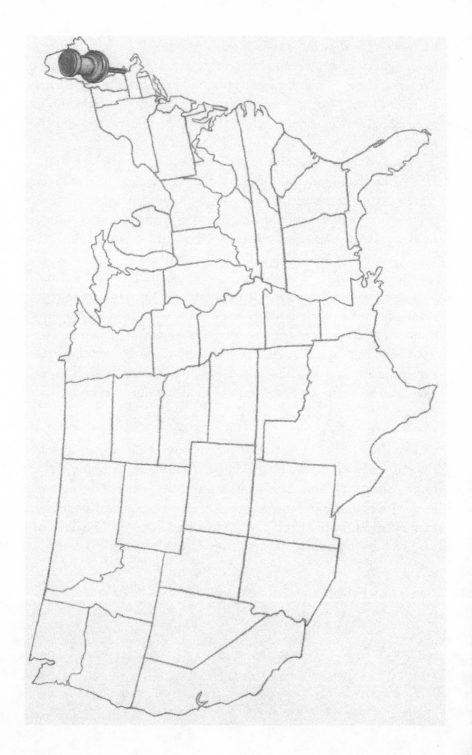

Violet

By the time we reach Boston, I've managed to write down the story of Nora's time in Sioux Falls. I started at the beginning of my time there when Oliver and I rolled into town. Reliving the days there made me laugh a little and cry a lot. I feel ashamed for leaving them and fleeing like a coward. The way I miss them is tainted by my guilt which has manifested into an achy pit in my stomach that I'm starting to think may become permanent.

When I finished recounting Nora's story, I started trying to write about Ocean Park and the night I left town. It's been less than a month, but I have been having trouble remembering the details. It's almost as if the memories aren't my own, like the choices weren't mine. It's like when you're walking and get lost in thought and suddenly refocus and wonder how you got across the street; but instead of lasting a few moments, it seems to have lasted days. Weeks.

Well, I'm paying attention now. As we enter the Boston city limits, I take in the scenery. Tall brick houses in crowded rows line a neighborhood street. I see a group of little boys playing hockey in the afternoon sun. They yell, "*Cahhhh!*" in unison (which I'm assuming means car) and scramble to move their makeshift net out of the street to allow a yellow taxi cab by. Then they make quick work of setting up their street rink and resume what appears to be a seriously competitive game.

We turn a corner and I see store fronts. On the right-hand side, I see a little café with a couple of tables outside occupied by ladies surely sharing some afternoon gossip over coffee. A rare book shop, a clothing boutique, a hair salon. A glowing sign in the window of the salon catches my eye just as the top line of it burns out. From "Walk-ins Welcome" to "ins Welcome" in a flash. Four points. Just below the faulty sign, there is a poster of a model with flame red hair. Instinctively, I stand up.

"Stop!" I shout. "Please stop the bus. I need to get off!"

"We're almost to the station, Ma'am," says the driver.

In a panic, I search for a quick lie.

"*Tell him you're sick,*" says a voice from behind me, though there is only a wall there.

"I'm...I'm going to be s-s-s-sick!" I shout.

The bus brakes squeal in protest as the driver pulls to the curb and opens the door. I grab my backpack and my journal and run for it.

"Ah cah-mahn!" a frustrated passenger grumbles in a thick New England accent as I hurry past.

"No need to wait for me," I call over my shoulder as I hop off the last step onto the curb.

I'm just a few doors down from the salon and walk quickly as I hear the bus pull away from the curb. I'm feeling suddenly very aware of my appearance and want to hide my face. I stop at the poster of the red-haired model in the window. A deep coppery-orange with highlights of marigold and lowlights in a brick red make it almost impossible to notice her face. I can't help but smile. A woman greets me from the open door.

"Hey, thay-ah," she says in a gruff voice that doesn't match her petite frame. "You need a cut?"

"Can you make me look like this?" I ask, gesturing to the poster.

"You bett-ah believe it," she winks.

I can't tell if she's placating me or if they just get this question a lot. No matter. I walk in, and she shows me to a chair.

An hour and a half later, I have a new look and a new friend. My stylist has been filling me in on all the best spots to visit in Boston. I've already decided I'm not staying in town for a single minute longer than I have to, but I don't have the heart to tell her so. She spins me around to face the mirror.

"Wow," I say out loud.

"Yep! You're a bona fide ginger now, Vi," she says proudly. "Ya look like a million bucks."

"Thank you," I whisper. Violet Shepard's reflection stares back at me from the mirror. Wavy red locks in every shade of the spectrum dance around my face as I slowly shake my head from side to side. Now this is a real change. She gave me a few hair extensions. Though I was skeptical, they actually blend in nicely. My hair is about a foot longer than it was when I walked in.

I pay the receptionist and then head to the restroom to freshen up. I wash my face and start over with fresh makeup. Charcoal gray eyeshadow and extra mascara, a little bit of pink blush, and my nude lip-gloss. No one will recognize Nova in this face. I don't.

I step back and survey my outfit. From the neck up, I'm definitely Violet. I walk out of the salon to my left to the boutique we passed on the way. It's just a few doors down. This place is very girly. Not Nova's style, that's for sure. I grab a few things quickly and head to the dressing room. With the help of a salesgirl, I pick out a couple of blouses, a new pair of shiny black heels, and some gold bangle bracelets. I put my old beat-up Converse in the trashcan and trade my t-shirt for a turquoise button-up blouse. With my dark jeans and heels, it looks almost dressy. I throw my black jacket back on over it, slip on my bracelets, and step back to look at the finished product in the mirror. I laugh out loud. I look like some kind of fancy city girl in this outfit. The funny thing is, it suits me. It suits Violet.

I thank the salesgirl and ask for directions to the train station. It's just a few blocks south.

"Take a left at the coffee shop and you'll see the sign. Can't miss it!"

I step out of the boutique, trip over the door jamb, and go sprawling onto the sidewalk with a thud. These heels are going to take some getting used to. I look around, expecting passersby to offer help me up, but no one is even looking at me. As I slowly move to sit up, a man in a suit talking on his cell phone steps right over me.

"*Welcome to the big city,*" a voice chuffs in my ear. I turn my head and see no one. I stand up, brush myself off, and keep walking. I keep checking behind me as I go. I don't see anyone, but I can't seem to shake the feeling that I'm being followed. There is a familiar melody coming from somewhere over my shoulder. Someone is singing softly...

Every trip you take every bone you break
I'll be watching yoooouuuu

I make it to the train station without further incident. There are a few trains leaving soon. Providence, Rhode Island. *No. Too close.* Chicago. *Nope. Wrong way.* Mystic, Connecticut. *Hmmm. Never heard of it.* There are two women ahead of me in line. I hear them chatting excitedly about their trip.

"Oh, the fall foliage is so gorgeous."

"Stunning."

"I think it will still be warm enough to get down to the beach too."

At the word beach, images of home come pouring into my mind. Sunrise on the west coast is pretty amazing. I wonder what it's like on the east coast.

"Excuse me, would you mind buying my ticket along with yours? I need to run to the r-r-restroom," I stammer, handing the woman in front of me a handful of cash and darting away. She watches me, bewildered.

"Next," says the ticket agent.

"Three for Mystic," says the woman.

Evan

Billings, Montana, September 12; Just Before Dawn.

A jet black Ford Mustang had been strategically parked just off the highway in the tall grass. If you weren't looking for it, you would have missed it under the cover of night. Reclined in the driver's seat, Evan slept restlessly. His dreams were vivid and intense. Dreams of Nora running and afraid. Dreams of Annabelle crying for her grandfather. Among the flashes from dreamscape to anxious dreamscape, he dreamt he was a shepherd herding his flock aimlessly through a vast hilly landscape. There must have been thirty sheep there, some snoozing in the warm sun, some grazing on the lush grasses of the valley floor. This place was familiar and comforting. A reprise from a flood of nightmarish circumstances.

It wasn't until Evan saw her standing on the hilltop in the distance that he really remembered this place. Like a dam bursting, memories of her came flooding through him. He knew her. He'd always known her. He loved her. He'd always loved Nova. Now she was Nora. How had he not recognized her? He'd have known her anywhere. How could she be real? How could any of this be real? He had to talk to her. Maybe she could explain all of this. He started heading toward her. First walking, then into a sprint.

Sheep eyed him curiously as he passed them. Nova still hadn't spotted him.

"Nora!" he shouted.

She couldn't hear him.

"Nova!" he tried. She was still too far away.

113

He had nearly reached her when the sound of a loud car horn startled him awake. He was back in his car, panting and covered in sweat as though he'd really been running.

"No!" he shouted, banging his fists frustratedly on the steering wheel. He tried to close his eyes and get back to his dream. Back to her. Alas, the portal had closed. His heart was racing. He resigned, knowing sleep wasn't possible tonight, and got back on the highway headed west. He needed answers and he needed them now.

Violet & Lyla

Mystic, Connecticut, September 12

*T*he train ride from Boston to Mystic took barely over an hour. I step off the car onto the platform still a bit nervous. I'm not sure I've gone far enough from Boston. If the police figure out that I took a bus, they'll know it had to be one of the two, either to Seattle or Boston. If they know I came to Boston, they might be able to figure out that I took a train next.

I managed to pay cash for the train, but I don't know if it's enough. Maybe the bus driver will rat me out and tell them that I got off at a hair salon. At least there won't be surveillance footage of me at the station in Boston. *Ugh! What have I gotten myself into?*

Still unsettled, I start walking. As I approach Main Street, I can't help but pause and take it all in. The little downtown is adorable. As much as I've grown to hate Ocean Park, I still have a soft spot for small towns. This one has a ton of character. It looks like a fairytale town and a fishing village all rolled into one.

Nearly all of the shops and restaurants seem to incorporate the town's name in them. Some cleverly like The Mystic Florist, which makes me wonder if you can get your palm read while you wait for a bouquet or Mystical Toys of Mystic. Kid-sized crystal balls perhaps? As I walk past Mystic Pizza, though the heavenly smell wafting from the building leads me to believe that they have a packed house for a reason.

As I stroll across the Mystic river bridge, I stop to watch the boats lazily floating in the warm afternoon sun. I know I should keep moving, but I'm feeling very unmotivated. I spot a park across the water and head that way. It couldn't hurt to rest awhile. I need to sort out my thoughts and figure out a plan. I make my way to the park and across the grassy meadow as fast as my fancy shoes will carry me. After sinking a heel into the soft earth for the third time in a row, I kick off my shoes and walk barefoot. The cool grass feels amazing between my toes.

I spot a giant shade tree and jog toward it. As safe as I feel in this little town, I still can't be too careful. I walk around to the backside of the wide trunk so I'm out of sight should anyone come to this part of the park. I take off my jacket and lay down, using my backpack for a pillow. The sun is starting to set now, but the breeze off the water is still warm and soothing.

I begin to collect my thoughts. I feel like I can stop running now. Unless I procure a boat, I've pretty much gone as far east as I can go.

"*Now what?*" says an annoying voice.

It has a point, though. I'm almost completely out of money after my makeover and tickets to get here. I can probably afford one night in a cheap motel or dinner…but not both. I won't last long at this rate. My stomach growls loudly in agreement. *Seriously, though, what am I thinking? This is so unlike me. My mom must be sick with worry by now. She probably thinks I've died or something.* I sit up and pull my cell phone out of my backpack. I'm about to turn it on when a thought enters my head. *Can my signal be traced? Will all this have been for nothing because I'm having a weak moment and missing my mommy?*

I throw my phone back into the bag. *Wait, no. I need to call her. Let her know I'm okay. Heck, maybe she'll understand. Maybe she'll wire me some money even.* I push the power button. As my phone begins to boot up, I lose my grip somehow. Rather than falling to the grass below, it flies from my hands and tumbles across the field toward the water. I chase after it in a panic. It stops just a few feet shy of the riverbank.

"Oh, thank God!" I sigh aloud.

As I reach down to grab it, it jumps out of my reach as if by magic and drops into the water with a plop. The current carries it quickly away as I watch it sink.

"What the hell?" I say to no one in particular. My eyes are filling up with tears. I think I'm going to cry. Now what am I supposed to do? I watch the spot on the water where my phone sank for a few moments as I try to pull myself together. Now isn't the time to fall apart.

As I turn to head back toward my tree, a woman has appeared and is sitting in the meadow on a plush patchwork quilt. She catches my eye and waves. She flashes me a bright grin from between deep dimples underneath a mess of gold and silver hair all piled atop her head. I look behind me to see if there is someone else she could be waving at. *Nope. Nothing behind me...aside from stupid phone-eating water.*

I slowly turn to look back at her. She smiles and waves again. Tentatively, I wave back. She motions for me to come over, patting a blank spot on her quilt. "Come!" she says giddily. "Join me, please!"

Under normal circumstances, I would run the other direction. She might be totally nuts, and I'm not a big proponent of talking to strangers as a general rule. I stand frozen, pondering...watching her watching me. She's sitting there patiently waiting. It's as if she isn't expecting a quick answer. She busies herself unpacking the contents of her picnic basket. She seems nice enough, right? It looks like she's got quite a spread there.

My stomach growls audibly as she pulls enough food to feed a small village out onto the quilt. I see cheese, a baguette, and is that jam? She pulls out a thermos and pours herself a glass of wine. I'm halfway across the meadow to her before I even realize that my feet are moving.

"Oh, how wonderful!" she says as she sees me approach. Her wide smile seems to stay on her face, even when she changes expressions. Deep soft laugh lines are well worn into her plump cheeks and settled in around her eyes. She must have lead a happy life. "Sit! Sit, dear! You must be hungry, mustn't you? Look at those skinny little legs of yours." She indulges in a hearty laugh right from the pit her belly. Obediently, I sit down in front of her and accept the glass she hands me. "Grapes from our vineyard on the Borough," she says proudly.

I take a cautious sip to be polite. "Wow. This is really amazing," I say astonished. "I've never had anything quite like it."

"Well, you wouldn't have, would you?" She shakes her head in a giggle. "I'll tell you what. I'll give you a bottle or two. It's the least I can do to repay you for keeping me company."

"Thank you, ma'am, but that really isn't necessary."

"Oh, don't be silly, now! It's impolite to refuse such a gesture. I insist. Now, I just live over in Stonington Borough. Do you know the area?"

"I don't, I'm afraid."

"Well, come along with me then, and I'll show you," she says as she hops up to collect her things. "It's just around the corner, really." She breaks off a hunk of the baguette and hands it to me with a wink before tossing the rest into the picnic basket. "Help me with the quilt, won't you, dear?"

We shake out the blanket and fold it up neatly.

"Off we go then!" she chirps and nearly skips her way toward the parking lot where a checkered taxi cab has just pulled in.

"Oh, but I couldn't possibly…" I start, but she's too far ahead to hear me now.

I grab my things from under the shade tree and jog to catch up. I probably shouldn't follow this strange woman into her cab, but desperate times call for desperate measures. I mean, I've known her all of ten seconds…but it's not like I have anything better to do. I resign to the idea of following her home and then finding a place to stay nearby. If she's a psycho killer or something, I can probably outrun her anyway.

I slip my heels on and click-clack across the parking lot to the cab. I try to pick up the pace and am reminded of my weakened ankle. It collapses under me as I all but fall into the backseat of the taxi. My left shoe flies off on the process. Real graceful. "Not to worry, dear," she says sweetly. "We should have another pair of shoes just your size."

"Oh, thank you…but that's not necessary," I assure her as I reach for my shoe. "Oh shoot," I say. "I broke a heel!" I collect my destroyed shoe from the ground and close the door behind me. Smart move, throwing my only other pair of shoes in the trash can in

Boston. Ugh! I eye the woman suspiciously as she grins at me. "Wait a minute. How did you—"

"My goodness! Where *are* my manners!" she says abruptly. "I didn't properly introduce myself. I'm Eloise. It's a pleasure to make your acquaintance." She shoves her tiny hand into mine and shakes it firmly.

"I'm...I'm, um, I..." *Crap what was my fake name again? I'm so over this whole lying thing! Violet, right. Violet.*

Eloise locks eyes with me and I lose myself for just a moment.

"I'm..." I'm literally incapable of looking her in the eyes and, "lying," I say.

"I'm sorry, what did you say your name is?" she asked.

"I'm lie...um, L-L-Lyla," I say, looking at my lap. What a train-wreck. *I'm lying? Really? That's the best I can do? Have I learned nothing so far?* A voice just over my shoulder is only halfway trying to stifle a laugh.

"Lyla. Such a lovely name," she says, thoughtfully studying me. "It suits you."

"Thank you," I say to my knees. She's right, though. It does suit me. *Lie-Luh. I'm such an idiot!*

Our cab ride is pleasant. Eloise tells me about growing up in the Borough and how much things have changed over the years. "Well, of course, everything really changed when the railway came to town..." Listening to her story, I'd think she was hundreds of years old. It's like she's from another time. She must be exaggerating, I'm sure.

In about five minutes, we roll into the little coastal town of Stonington. It looks like something out of a movie. New England charm meets storybook village.

"It's just up ahead there on the left. You can let us out at the end of the drive," Eloise cheerfully instructs the driver.

Upon arrival, you would be hard-pressed to find a house on the property at all. Most of the homes in the village look like something out of a 1950s idyllic sitcom. Each home has stereotypical curb appeal equipped with impeccably manicured lawns, ornamental hedges, and picket fences. The house next door even has ornate sky-blue shutters and tulip-filled planter boxes at every window as if proving a point. Directly across the street, a golden retriever eyes us lazily with mild annoyance while basking in the afternoon sun.

To say that Eloise's humongous lot stuck out among the rest would be a gross understatement. Big houses all close together, and then this. The winding driveway looks like an accidental brush stroke interrupting the sprawling rows of neatly planted crops. From corn to watermelon and a rainbow of leafy vegetables, it looks like she could feed the whole coastline. Nestled behind the gardens sits a mismatched collection of greenhouses in an array of different shapes, sizes, and hues. Overall, the effect looks like a large-scale replica of her patchwork quilt.

I make my way up the drive behind a spry Eloise as fast as my broken shoe can carry me and notice that one of the greenhouses is set up for tea. It's been converted into something of a sitting room. The walls are lined with short wide bookshelves so as not to block the sunlight. From here, many of the books look tattered and ancient. I make a mental note to snoop for treasure among the dusty volumes, if I get the chance.

A wrought iron cafe table and chairs sit, waiting in the center of the building. The sitting room is connected to the main house by a long arching trellis covered in lush cascading wisteria. The shock of vibrant purple blooms looks like tiny bunches of champagne grapes against the deep green vines. They almost completely conceal the window at the backdoor where a huddle of women has been watching us quite curiously. They see me see them and scatter like leaves on the wind. Suddenly, I'm feeling uneasy about this.

A few moments later, we make our way to the front door, though a little worse for the wear. It hasn't occurred to me to question Eloise's motivation for inviting me here. *Was I wrong to assume positive intent? Why am I so at ease with this stranger?* This seems to have become a theme for me. I hesitate before following her in the front door. *Was she just being polite? Am I imposing?* Just as I'm about to turn on my broken heel and head back down the driveway, the door opens, and I'm pulled in by a woman who suddenly doesn't feel like a stranger at all.

Evan & Jeanette

Astoria, Oregon, September 12

*I*t was dusk as Evan began the northbound crossing over the Astoria-Megler bridge. The mouth of the mighty Columbia river acts as a state line between Oregon and Washington. The water seemed agitated. Evan took this as a sign of foreboding and felt an uneasiness in the pit of his stomach. After an accidental southern detour, he'd decided to buy a real map. He'd driven nearly straight through from Sioux Falls.

The potent cocktail of sleep deprivation and exhaustion were proving to be just enough to let the ghosts and ghouls hidden along the blurred lines of reality seep in at the edges of his vision. Shadows out of the corner of his eye. Whispers in the dark. The glare of the oncoming headlights was nearly more than he could bear. He began to doze off, nearly swerving head-on into a long-haul truck. Long blinks. Heavy eyelids. The truck driver blew his horn. The sound remained long after the truck had passed, the chopping wind cutting through it in arpeggios. It faded away, but not completely. Not for what seemed like an eternity to Evan.

He had finally decided to pull over and rest when he realized how close he was. He saw the sign pointing left at the end of the bridge to Ilwaco and remembered seeing that town name on the map. It couldn't be much farther now. Wasn't that just a few miles away from Ocean Park? He pulled over next to the sign to get out and stretch for a moment. The salty sea air reinvigorated him.

"Now is not the time to fall apart," he said to the night.

He got back into his jet-black car and continued around the edge of the peninsula. He found a radio station playing top-40 pop and cranked up the volume. He passed through Ilwaco in a blink. He approached the town's single stop light, not even bothering to pause, and took the right turn toward Long Beach hard and fast. His tires squealed in protest. With the pedal to the floor, he passed a small hospital in a blur… and then a school…with a red lighted sign…with Nova's name on it? Evan practically ran his Mustang into a ditch and jumped out of the car. He ran at full speed back to the sign in front of Ilwaco High.

"We're praying for Nova," it said simply. Four words to change everything.

He stood there dumfounded. He'd driven all this way to find answers under the assumption that there would in fact be answers to find. Is it possible that these people were all just as clueless as he was? He walked back to his car and drove it a few more yards. He decided that he was too tired to face this new possibility tonight and pulled into the parking lot at Black Lake. He clicked off the engine and fell instantly asleep in the driver's seat.

* * * * *

Evan awoke to the predawn light peeking in through his windshield. The warm pinks, oranges and golds danced on the surface of Black Lake like wildfire. Evan slowly opened his eyes and got his bearings. He stared out at the aptly named lake, marveling for a moment at its inky color. He'd never seen anything quite like it. As he pulled out of the parking lot, he resolved to take in his surroundings on this trip. After all, it was his first time to the west coast. Rather than taking a right to head toward Ocean Park, he backtracked to the high school. With inconsistent memories from the night before, he wanted to make sure he'd seen what he'd seen. Sure enough, right there in bright red lights, the sign read, "We're praying for Nova."

Evan flipped a U-turn and headed the Mustang north. He wasn't sure what to think now. Did these people think she'd been kidnapped or something? He'd figured she must have run away. In his experience, most runaways were leaving something far worse behind them. As he passed into a "blink and you'll miss it" town called Seaview, he couldn't help but worry. First it was a boxy white shack that had been turned into a business advertising the sale of fresh seafood. Their shabby little reader board read "Crab, Tuna. Bring Nova Home."

Next was a brew house on the right hand side of the highway. It looked abruptly modern amidst a row of weather-tattered buildings. The sign read, "Our thoughts are with you, Nova."

Sign after sign as Evan made his way along the highway through Seaview and into Long Beach, though the town name had changed, the scene remained the same. The grocery store, the ice-cream shop, the tavern—all displaying thoughts, prayers, and well wishes in solidarity for Nova.

By the time he rolled into Ocean Park, he felt numb. Maybe it was the crisp morning air whipping in through the window and across his white-knuckled grip on the steering wheel. Maybe it was because he had been holding his breath and clenching every muscle in his body for an indeterminable amount of time. Evan had never dealt well with ambiguity. Today, he was plummeting head-first into the unknown.

Though every single nerve in his body was urging him to turn his car around, go home, and try to forget about this girl, he wouldn't even consider it. An innate primal instinct to protect her controlled his impulses and lead him right to the parking lot of Jeanette's Café. He'd seen a woman on TV being interviewed in front of it with big brown eyes matching Nova's. A relative, he was sure. He was out of the car and halfway through the open door before he realized he had not formulated a plan.

The wooden wind chime hanging from the door frame jangled like a stale xylophone. In an instant, all eyes were on Evan. "Good morning!" called a cheerful woman from behind the counter. A bright familiar smile stretched across the lower half of her face, managing to avoid her eyes completely. It seemed genuine enough...not like the creepy smile you'd see on the face of a salesman that looks like it was clipped out of a magazine and painted on with craft glue. That kind of smile doesn't reach the eyes because it's a fake. This one, the smile on the face of this woman, was real. Her eyes were just too weary to participate. The contrast in her expression made it impossible to hold her gaze.

Evan knew right away he was looking at Nova's mother. Same eyes—big, brown, and searching. Same smile, the kind of smile that makes you smile back. Same sort of messy hair, though Jeanette's was a deep chocolate brown to match her tired eyes. Lightning silver streaks gave her depth and betrayed the youthful story her smooth skin was telling.

Evan felt self-conscious. He slunk into the chair at the end of the counter and busied himself looking at the menu. Jeanette eyed the unkempt stranger suspiciously. Sensing that he didn't want to chat, she set a mug down in front of him, filled it with piping hot coffee, and walked away.

Out of the corner of Evan's eye, he saw a newspaper clipping taped to the wall above the coffee brewer. The headline read, "The Search for Nova Daniels." Below was a ridiculous picture of Nova. Evan couldn't help but chuckle. It was her face all right, but it looked like something out of a cheesy catalog selling argyle sweaters and boat shoes.

He would have to remember to give her a hard time about it… if he ever got the chance.

"Hi there," said a gruff voice next to him. The man attached was tall and bearded, wearing a flannel shirt and tan coveralls. He looked a bit like a lumberjack to Evan, though he said he was a fisherman. "It's a big business in these parts," he'd told Evan. He did not, however, pick up on the fact that Evan didn't want to chat. Over corned-beef hash, he gave Evan the not-so-brief history of the peninsula. Evan did his best to pay attention.

"You from around here?" asked the fisherman through a mouth full of half-chewed toast.

"No, just passing through, really," Evan tried.

Dave nearly choked while laughing through his overstuffed mouth. "You can't really pass through. Much further, and you'll be drivin' in the sea."

Evan watched him with mild curiosity as he turned pink from laughing.

Jeanette was watching Evan now. *Could this be him?* she thought.

By the time Evan looked up and the fisherman had collected himself, Jeanette was across the café, refilling coffee cups.

"So what's that all about?" Evan asked, trying to sound casual. He was pointing at the newspaper clipping.

"Oh, Nova." The dramatic fisherman now lowered his voice to a whisper, pausing to look around, making sure they couldn't be overheard. "She's the daughter of the owner of this place. Kidnapped in the night or something they say. Such a tragedy." The fisherman donned a contrived look of sadness and shook his head slowly. Looking around again, he whispered to Evan, "If you're askin' me, I think she offed herself."

"What?" said Evan, shocked.

"You ain't never met a sadder sack. I'll tell you what. That is the darn sorriest girl I ever seen. Always mopin' around here, makin' her momma worry." The fisherman looked at Jeanette with pity in his eyes.

Evan spent the rest of the day at Jeanette's Café. He'd met about a dozen locals that had shared with him their varying theories on Nova's disappearance. Though he'd heard everything from alien abduction to running off to join the circus, a theme had developed. It seemed that most people thought she'd been capable of hurting herself/myself.

Jeanette had left right after the breakfast rush. The fisherman had told him that was her new routine. Instead of spending her days here, she spent most of her time alone in her house, afraid to be away from the phone in case Nova should try to reach her.

Evan took a walk outside to be alone with his thoughts. He walked the three blocks from the café to the windy shore of the ocean. Rather than marveling at his first real-life Pacific Ocean view, he let his mind wander to Nova. The girl he knew was full of life. She was funny, kindhearted, easy to get to know, argumentative, clumsy. She seemed happy. Evan did not know this version of Nova. The Nova he knew was definitely not capable of hurting herself. She certainly wasn't capable of leaving a mother who loved her to worry this way without so much as even a clue to follow.

* * * * *

Jeanette had left the café just before lunch, careful not to let the stranger notice her as she slipped past him and quietly out the door.

125

She practically jogged the quick blocks to her sunny Victorian house. She took the key from above the porch light and hurried inside. The letter was held by a heart-shaped magnet to the side of the fridge with the others, just out of sight. It was the fifth letter she'd received with no return address. All of the others had been written in riddled poetry, but still made some kind of sense—poems suggesting that Nova was okay and that she'd return home. Something about a journey that needed to be taken.

Jeanette had decided that probably meant that she was on a trip but alive. Some things she couldn't make sense of like something about freedom from the shackles of what cannot be seen. Some more specific, like a poem rhyming Sioux Falls with wherewithal. Jeanette had called the authorities immediately when she'd seen that one. They asked her who tipped her off. She said she just had a hunch.

The cops had searched for Nova in Sioux Falls to no avail. Someone matching the description had been identified, but there was no way to know for sure if it had been her. Jeanette feared they had just scared her off…or maybe scared away whoever was holding her. She tried searching the Internet for clues as to who the author of these letters might be. Something in her knew it wasn't her daughter's captor; rather, someone who was looking out for her.

By this point, she had read each letter over a hundred times, pouring over each word and trying to make sense of them. Most of them left her with a feeling of hope. All but this last one. The shortest. She'd read it so many times that the stiff parchment paper had become soft like cloth. Words were fading away where the folds were. It didn't matter, though. She knew it by heart:

> *Don't look for me or where I may be,*
> *For I'm not the one who holds the key.*
> *The new moon brings a man from afar.*
> *You'll know him just by his guitar.*
> *He'll look to you to show him the way through cover of night,*
> *not light of day,*
> *For he can break the spell she's under where shepherds roam*
> *and lost sheep wander.*

Jeanette had noticed the new moon two nights ago. She hadn't slept since, waiting and keeping her eyes peeled for any sign of a stranger in town. So far, she'd seen the same regular faces she saw every day in the café. Every day until today. She'd been so excited to see a new face at her counter. It was the first time she'd felt hopeful in weeks. It wasn't until the next morning that she knew for sure.

On her predawn walk into work to start her morning baking, she'd noticed the black Mustang parked around the corner. By the foggy glass, she had suspected that someone was sleeping in the car. Later in the morning, she just happened to be taking a bag of trash out along the side of the building when he got out of the car to stretch. As he turned to the side and yawned, arms reached long like a cat's, she saw the neck of a guitar on the backseat. The morning sunlight flickered off of the steel strings as if calling her attention to them.

She dropped her bag in surprise. Evan locked eyes with Jeanette. Recognition sparked between them. He had no doubt in that moment that she had been expecting him.

Part 2: Becoming

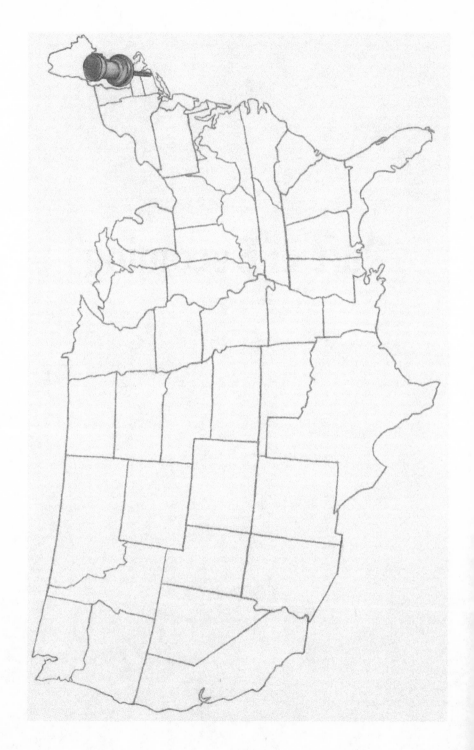

Lyla

*T*hough I know there are others in the house, no one comes to greet us. Eloise hasn't stopped talking since we walked in. I haven't absorbed a single word, but I don't have the heart to look away from her enthusiastic prattle. Robotically, I aim my best blank stare her way. I'm sitting in an overstuffed armchair in front of the big stone fireplace in the center of her cramped little living room.

Though the day was warm, Eloise said the evening air was chilly and insisted on building the fire for me. She has handed me a cup of jasmine tea and is running back and forth from the adjacent dining room, bringing chairs with her and arranging them in a half circle, all facing the fireplace…all facing me. *Why do I get the feeling I'm about to be interrogated?*

I'm suddenly uncomfortable. Maybe I should have been the whole time. I stand up and set my teacup down on the side table. "Well, thank you so much for the tea, but I'd better get going." I call into the dining room where Eloise has disappeared once again.

"Oh, goodness no!" she says, alarmed. "You have no place to go. Just sit right down and enjoy that tea. You'll catch your death in the sea air at night!"

We stand looking at each other. We seem to have come to an impasse. I'm not sure how she can say so confidently that I have nowhere to go, but I don't want to ask her. There are a lot of things that have happened these past couple of hours that I don't want to ask about. She's not going to let me leave without a good excuse… and quite frankly, I don't know what else to do. For the first time since I left Ocean Park, I'm more than a little bit scared. She must have known what I was going to decide before I even decided it. In the time it takes me to sit back down in my big chair, she's fetched a tray of cheese and crackers.

"I'd like to introduce you to my...housemates," she says. "*Ladies!*" she shouts to the ceiling. I hear the *click, click, click* of several sets of heeled shoes coming down the hardwood hallway. "Come! Meet our guest!" Another set of shoes is clicking down the stairway. I can't even count the number of footsteps. It sounds like a fashionable stampede. My heart is racing.

The first woman into the living room is unlike anyone I've ever seen. She's tall, maybe six feet, skin the color of rich dark chocolate, with a shock of stark white hair that falls stick straight all the way down her back to her elbows. Her eyes are a stormy gray, like the color of ice caps on the sea. She's wearing a black party dress with white polka dots all over it and a pair of blood red leather pumps. It's impossible to determine her age as she has so many conflicting characteristics. Somewhere between thirty and seventy.

"Suzanne, I'd like you to meet Lyla. Lyla, Suzanne."

"Hello," I say weakly. I feel like a field mouse under the sharp gaze of a hawk as it corners its prey. She is looking right into my very soul. I can feel her gaze and it makes me want to crawl out of my skin.

"Charmed," says Suzanne. She takes a step back to lean against the wall behind her and proceeds to stare me down. I shrink into the chair.

Next into the room is a petite athletic looking woman with angular features on a strikingly beautiful face. I'm guessing she's in her thirties. Long dark brown hair in thick waves hangs over her shoulders. She's dressed similarly to me in dark jeans and a blouse. Unlike me, though, she exudes confidence. No matter what outfit I have on, I don't have that. That and she's got shoes on. My cheeks flush with embarrassment as I remember my bare feet. I look over my shoulder at my beautiful broken shoe in the entryway and scoot my cold toes closer to the fire.

"Hi, Lyla, I'm Elaina," she says casually in a New Jersey accent and sits down next to me with a wink.

Next, two women walk in together. The first is maybe Eloise's age, which I'm guessing to be close to sixty. She's blonde and blue-eyed, slim and elegant. She's dressed in tan slacks and a lavender sweater set. On her arm is a woman who just looks like an older version of her. Same face, but maybe aged ten years or so. She's leaning on the younger woman for support, though as far as I can see, she's capable of walking just fine on her own.

"Lyla, this is Mary-Anne..." she starts, motioning to the younger version, "...and her mother, Mae."

Mother? Good genetics in that family, I guess. "Hi there," I offer.

Mary-Anne helps Mae into a chair across from me and sits down herself.

"Carolyn!" Eloise calls.

I hear a crash of pots and pans accompanied by some muffled swear words. A moment later, a woman hurries in to join us. She's Eloise's height with hair the color of honey. Kind blue eyes peek through her black-rimmed almond shaped glasses. She's wearing an apron and covered pretty much head to toe in what appears to be some sort of batter.

"Hi, Lyla!" she says breathlessly.

"Hey," I offer back.

Carolyn comes to sit down on my other side. She smells like birthday cake. My stomach growls at her as I reach for the snack tray. I chew my cracker, regarding each woman thoughtfully. It's not every day you find six grown women living together in one house. I wonder what their deal is.

"I don't like this. You need to get the hell out of here," a voice growls in my ear.

Suzanne steps out from her spot against the wall abruptly and marches right up to me. She looks just over my shoulder and sternly says, "Well, I think it's high time you let her decide for herself. Not another word out of you." The expression on her face is nothing short of menacing.

I look up at her, utterly stupefied. *Is she scolding the voice in my head? Can she hear my thoughts or something?*

"Well, this is quite a development," Eloise says nervously. "Suzanne, why don't you sit down and give Lyla her space? We don't want to frighten the girl now, do we?"

Um. It's a little late for that. Who are these women?

"Maybe she *needs* to be frightened!" argues Suzanne, watching me with a scowl.

"That's not necessary," Elaina pipes in. "Seriously, can't she at least finish her tea before we start fighting her battles for her?"

"We mustn't say too much now, ladies!" Eloise chirps, though she is unheard over the sea of voices.

"She's not a child," Mae adds.

"Isn't she, though?" Mary-Anne retorts.

"She has no idea!" Eloise's cheeks are turning bright red. Her eyes full of panic. She has obviously lost complete control of this situation, whatever it is.

"You don't know that!" I hear Mae say.

"She doesn't know," Elaina replies matter-of-factly.

Suzanne, who has been watching me pointedly while the others bicker, decides to speak up.

"Quiet. That's enough. So, tell us. Lyla, is it?" She pauses to wait for my reply, though I suspect she is well aware that my name is not Lyla.

"Yes. Ly-Ly-Lyla," I sputter.

"So tell us, Lyla, how long exactly have you been letting this nasty entity run your life?"

At that, the women are in an uproar. Six women shouting at top volume.

"Suzanne! You're being reckless!"

"You're going to scare the poor child to death!"

"What were you thinking?"

What does she mean by entity? Not a ghost or something, right? I mean, ghosts aren't even real. Everyone knows that. Besides, I'm not a little kid anymore. I know better.

Their words are all lost in a jumble of sound. Everyone is still shouting with the exception of Suzanne. I meet her gaze as we quietly wait for the waves of chatter to subside. As all eyes settle on me, all I can say is, "I don't know what you mean".

The room begins to spin. I'm feeling like I might be flung like a rock from a slingshot right out through the roof. I try to steady my vision and feel myself sliding out of the armchair toward the floor.

"She's going to faint!" I hear Eloise cry before the room fades to black.

* * * * *

I'm transported instantaneously to the valley that I know all too well. I find myself sitting cross-legged in the tall grass, sheep grazing in the distance. I'm disappointed to see that Evan is nowhere in sight. I'm not ready to see him here, but I need him. This is all becoming too much.

I look down onto my lap and see a pad of paper and a pen that seems to have manifested from nothing. I decide to write a note to leave for Evan.

Dear Evan,

It's such a mess. I'm somewhere in Connecticut, I think. Near the water. I met a woman who has some really intense roommates. I'm scared, Evan. Nothing makes any sense. I wish you were here with me.

Also, I'm sorry. I miss you. I miss Annabelle and Kate too.

Sorry, Nora Nova.

I set the pen down just in time to watch the bright greens of the rolling hills begin to melt away as Eloise's sitting room shifts back into focus.

Evan & Jeanette

Ocean Park, Washington, September 13

Jeanette and Evan just stared at each other from across the parking lot for a moment, each sizing up the other.

"Do you know me?" asked Jeanette. "Do you know my daughter?" she added.

"I know your daughter. At least, I thought I knew her," said Evan.

"How?" Jeanette asked.

"I'm her...she's my...friend." Evan stumbled over his words. "I'm Evan."

Jeanette felt her eyes well up with tears. She didn't remember ever hearing anyone her daughter's own age refer to themselves as her friend.

"Jeanette." She closed the distance between them to offer him a handshake. It felt foreign. What a strange time for formality.

"Do you know where she is now?" she asked him.

"No. I was hoping you could tell me."

They stood there, letting the silence sink in.

"Well, you must be hungry," said Jeanette. "Come on in and let's get you some breakfast."

Evan and Jeanette spent the morning in the café getting acquainted. Evan told Jeanette about meeting Nora and the life she had built for herself in South Dakota. He told her about his makeshift family of displaced souls, namely about his littlest charge, Annabelle.

In return, Jeanette told Evan her story. How she and Nova started a new life in Ocean Park. How she'd struggled to keep the café in business during hard economic times. How the community had come together to support her. This was exactly the kind of place she had dreamed of raising her daughter. Why was it never enough?

Evan could tell that Jeanette loved her daughter deeply, yet he found it so troubling that she seemed to be describing someone altogether different from the girl he knew.

"She goes on these extra-long walks in the middle of the night. She has for years. She waits until she thinks I'm sound asleep and then sneaks out. When she was younger, I would let her get a head start and then follow her, you know, just to make sure she was okay. She never saw me. I had to be so careful for fear she'd never forgive the invasion of privacy. I wasn't really afraid for her safety out here. I guess, somehow, I just thought it would help me get closer to her. When she was fifteen or so, I stopped following."

She paused, sighing.

"We've been strangers for many years. On some level, I have always felt like she's punishing me. I just don't know why. I catch glimpses of love in her eyes…but then it's gone. It's as if she won't let herself let me in." Jeanette spoke through a stream of silent tears.

Evan reached across the table and took her hand. It's all he knew to do.

"I'm sorry," she said, suddenly embarrassed. "I just haven't had anyone to talk to about it, I guess." Wiping tears away, she moved to stand up.

"It's okay," Evan reassured her, "I know the feeling."

She sat back down regarding him thoughtfully. "So, what's your plan?" she asked him. "Now that you're here, what will you do?"

"I haven't gotten that far," he said, exasperated. "I thought I'd come here and find answers. Something to tell me where she's gone. A clue of some kind." He paused, hearing the desperation in his own voice. "I wasn't expecting to find…well…you."

In that moment, Jeanette made the decision to trust Evan. "You love her, don't you?" she asked.

Evan was speechless. He wasn't prepared to answer that question…not even to himself. His eyes told her everything she needed to know.

"I'll tell you what," Jeanette began, giving Evan the chance to let out the breath he'd been holding. "You can stay with me. I made up the guest room, and it's all yours."

"Oh, that's so kind, really, but I couldn't impose." Evan was not used to being the recipient of charity.

"I insist," she said. "Besides, I might have the clue you're looking for."

* * * * *

Evan unpacked quickly, though there really wasn't much to unpack. Aside from the gray plaid shirt he was wearing, he only had one other with him. A long-sleeved thermal shirt in olive green. It was Annabelle's favorite. She said it matched his eyes. He tossed that along with a couple of white undershirts, one pair of jeans, and a few pairs of socks and boxer shorts into the drawer Jeanette had emptied for him. He hung his black motorcycle jacket on the post of the headboard on the cozy daybed and half jogged into the kitchen to see what "clue" Jeanette had to show him.

They sat at the built-in table in the corner of the big kitchen that fit snuggly into a wrap-around window overlooking the backyard. Jeanette took out Eloise's letters one by one and read them to Evan. She offered up her interpretations of each as she went.

So far, Evan had agreed with her logic. The one about a kind stranger with the heart of a gypsy explained how she must have gotten to Sioux Falls. He had wondered how she'd made it so far without being caught. He must have taken her the whole way.

"This last one is the only one that I just can't figure out," Jeanette said. "Does this mean anything to you?"

Evan read the worn letter silently:

Don't look for me or where I may be,
For I'm not the one who holds the key.
The new moon brings a man from afar.
You'll know him just by his guitar.
He'll look to you to show him the way

through cover of night, not light of day,
for he can break the spell she's under
where shepherds roam and lost sheep wander.

"You're white as a ghost," Jeanette said, shocked. "Are you okay? Was it something in the letter?"

Evan's mind was racing. Who could have written this? He had never told anyone about his dreams of Nova. Nova, the girl he grew up with, the only one who'd been with him always in a life filled with loss and grief. His constant. His dream girl. The girl that was somehow miraculously real, whom he'd let slip right through his fingertips. He had never spoken of it to anyone. Not even to Nova. He had known her the first moment he saw her when she'd nearly stepped on him in her rush to get to the diner that day. His dream girl, in real life.

"It's me," he said so quietly that Jeanette almost missed it.

"The guitar. I knew it was you when I saw that guitar in your car this morning!" she said excitedly.

"Not the guitar. I mean, yes. That too…but it's all me. I know where to find Nova."

Lyla

Stonington Borough, Connecticut, September 30

*I*t's been more than two weeks since I arrived at the Borough house. Time has been going by in a flash. It's almost as if I'm missing bits and pieces. Eloise refused to let me leave when I couldn't come up with an explanation as to where I would go. She set me up in a guest room just down the hall from her own bedroom. I'm not sure why this mystery of a woman decided to take me under her wing, but I'm thankful just the same. I haven't seen the other women much since the first night, aside from Carolyn who is pretty much always in the kitchen. I have a feeling they've all been avoiding me, but honestly, Eloise has kept me too busy to give it much thought.

We've been back and forth picking apples, berries, and lettuces to go to the farmer's market and working in the antiques shop in the Borough. The shop is actually owned by Carolyn, but apparently she's been neglecting it ever since the harvest began so she can devote herself to canning, making preserves, pies, and tarts—and a freezer full of other goodies for the winter. I don't mind, though. I love my time in the shop.

We don't see many customers, so I get a lot of time to explore while Eloise dusts and organizes. The showroom is a veritable treasure trove of trinkets just waiting to be discovered. I love imagining where different items came from and who might have owned them. A jeweled hair clip fit for a movie star, a jewelry box adorned in ivory and rubies, a red velvet chase lounge—a million untold stories are hidden in this place. Sometimes I touch an object and imagine an entire scene. It's like I can tell where it came from and see who owned it. Obviously, that's impossible, of course. Still, it's fun to let my imagination wander.

Business has picked up a bit this week as the changing fall colors bring hordes of tourists to New England. I can't help but be nervous that someone will recognize me here. As the door chimes jingle, I reach for a tube of red lipstick and apply it generously. I decide that makeup is my best disguise. Nova has never owned lipstick. Lyla, on the other hand, fiery red hair and a style to match.

"Hello and welcome." I smile my best salesgirl smile in the direction of the disheveled couple that has just entered the shop.

"Windy!" the woman says in a British accent.

I relax instantly. I'm certain no one is looking for me on the other side of the pond.

"I nearly blew away out there!" she says to the man who has come in with her.

"Let me know if you have questions about anything," I say as they make their way toward the back of the shop to admire a large seascape painting.

"Lyla, dear," Eloise chirps from behind me. "Would you mind, terribly, closing up for me this afternoon? I have a few errands to run."

"Oh, of course. Not a problem."

"I can come back and walk home with you after!" she says happily.

"Eloise, that's not necessary. It's four blocks. I think I can manage to make it on my own." I give her a reassuring smile. "Thank you, though."

"Of course, of course! You're a grown woman!" she says with a giggle.

I decide to lock up after my customers and take a stroll. I haven't really explored the Borough yet. I just haven't been very curious. I guess if you've lived in one small coastal town, you've lived in them all. That said, though, Stonington couldn't be more different from Ocean Park.

Proximity to the sea and friendly residents are where the similarities end. In the Northwest, the beach towns are so run down.

Poverty abounds. The families struggle to make ends meet, and jobs are few and far between. They'd all do better to move into a city and find a stronger economy, but they would never leave each other. The sense of community is worth it to them. In the Northeast, the beach towns are affluent. Rather than oyster farms and mobile homes, it's nautical themed mansions and exclusive yacht clubs.

Stonington is kind of the sweet spot of the eastern seaboard, if you ask me. Historic homes and a sprawling marina, but without some of the snobbery that old money can bring. I decide to go for a walk to window shop a bit. I walk across the street to the coffee shop to get a warm cup of tea to keep my hands from getting cold. Living in the Northwest, I've been spoiled with great coffee. I can't find a decent latte in the Borough to save my life, but it's pretty hard to screw up tea. Lyla is more of a tea person anyway, I think.

Though I'm blocks from the beach, the sound of sand crunching under my feet is constant on the concrete. A parked car in front of me has a bumper sticker that reads, "Life's too short to own an ugly boat." That alone speaks volumes about the differences between the two northern coasts. The last bumper sticker I saw in Ocean Park said, "There's a paper shortage, wipe your ass with a spotted owl." There is a kind of optimism and a lust for life here that doesn't exist where I'm from. I'm so used to cynics, I almost forgot there was another point of view. I can't help but smile.

I see a café called Noah's on the left. As I approach, the door opens, and a group of people walk out laughing and talking. The heavenly aroma of clam chowder wafts out of the doorway into the crisp fall air. I decide that a late lunch is in order and slip in before the door has a chance to swing closed. Inside, I see a rectangular bar at the back. The bartender waves at me like I'm an old friend and motions for me to come over. I take two steps and then pause to look over my shoulder, just making sure she means me. I grab a stool with my back to the wall of the room so I can people watch.

"What can I getcha?" the bartender asks.

"Is that clam chowder I smelled on the way in?"

"Must be!" she says.

"I'll take a bowl."

"You bet. A glass of Pinot Gris to go with?" she asks. "It's on special."

It seems like I ought to have my first real drink. I've never really been interested in alcohol, but I bet that Lyla is the type of girl that drinks white wine.

"*That's a bad idea*," says a voice from directly behind me. I start to turn to see who it is when I remember my back is to a wall.

"Oh, I'm not twenty-one," I reply shyly. She shrugs and heads through the double doors to the kitchen.

The bartender is back in a flash. "Here you go, hun," she says, setting down a steaming bowl of clam chowder in front of me. It smells even better up close. She sets a glass of white wine down for the waitress and turns her back. With a swift movement that I can't explain, I push the glass of wine over the end of the bar, crashing to the floor. The bartender jumps as the glass shatters into a million pieces. Startled, she turns to look at me. "Are you okay?" she says.

"Yes," I whisper. She's looking at me expectantly, waiting for an explanation as to what happened I'm sure. I don't have one. "I'm sorry," I offer.

"Don't worry about it," she says, pouring another and setting it down nearby.

"*No! No! No!*" shouts the voice behind me, so loud that it leaves a ringing in my ears. No one else seems to have heard it.

"Long day?" the bartender asks, making small talk.

"I guess so." I smile.

"Are you new in town?" she asks.

Oh great. The questions begin. Not knowing what to say that won't make me stutter like an idiot, I reply, "I'm Lyla." *Nice, no stutter. I guess I really am Lyla here.* She's not a lie anymore.

"Oh, hi. I'm Courtney. Nice to meet you."

Courtney and I are fast friends. She's from the area and is a wealth of knowledge about the Borough. It's after five by the time I notice the clock. Eloise will be worried.

"Well, I'd better head out," I say. "If you're going to the farmer's market on Saturday, I'll be there selling some pretty fantastic watermelons!"

"Wow! It's a little late in the season for melons, isn't it?" Courtney asks.

I shrug. I have no idea what crops grow when, but I guess it does seem a little odd that everything seems to be ripening at once.

"Okay, I'll come by and say hi. Maybe we can go grab coffee or something."

"I'd like that," I say, grateful to have met someone close to my own age, at least. I wave behind me on my way out the door and head back toward the Borough house.

Eloise

Stonington Borough, Connecticut, September 30

*E*loise had retreated to the back of the antique shop to dust the shelves when she'd caught a glimpse of an ancient looking book of poetry. Giddy with excitement, she'd plucked it from the crowded shelf and plopped herself down onto an oriental loveseat trimmed in gaudy gold medallions and fringe so she could examine it more closely. It only took moments for her to nod off. It seemed the older she got, the more quickly she fell asleep at the most inopportune of times. Mr. Cato, the cat that lived in the shop, took this opportunity to curl up next to her. He lived for stolen moments cuddled up with Eloise.

The vision came immediately. To Mr. Cato's chagrin, she awoke just a few minutes later to the sound of the door chimes. "Windy," she heard a woman's voice say in a British accent. Eloise was glad that Lyla was there to help the customer. She reached into her purse for a paper and pen and hastily began scribbling. She'd had a very brief vision. Vague this time. Still, though, she felt a sense of urgency to share what she knew right away. The post office would be collecting for the last time today in less than a half an hour.

> *He'll take the reins while she slumbers.*
> *She'll succumb, like a spell she's under,*
> *losing herself beneath his will*
> *absent, though she's in there still*

The details have not come to me.
His intention's all that I can see.
He's crouching now like cowards do.
Time will tell what he's up to.

* * * * *

Eloise was relieved to find that she'd beaten Lyla back home. This would give her a little bit of time to consult with the others about what she had foreseen. Though Eloise herself was a powerful sibyl, each of the women of the circle had her own special gifts.

Suzanne is a shaman of sorts. Her ancestors from the spiritual plane can come through using her energy. The magic of the old world still flows through her. She also has a knack for glamour spells. Suzanne is nothing if not fashionable.

Elaina uses the study of astrology to divine information. She lets the waxing and waning of the moon guide her practice and gleans the details from her tarot cards. Sometimes, she sets up a table in the Borough to do tarot readings for the tourists. She says it keeps her in practice, but Eloise thinks she just likes the attention.

Mae is a medium. Spirits come to her in all their forms for help and to provide guidance. Mary-Anne, of course, is an herbalist and conjurer. Her herb garden is her pride and joy. She can concoct a spell for nearly anything.

Then there is Carolyn. The women call her their kitchen witch. She can send intention through food. If you've ever heard someone say that their chicken soup can heal what ails you, only to wake up with the same affliction in the morning, you've never had a soup made by Carolyn. The night that Lyla came to the Borough house, Carolyn had made her famous truth tray, cookies meant to alleviate one's inhibitions. Homemade crackers meant to coax the inner truth from one's lips. Peanut butter fudge to quell the fear of knowing one's own truth.

Eloise was still reeling from the vision she'd had. Though there hadn't been much information, she felt a deep inkling of trouble ahead. She sat down at the head of the dining table and reached for the silver tea set in front of her. A dainty silver bell sat next to the tea pot. Though she rang it with vigor, the delicate sound was barely audible in the open room. She couldn't help but smile.

No matter where the others were on the grounds, she knew it would be but a matter of moments before they joined her. Mary-Anne had given the little bell the power to call to all of the women whenever a gathering was in order.

Carolyn had emerged from the kitchen with plates of tea cakes and cookies and was busily placing them around the table as the last of the women took their seats. Carolyn sat down quickly causing a puff of flour to rise from the fabric of her apron and surround her face. It made her look like she was in a tiny patch of fog for an instant. Eloise giggled nervously.

"Well, we're all here," Elaina said impatiently. "Who calls this gathering?"

"I do," Eloise confessed. "It's Lyla. She's in trouble. It's almost time."

As Eloise recounted the vague details of her vision, the women offered scenarios.

"We knew she was in trouble from the get-go. It's that ghost that's hanging around her."

Suzanne had not spoken a word. "I will talk to the ancestors to see what they can find out about him," she said with a scowl.

"He doesn't seem to fear us," Mary-Anne mused. "He knows we have been aware of his presence from the first night, yet he has made no move to conceal himself."

"He also hasn't tried to communicate with any of us, though, which leads me to believe that he has something to hide," Mae added.

"Maybe he's playing dead, thinking we'll just forget about him," joked Carolyn.

"She's coming!" Eloise said with a start. She had seen a flash of Lyla coming up the drive to the Borough. "Let's just agree to focus our collective energies on trying to suss him out. I have a feeling we have much to worry about."

"Agreed," they said in unison.

Lyla

*A*s I walk up the long driveway to the Borough house, I can't help but marvel at how quickly this place has begun to feel like home. My feet carry me by heart as though I've walked this path a thousand times. Eloise has been keeping me so busy that I really haven't thought much about my other life. My other lives. Nora and Nova. Even Violet. They seem like something out of a dream. It's as if this life in this moment is the one I've been living all along. Like I am Lyla and she is me. Every time something triggers a memory that this is all a lie, I have this voice in my head telling me to focus on the here and now.

Evan is the only thing that ever shatters the illusion. Every night since I've been here, I think of him. It's like I'm willing myself to dream of him. Like if I concentrate hard enough, I'll transport myself into our valley. *If I could just talk to him and try to explain, maybe he would understand. Who am I kidding, though, really? How could he forgive me after all the lies I've told? I walked out on Kate and Annabelle. My mother. I've let so many people down.*

"*He won't want you now,*" says a voice in the back of my mind. "*No one will.*"

My face feels damp. I touch my cheek and realize I'm crying. Eloise opens the door and snaps me out of it.

"Oh, sweet girl, are you crying?" she asks lovingly.

"No, just s-s-something in my eye," I attempt.

I walk into the foyer and notice that all of the women of the house are sitting around the dining table. It's the first time I've seen them together since the night I arrived. None of them says a word,

148

yet they're all looking at me conspicuously. I suddenly feel so vulnerable. It's like that dream where you're standing in front of your entire high school naked.

"Um. Hi, everyone," I say, more quietly than I intended.

"Hi, Lyla," they say all together. All but Suzanne who is glaring at me. We make eye contact for an awkward moment.

"*It's time to go upstairs,*" says a voice in my head.

"Well, I think I'll go upstairs now. Nice to see you all," I say politely and turn toward the stairs.

"Nonsense," says Suzanne sternly. She pats the seat of the empty chair next to her. "Come and join us for some wine and dessert."

Sounds delicious actually. I've been wanting a glass of wine since Noah's. I move to head over to the table and feel my hips rotate back toward the staircase. I fight against the involuntary movement and turn again, toward the table. It's like I only have so much control… like my free will is on the fritz or something. All but tripping, I force my body to move to the chair and sit down next to Suzanne. The whole fiasco only took a few seconds, but I can tell that the women think it was strange. They exchange suspicious glances.

Carolyn breaks the silence. "Here, dear. Have a macaroon."

"Thank you," I say, gratefully.

She pours me a glass of red wine. I pick up the glass and inhale deeply, expecting the familiar fragrant aroma of the wine made from the grapes here on the property. Instead, it smells putrid and sour, like death mixed with rotting seafood and a bunch of farts. I hide my disgust and slowly slide the glass away. Clearly, Carolyn made a bad batch. *Yikes. I don't have the heart to complain. I guess no one else does either, because they are all drinking it as if it's not completely nasty. That's a whole new level of loyalty!*

We spend the next hour making small talk. Carolyn regales us with stories from the antique shop. We all know that Mr. Cato runs the show there. The rest of us are simply guests in his domain. Elaina talks about plans for the weekend. She'll be helping us out at the farmer's market. We decided to add a second table, because of the extra-large harvest, and agree that we could definitely use an extra set of hands. They all ask me how I'm settling in.

"I made a friend today," I say proudly.

"Well, that is wonderful dear!" chirps Eloise.

"I mean, it's not a big deal. She might stop by the farmer's market, though."

"You'll just leave her like you leave everyone else," says a voice somewhere close by. I wince as if I've been slapped.

"Are you okay?" Eloise looks concerned.

Suzanne looks angry. She's scowling…not at me necessarily, but just past me. I can tell it is taking everything she's got not to say whatever it is she's dying to say.

"What is it?" I ask her timidly.

Though she's been nothing but nice to me, deep down, I am a little afraid of her. She looks at me intensely. Eyes like ice. Unmoving. I can feel it.

"It's time to go upstairs now. You've had a long day and you're tired," I hear a voice say.

"Well, I guess I'll head upstairs now. It's been a long day," I say and stand up. "Thank you for dessert." I smile at Carolyn and head up the stairs much faster than I mean to.

Evan & Jeanette

Ocean Park, Washington, November 2

The letter had come express mail yesterday, but already between the two of them, Evan and Jeanette must have read it dozens of times.

He'll take the reins while she slumbers.
She'll succumb, like a spell she's under
losing herself beneath his will
absent, though she's in there still

The details have not come to me.
His intention's all that I can see.
He's crouching now like cowards do,
Time will tell what he's up to.

Evan had decided to pack his bag again, just in case he needed to leave in a hurry. Though he still had no idea what the letter meant, he knew that Nova was in trouble.

He'd been picking up shifts at the café to help Jeanette out and to keep himself from going stir crazy. He'd been on the phone with Kate most days, just getting tips on how to be more of a help than a nuisance to Jeanette. Kate had told him he was helpless, but she liked talking to him just the same. She was just as worried about Nora as he was about Nova, though she was still too hurt to admit to it.

Evan was desperate to help Nova, but he had no idea how. He hated the feeling of helplessness, especially where Nova was concerned. Every night at bedtime, he closed his eyes and concentrated on the meadow where he knew she'd be. He tried thinking of her, thinking of his sheep, thinking of the green of the grass and the blue of the sky. Yet, every night, he found himself dreamless.

This morning, Evan had awoken early and called Kate right away. He knew she'd already be up and he needed to take his mind off of spending yet another night without seeing Nova. They talked for an hour. Kate caught him up on all things Annabelle. "Her teachers say she's a star student and she has made some friends."

Evan was relieved to hear that she's finding some sense of normalcy in all this. Between Kate, Hank, and Jerry, she had everything she needed.

"Seriously, Evan. You worry too much." Kate told him. "We've got it covered. You just focus on what you're there to do…"

Even now, Kate still couldn't bring herself to say Nora's name, let alone Nova's. She felt her anger fading away and was clinging on to what was left of it. If she could stay mad, then she wouldn't have to miss her. Somehow, missing her felt unbearable to Kate.

"Well, I think I'll go in early and see if I can help Jeanette with the morning baking," Evan said.

"Are you kidding me?" Kate giggled. "You are absolutely no help in the kitchen. Sorry to tell ya. Why don't you just go back to sleep for a while and stay out of her way."

"Thanks for the vote of confidence," he replied, acting hurt.

"Hey, I just call 'em like I see 'em," she said.

"Ah, now, there's the bratty little sister I never wanted in true form," he joked.

"Love you too, Ev," she said. "Keep me posted on…you know."

"Will do, Kay."

He hung up the phone and laid back down. Though he had every intention of going in to the café early just to spite Kate, a wave of exhaustion washed over him. He decided to just close his eyes for a few minutes. *Maybe just until the sun comes up*, he thought.

Within seconds, his eyes filled with the shocking brightness of a midday sun. He squinted and tried to blink away the purple spots in his vision left behind by the light. When the world returned to focus, he found himself in a meadow. He looked down at himself and saw that the familiar tan linen smock hung loosely over his chest and down to his knees where his boxer shorts were just moments before. He raised his head slowly, almost afraid of what he might see. Afraid of not seeing Nova here. Nervous about having to come face-to-face with her and not knowing what to say.

As his gaze found the pasture, he saw that it was empty. His heart sank. Several of his sheep grazed on a hilltop in the distance. He started turning slowly, scanning every inch of the valley for her. As he rotated, he found more and more space devoid of Nova. He felt like screaming. What was the point of this place without her? Would fate be so cruel as to keep him from her like this when she needed him most? When he needed her most? He took a step and heard something crunch beneath his foot. He bent down and found a folded up sheet of notebook paper. He opened it so quickly, it nearly ripped apart.

Dear Evan,

It's such a mess. I'm somewhere in Connecticut, I think. Near the water. I met a woman who has some really intense roommates. I'm scared, Evan. Nothing makes any sense. I wish you were here with me.

Also, I'm sorry. I miss you. I miss Annabelle and Kate too.

Sorry,
Nova

Evan's hands were shaking. He dropped to his knees. Trying to make sense of it all was pointless. There was no logical explanation for this place. This meadow. This world he'd seemingly created as a place of peace from his favorite story book when he was a little boy. The place where he'd met Nova all those years ago. Never in a million years would he have imagined that any of it was real. Even now, he questioned his own sanity.

Yet here he was, holding a very tangible letter in his hand. He folded the letter back in half and clumsily gave himself a deep paper cut on the thumb of his right hand. It hurt, a very real pain that made this world fade to black at the corners.

"No!" he heard himself yell as he held onto the idea of this place as tightly as he could. He felt the air change, as if he himself might drift away. He lay his hands on the cool grass to ground himself and felt something under his palm. A pen. He sat back up and quickly began writing on the back of Nova's letter.

Nova,

Please just tell me how to help you. There is no reason to hide. Your mom has called off the police. You're safe. Just tell me how to find you.

He paused, unsure how to sign it. Sincerely? That seemed ridiculous. He realized that now was not the time to hold back.

love,
Evan

He had barely set the pen down when the sun faded to gray and he was back in the early light of Jeanette's spare room. He ran his hands across his face, trying to get a hold of himself. He felt a warm dampness on his cheek and pulled his hands back to examine them. Dark blood ran slowly from a deep cut in his right thumb. A paper cut. He jumped up to go into the bathroom and clean himself off.

His reflection in the bathroom vanity startled him. He looked like a warrior. Cheeks pink from the warmth of the sun. A crimson streak ran from the bridge of his nose to his cheekbone. As he splashed warm water onto his face and watched the remnants of dried blood wash down the drain, he acknowledged for the first time that this was all very much real.

Lyla

Stonington Borough, Connecticut, November 9

*I*t's the day of the farmer's market, and I have a million things to do before it opens. The first order of business is cutting these stupid hair extensions out. I don't know what I was thinking with these, I mean, aside from running from the law and all. They are totally impractical. I can't put my hair up into a decent ponytail, and it's so long that it gets in the way constantly. I snuck a pair of Eloise's sewing scissors out of the sewing room and am cutting out the last few strands in the mirror above my dresser when I hear a knock at my door.

"Lyla, dear?"

On no, it's Eloise. She'll kill me if she sees me using these scissors on my hair. "Just a sec!"

"Okay, dear. It looks like the peaches are ready. Could I trouble you to help me pick a basket or two to take with us?"

"Be right down!"

I cut the last of the extensions out and push them all off the dresser top into the waste basket. I pull on my jeans and the Stonington sweatshirt I picked up from the coffee shop. With one last glance in the mirror before I run out the door, I stop short. No makeup. Sweatshirt. Hair still reds and ambers, now shorter and messy. I look way too much like Nova.

I grab my cosmetics bag and apply some mascara and lipstick before pulling my hair back into a loose bun.

"Better," I say to the mirror and run down the stairs to meet Eloise in the orchard.

She looked ridiculous standing on her tiptoes on the step ladder with layers of skirt and petticoat draped precariously over one arm.

"Eloise? Can I help?" I ask, testing the waters.

Eloise is very independent and seems to be extremely sensitive whenever anyone implies that she can't do something on her own. She definitely is one of the most capable people I've ever known, but she's also got to be near seventy.

Eloise sizes me up, I think trying to decide whether I'm asking to help or implying that she needs help. Satisfied, she climbs down from the ladder and motions to it.

"As you wish, my dear," she says with a wink. "Just a bushel or so if you would, and then we best get going. I'll go pack up the artichokes!"

She ran off before I could ask what a bushel was. Well, I decide a big basket full would do and haul it over to the wagon. We're walking distance from the town dock, so most Saturdays, we load our goods into red wagons to pull behind us. When I get to the driveway, I see that there are three wagons. I assume Elaina will be joining us today.

Carolyn is at the antique store today. She says Mr. Cato gets complacent if she isn't there herself on occasion. Mae and Mary-Anne never come to the market. Neither does Suzanne, thankfully. Though I feel like I've built relationships with all of the women in the house, I am still never comfortable around Suzanne.

"Oh lovely, dear!" says Eloise as she sees me walk up. "Just put the peaches in the first wagon and we're ready to go!"

"There are three today," I observe. "Who else is—"

"Well, let's get going, ladies. I haven't got all day." Suzanne has come up behind us. Where Eloise and I are both dressed for the weather, Suzanne has chosen a tangerine colored silk blouse and dark gray high-waisted slacks. While I'm wearing hand-me-down tennis shoes and Eloise dons her standard orthopedic Mary-Janes, Suzanne has chosen black snake-skin stiletto heels. How she can even stay on her feet on the gravel driveway is beyond me. Eloise sees my baffled expression.

"Suzanne will be coming along to help out today. Elaina is doing a reading for a client, and we have more than we can handle on our own."

"Perfect," is all I can manage to say. She's right, though. We need the help. There are only a couple of weeks left of the market for the season, and we're still harvesting almost everything. Today, our wagons are overflowing with peaches, artichokes, cherries, herbs, honey, bottles of wine (hopefully not the bad batch), cucumbers, arugula, and kale. Though I'm certainly no expert on farming, I can't help but wonder if it's normal for these things to be growing this time of year. Aren't peaches a summer thing?

We make our way to the market quickly. I have to jog part of the way to keep up with Eloise and Suzanne. When we arrive, the market is already open and crowded. Conversations and laughter fill the air. That is, until we approach. An eerie silence falls over the crowd in a slow moving wave as one person, then another, notices us. Eloise gets looks of reverence from one person, then another. while Suzanne gets looks of fright. At least I'm not the only one who is terrified of her.

I'm used to it by now. It's the same thing every week. It's like people are afraid of the women for some reason. I've heard some really funny ideas. People think they are in a cult or that they practice witchcraft or something. It's ridiculous. I mean, I get it on some level. In the beginning, I found it odd that six women were living together, but I don't anymore. It seems like any other family to me. When I asked Eloise why they don't just tell people they aren't worshipping the devil or something, she just laughed. "People will think what they want to," she says.

Anyway, it never seemed to be bad for business. We sell out almost every week. We always seem to have things no one else is selling, which helps.

"Hey, Lyla!"

I turn around to see Courtney, my only friend in the Borough outside of our house. "Hey, Court."

"I'm headed to Noah's to help with the brunch rush. Want to grab coffee after the market?"

"Sure! I'll meet you over there," I say. I could use some time out of the house. The days have been passing quickly. It's almost as if I'm missing chunks of time. Some days seem to drag on forever while others... I can't explain it, but it's like I just miss parts. Like

I'll finish breakfast and then suddenly, Carolyn is in the kitchen making dinner.

Spending time with Courtney makes me feel normal, which sounds great after the week I've had. Whoever said living on a farm was relaxing has never lived at the Borough house. Between harvesting and picking up shifts at the antique shop, I barely have time to sleep.

As I finish setting out the produce on the display table, I hear whispering behind me. I can't make out the words and turn to see who's there. Nothing. As I turn back around, I lock eyes with Suzanne. She is staring at me intensely. I hear the whisper again. I feel dizzy.

"Lyla?" I hear Eloise calling my name. "Lyla, honey, can you hear me?"

"Yes," I say, though I feel a little groggy.

"Honey, let's get going. We're all packed up. We sold everything! Can you believe it?"

"Wait. We...what?" I'm confused. I look around and see that our table is empty. The little chalkboards we use to display our pricing are packed neatly back into Eloise's wagon. The noisy crowd that was here just moments ago has vanished.

"I still can't believe you sold all the wine to our very first customer! We'll have to crush grapes tonight!" she says cheerfully.

"I... I what?"

"Oh, don't be so modest, Lyla! You have a real knack for sales. Don't let Carolyn see you do that or she'll never let you out of that shop!" Eloise giggled.

"I won't," I say doubtfully.

Suzanne hasn't said a word. She's watching me with unwavering focus.

"Ellie, let's go and let Lyla see her friend," she says.

"Oh, yeah. I'm going to meet Courtney for a while if you don't need me," I say, remembering our plans.

"Oh, dear! See you at home later on then," Eloise says reluctantly. She and Suzanne grab the wagons and start their quick walk back toward the Borough.

It takes me a moment to move. *Is there something wrong with me? I seriously don't remember anything from the last three hours.* I was setting up, and then it was over. *I obviously need to get more rest. Maybe all the lies are catching up with me or something. I could definitely use some coffee, though, that's for sure.*

* * * * *

As I walk up to Noah's, the neon "Open" sign flares brightly and then bursts, burning out and sending minuscule fragments of glass cascading down the inside of the window. The customer sitting at the table in the window jumps up, tipping the table over with him, and sending plates and glasses flying. I'm frozen, just watching the scene unfold. Courtney runs over to help the man and clean up the mess. She catches sight of me and mouths, "Give me a minute."

I nod. My heart is racing.

"*Oops!*" says a voice somewhere close by. It's followed by faint laughter.

"Four points, I guess," I say to no one in particular.

I'm pacing back and forth next to Noah's, trying to figure out where my day went. I've been losing time lately, but not like today. At first, I thought I was just sort of losing focus. Now I wonder if there is a more complicated explanation. I guess karmatically speaking, it would serve me right to end up with some sort of inoperable brain tumor or something. I've certainly earned a bit of bad luck, I suppose.

"Hey, Lyla," Courtney says as she walks out to meet me. "How was the market?"

"It was..." *I am at a loss.* I don't remember a thing from the market aside from setting up and tearing down. "Well, we sold everything, so I'd call it a success."

"Wow! That's great. You guys had quite a haul."

"Yeah. That's nothing compared to what's in the gardens. We might need another table next week," I say.

"Well, it's nice that you had time to get down to the marina. I saw you down on the docks earlier. Do you have a boat in the harbor?" she asks.

What? The docks? I've never been down into the marina. She must have seen someone who looks like me. Though, this is a small town.

"I don't…um…no," I try.

"I tried calling your name but you must not have heard me," Courtney says.

Was I on the docks? I know I lost a few hours today. Was I sleep walking or something? "Oh yeah. I didn't hear you, I guess."

"It's no big deal." She's eying me with concern. "Are you okay, Lyla? Seriously. You look like you've seen a ghost or something."

My hands have gone cold.

"*Everything is fine. Don't be paranoid,*" says a voice just over my left shoulder.

I'm staring blankly ahead. It's like it all just hit me at once. The docks today. The other day, Eloise said she'd seen me in the orchard when I could have sworn I was napping. I thought she was just seeing things, but then I found mud on my shoes. *What is happening to me?*

"*Nothing is happening to you. Snap out of it, you're weirding your friend out. You don't want to scare off your only friend now, do you?*"

"Lyla?"

Courtney's hand on my shoulder snaps me out of it. "Sorry, I'm fine. I could definitely go for a cup of coffee, though."

"Okay, let's walk up to the coffee shop," she says.

I groan. She knows how much I hate their coffee.

"Oh, c'mon! My treat!"

Courtney's apparent good mood is contagious. She entertains me with hilarious stories from the bar over coffee. I find myself actually enjoying my cup. Maybe Lyla would like this coffee. I mean, she didn't grow up in the Pacific Northwest, totally spoiled with a coffee roaster within walking distance. She wouldn't think twice about an overpriced, over-sweetened latte. A Connecticut latte. I take another sip. Even better than the last one.

"So, what were you doing in the marina anyway?" Courtney asks.

"I don't know," I say honestly. "I have never been on a boat before."

"*What!* You're kidding me! How is it humanly possible to grow up in New England without ever having been on a boat?" She looks at me in utter disbelief.

Great. This is exactly why I shouldn't bother building relationships here. It's all based on lies. I don't even have a good backstory for Lyla. I'm racking my brain for a good response, just willing my watered-down coffee to kick in and get my mind going. Mercifully, she doesn't wait for an answer.

"Well, we're going to fix that right now," she says matter-of-factly as she pulls out her phone. "Hey, it's Court. What are you doing right now?" She grins at me while listening to the reply of whoever is on the phone. "I'm having coffee with a friend who has literally *never* been on a boat before." She giggles. "I know, right? Do you have time? Just once around the harbor is fine. Uh-huh. Okay. See you in five."

"See who in five?" I ask.

"Just a coworker of mine. He's got a little fishing boat in the marina. Not a fancy sailboat or yacht, but he putts around the harbor almost every night."

"I don't need fancy," I say, motioning to my sweatshirt and jeans.

"Well, it will be perfect. Now that the days are getting shorter, we'll be out at the point just in time for sunset. Who knows how many more sunny days we'll get? We'd better take advantage of it."

"That's really nice of you, Courtney, but really…you don't have to—"

"Don't you dare try and get out of it! It's totally no big deal. Besides, it will be fun! Unless you're dying to stay here and have more of this delicious coffee."

We share a giggle like old friends.

The Circle

Stonington Borough, Connecticut, November 9

The women of the circle were all home but were spread out all over the property when Eloise rang the silver bell. Mae was in the greenhouse under a blanket rereading Dickens for the umpteenth time while Mary-Anne was tying up bundles of herbs with twine to hang dry. Carolyn was in the cellar labeling wine bottles from the latest batch. Elaina was just returning from a run and was enjoying some cool-down stretches in the orchard.

As clearly as if it had been right next to them, they all heard the soft jingle of the enchanted bell. They each dropped what they were doing to head to the dining room. All with the exception of Suzanne.

Suzanne was in the attic. She had climbed the little retractable ladder and then pulled it up behind her, shutting the trap door quietly. The last thing she needed was an interruption when she was planning a conversation with the ancestors. Devoid of her typical high fashion ensemble, she wore a modest hooded robe the muted color of raw linen. She sat barefoot and cross-legged on the hardwood floor. Votive candles were arranged carefully in the shape of a crescent around her. She used the crescent to pay homage to the ancient gods and bring forth the spirits of her own ancient relatives. It pleased the ancestors to see a display of such honor. That she would humble herself in their sight would show them further still that she came with no vanity or selfishness in her heart. Around her neck she wore an amulet of amethyst. She clutched the stone tightly in her hands as she closed her eyes to call the ancestors in.

"Mother if you hear me, sit with me this night. Share with me your light that it may draw to us the spirits of our mothers before us."

She concentrated on a white light surrounding herself. She felt her mother's spirit join her in the glowing crescent. In a flash, she transformed—a confident woman to a tiny babe in her mother's loving arms. She closed her eyes to let the sensation envelop her and took a deep breath.

"Great Mothers before us, hear me now. Enter into this crescent and speak freely of what you know and what you have foreseen. Share your wisdom on this night as the moon rises. Guide my power as it pleases your great plan. Whisper to me how I might help our young visitor, for I am your daughter in spirit and in light."

A subtle wind rose in the attic, causing the little flames to dance excitedly.

"We hear your call, dear daughter."

Suzanne opened her eyes to see seven women standing before her. Though they were translucent, she could see them as clearly as if they were there in the flesh. Generations of her blood. Her family. She stood to face them.

"Why have you called us here this night?" her eldest ancestor inquired, her voice reverberating as if it were coming from down a long corridor rather than from mere inches away.

"Thank you, Mothers," she said with a slow bow of her head. "I call you in for guidance. I trust that you know of the young woman who has come to stay?"

"We do," said one of the ancient mothers. It was hard to tell who was speaking. They seemed to answer as one voice, the sound rushing over Suzanne like a warm wind making her feel safe and small. The beloved child fortified by the love of her matriarchs. She dropped to her knees, bowing her head again.

"Thank you, Great Mothers," Suzanne replied.

"She is in grave danger. She is but a pawn in her captor's game. He gains more control by the hour. Without intervention, she may be lost completely," warned the entangled voices of the ancient mothers.

"Yes. It's just as I feared. He is careful and cunning. He does not show himself to the women of the circle. Not since the first night," Suzanne told them.

"He has been planning this for many years," they said as one. "Inching his way in. Gaining her trust. Making her think his voice is that of her own subconscious mind. Leading her away from relationships that may influence her so that he may have sole control of her choices and actions."

"I don't understand," said Suzanne, looking at them now. All seven generations of her ancestors fixed their gazes upon her. She shuddered under the intensity. So much love, yet so much power. She felt a reverent fear begin to build in the pit of her stomach. She tried quickly to stifle it, knowing that if the Mothers sensed her fear, they may strike. "Forgive my ignorance, Mothers," she said, steadying her breath. She bowed her head again, focusing on the image of a white light surrounding her. Protection and strength.

"Dear child. Don't you see? Just as her mother took the child from its father, he would wish the same vengeance. He wants the mother to suffer. He has driven a wedge between she and her daughter. If he can't have her, neither shall her mother."

"I see," Suzanne said.

The Mothers continued. "Over time, he grew bored with his quest for revenge. His selfishness had caused his daughter to live a life of solitude. His soul is bound to hers, yet this life bored him. He desires adventure. His wanderlust rules him now. By the time he decided to take her, it was easy for him. He simply turned her feet away from home and planted the thought in her mind."

"So she is but a vehicle? What kind of a father would do that to his own daughter?" Suzanne was appalled. Though she had contemplated many theories, this truth was far more repulsive. "He's a parasite."

"Precisely, dear child."

"Great Mothers, how can I save her from this vile demon?" Suzanne asked, daring to look at them once more.

"Be patient, dear heart, for he is letting his guard down now. We see him losing focus and becoming careless. He feels it too. He fears that the addictions that plagued him in the flesh will weaken his hold on her now."

"That explains why she won't drink the wine," Suzanne realized aloud.

"Yes. He will be cautious, so be careful not to let on that you know of his presence. You cannot help her if she does not stay."

"Thank you, Great Mothers. I will convene with the circle. We will figure out a way to rid her of her father." Suzanne stood, ready to end the ceremony. "Thank you for imparting your great wisdom on your daughter as undeserving as I may be. Blessed be your journey back to the great beyond. I send love and light to illuminate your path."

"Be well, dear daughter. You fill our hearts with pride." The Mothers began to shimmer and fade. Suzanne's own mother came to stand before her daughter.

"I love you, my sweet Suzie."

"I love you, Mother."

"You are a light in the darkness, my girl. Know that there is one like that for your visitor as well. Should she find herself in darkness, he may be the way."

With that, the image of Suzanne's mother shimmered and then faded away. As the Great Mothers vanished completely, a cold bitter wind blew through the attic, extinguishing the crescent of candles and leaving Suzanne in darkness. She shivered, partly from the sudden drop in temperature, partly from residual fear. It was then that she noticed the persistent ringing of the bell.

* * * * *

"We need to talk about what happened today," Eloise said to the others with more seriousness in her voice than they had heard in recent memory. "It's Lyla. At the market…she was there…and then…" She trailed off at a loss for words.

"And then the ghost of her father possessed her body," said Suzanne who had emerged from the hallway.

The women of the circle didn't have to question how she knew this. They could tell by her robe that she had come from a meeting with the ancestors.

"That explains it," Eloise said, sounding again like her cheery self.

Suzanne told the others what she'd learned from the Great Mothers. As she talked about Lyla's father's desire to keep her from having a relationship with her mother, Mary-Anne let a few tears fall silently down her cheeks. "What a cruel fate to subject your own daughter to. Every girl needs a mother," she said, reaching for Mae's hand. Suzanne too began to cry, albeit silently. Feeling her mother's spirit so close caused her to relive the loss every time she called the ancestors. *A price worth paying*, she reasoned.

"I saw him the moment they walked in on the first night," said Mae. "It was clear that he wanted his presence to be kept a secret, so I have made no effort to communicate with him."

"That's good," said Suzanne. "The last thing we want to do is let him know we're onto him. We need a plan."

Lyla

Stonington Harbor, Connecticut, November 9

The wind seems to pick up as we push off from the dock. I'm wishing I'd worn something warmer. Apparently, Courtney's friend wants to get a little distance between us and the other boats before starting the engine. He's using one beat-up looking paddle to navigate us out. At first, I thought he was just being courteous, but now I'm thinking it's more like good ol' fashioned embarrassment. The weathered little boat seats the three of us comfortably but probably could not handle four. I imagine at one time the exterior was painted white. Now it's almost indescribable. It's like if sadness was a color. Still, there is something charming about it.

He starts the small motor at the back with a pull string. It comes to life on the third try, and an involuntary laugh escapes my lips. It sounds like a shrunken lawnmower or a blender or something, all high pitched and wound tight. Courtney catches my eye and mouths, "Don't say anything about the motor."

As it turns out, I don't have to say anything to totally offend someone. Not only am I a terrible liar, but I have zero ability to edit my facial expressions. Courtney's friend looks at me just as I'm beginning to turn pink in the face from trying not to laugh. He turns the motor's little rudder by hand to change direction and it squeals like a stuck pig. I can no longer control it. I'm not sure if I'm laughing more because the wimpy motor sounds so ridiculous or because they are both taking all of this so seriously. He scowls at me for a moment before giving in to the hilarity of it all. We giggle our way through Stonington Harbor and out into the sound. I see an island just to the south of us and start to ask what it is.

167

"Hey, what's that—"

"Shhhhhh! Wait for it. Waaaaait for it…" Courtney's friend shushes me dramatically.

"But I just wanted to ask—"

"*Shhhhhhhhh!* Just a little bit further. Wait for it! And…*now!*" He stands-up fast, precariously rocking the boat. He clears his throat theatrically, and in a very official voice, he starts. "Let me be the first to officially welcome you, Miss…oh crap! I don't even know your last name!" he says.

Um, I don't even know his first name. Now it's that awkward thing where I should already know, so it's sort of too late to ask. "It's… Da… Shepherd," I say.

"Right. Okay." Clearing his throat again, he says, "Let me officially welcome you to New York, Miss DeShepherd. As a proud New Yorker, I hope that you enjoy your time here." He bows deeply, taking off his baseball cap, waving it at me, in turn throwing himself off-balance and kicking the motor. The boat turns sharply and rocks hard while we all struggle to stay right-side up.

"Aaaaand welcome back to Connecticut!" Courtney says.

We laugh ourselves into a frenzy.

"Oh, wow, you are a terrible tour guide!" Courtney says jokingly to her friend. He seems a little bit hurt.

"Hey, I appreciate it. That was my first time to New York," I confess.

"What?" he says, genuinely shocked. "You've never been on a boat *and* you've never been to New York? Geez, Court, what cave did you find this one in?" he asks. "No, seriously."

"Well, I'm here now," I offer, hoping to end the questions before I am forced to try and lie to my only friend again.

"*This* is not New York," he says, making a wide sweeping motion with his arm like he's some kind of game show host.

"You just said it was," I say, now beginning to get irritated.

"You haven't seen New York until you've seen Manhattan, baby. Plain and simple."

"*He's got a point,*" adds a nagging voice in the wind.

"Well, it's on my list of places to see," I say dismissively. Realizing that I'm not about to get as excited as he wants me to be, he changes the subject. I guess I always figured if I got to the east coast, I'd head straight for NYC. Now that I'm here, though, I really have no desire to see it. I'm not sure if I've just built it up in my mind so much over the years that I don't think it has a chance of living up to my expectations or if I really am just a small town girl through and through.

"It will be sundown soon. Let's watch the sunset from Stonington Point." He aims the little vessel northward.

We ease back into the inlet, just in time to see the sky light up. The grayish afternoon sky looks like it's being attacked by neon flames. Electric orange, blazing pinks and reds, and just to the edge of my sight line, the top half of the sun winks our way.

"How funny. You can barely see the sun from here," I say, not fully aware that I'm thinking aloud. I don't think I'll ever get used to seeing the sunset without the sun in the middle of it. From the Borough house, I can't see it at all. I watch the colors fade over the orchard from my room and yearn for my peninsula sky. It's just not the same.

"What did you say?" asks Courtney.

"Oh, nothing important. Where to next…man?" I say to her friend. *Man? Ugh. Get me off this boat.* I am too awkward to function.

"Back to the marina," he says, bashfully.

"The boat doesn't have a light on it, and he is already on warning from the harbormaster not to crash into anything else," Courtney explains. "No drinking and putting, he says." She laughs.

"Shut up, Court! That was one time! Geez," he says, pink-cheeked.

"Um, someone is sensitive!" I add sarcastically.

As we maneuver back into the boat's little slip, he says, "Well, he didn't say anything about drinking when we're tied to the dock!" He pulls a bottle of cheap champagne out from under the seat.

"Hey! I guess this was a good idea after all!" Courtney says.

"Very funny, jerk face," says her friend with a wink.

"Um, were those sparks I just saw flying between you two? I'm pretty sure I detect a love connection."

"*Whaaaaaaat?*" he says, totally proving me right. He's looking at his shoes.

"Us? Whatever. I'm going to go get cups," Courtney says and hops out of the boat.

"Oh, wow. I'm right, aren't I?" I ask him. I'm so happy to have the attention on something other than me that I can't even help myself.

"Right about what?" he asks coyly.

"You are totally into her, aren't you?"

He cranes his neck to see if she's within earshot.

"You're fine. I just saw her board that big sail boat over there," I say, pointing across the small marina.

"Oh, yeah. That's her dad's schooner. I can't believe she even bothers hanging out on my stupid dinghy when she could be out on that."

"Well, I'm guessing she likes the company better here," I say. "Stop avoiding the question! You like her, don't you?"

"So what if I do?" he says dismissively.

"Does she know?" I pry.

"Do I know what?" Courtney says, expertly stepping back into the boat.

"Oh my God," he says under his breath.

"I've got cups!" she says, suddenly blushing.

She totally knows what we're talking about. Pink cheeks, clammy hands. *She likes him back, I know it!*

"Jake, do the thing!" she says.

"Oh! Jake," I say accidentally out loud.

"*Real smooth,*" says a very rude voice somewhere in the dusk.

"Yeah, Jake. Do the thing," I say, trying to make a quick recovery. I have no idea what the thing is, but at least I have a name.

Jake steps up onto the dock with the bottle of champagne and kneels down to face his boat. Swinging it like a baseball bat, he cracks the neck of the bottle open on the back of the stern. A geyser of carbonation erupts from the jagged opening as Courtney cheers.

"You guys are so nautical right now," I say sarcastically as Jake quickly pours the spilling alcohol into our plastic cups.

"*Don't drink that,*" a voice says.

Remembering my recent clumsiness, I clutch my yellow cup tightly.

"*I'm warning you!*" it says louder.

I raise the cup to my lips.

"*I said no, dammit!*" it says at an almost deafening yell.

I nearly drop my cup as a result.

Jake and Courtney are staring at me suspiciously. They clearly didn't hear what I heard.

"What, you're too fancy for my gas station champers?" Jake says.

"Um…we forgot to toast!" I say, trying to cover my unease. "To the happy couple!"

We clink our plastic cups as they both glare at me. I move to pull the cup to my lips and it suddenly weighs a ton. I am getting so sick of this. I fight and win, taking long slow gulps of the bubbly warm liquid.

"*Dammit! Stop immediately! I'm warning you!*"

Courtney and Jake are staring as I empty my cup.

"Thirsty there, little slugger?" Jake says playfully.

"More, please," I say, forcing my hand to offer him the cup to refill. I drink the next cup full even faster than the first and give myself the hiccups. I'm waiting for the bossy voice to return, but I hear nothing. In fact, for the first time in a very long time, the only voice in my head is mine! I feel like a fog has lifted.

"Good thing I brought two!" Jake says, pulling out a second bottle.

Courtney and I both applaud.

Lyla

The Borough House, Stonington, Connecticut, November 10, 2:22 a.m.

*T*he smoke of several bundles of white sage hangs heavy in the air. I only sort of remember getting home. I must have walked here by muscle memory from the town dock. After a bottle of champagne all to myself and almost equal amounts for Courtney and Jake, I started to feel like an unwanted third wheel. I'm pretty sure they're still back on Jake's tiny boat…falling in love. I giggle out loud at the thought as a hiccup escapes my lips. I'm still just standing…well, swaying in the entryway. I'm awkwardly trying to kick off my shoes when Carolyn peeks her head out of the kitchen, looking for the source of these giggles.

"Oh! Lyla! I didn't hear you come in." She looks anxious. Then much louder, she says, "I'm glad to see that *you're home, Lyla!*"

I giggle some more. "*Glad to see you too, Carolyn!*" I match her tone and volume and then giggle. We're both shouting like we're performing in a poorly-acted community theater play. Suddenly, the smoke from the sage becomes overwhelming, and my giggles turn to coughing.

"Oh no, dear!" Eloise has come in the room and is hurrying toward me. In the distance, I hear voices speaking low and steady, like the rhythm of a drum circle. *Is that Mary-Anne? Suzanne too maybe? What are they saying?*

Mae has entered the foyer and is staring at me with her arms folded. "Evening," I say with a hiccup in greeting.

"I can tell you're tired, dear. Let's get you up to bed," Eloise says, taking me by the hands.

"She's not tired," Mae says, obviously amused. "She's drunk!"

172

"Oh my gosh, no, I'm drunk," I say, pretty proud of my acting skills…until I realize that I may have left out an important word. I hiccup again followed by, "Errr… I mean…not drunk." *Yeah. That ought to be convincing.*

A bit out of confusion, a bit out of embarrassment, I let Eloise lead me up to my room. We pass the den on the way to the staircase. The door is open just a few inches, but the candlelight catches my eye. I see Suzanne and Mary-Anne sitting cross-legged on the floor, holding hands. They are talking in unison. It almost sounds like chanting. I am laughing so hard I snort. "Are they pretending to be witches or something?" The idea totally cracks me up. I've never seen grown women acting out silly fantasies before.

"Oh, you are just seeing things I think, dear!" Eloise chirps in my ear and all but shoves me past the door and up the stairs.

I fall asleep in my clothes before I even get my other shoe off.

* * * * *

The sunlight in the meadow is such a shock from the blackness of my dark bedroom that it sends shooting pain to my head. "Ouch!" I yell aloud. My complaint is answered by a chorus of sheep. As my vision clears, I see there are more present than normal, all eyeing me expectantly. Of course, Evan is nowhere to be found. It's been so long since I've seen him, I am starting to wonder if he's even real. I turn 360 degrees slowly, hoping in vain that he's here somewhere. By the time I've gone full circle, I'm crying uncontrollably. Maybe it's the champagne as it seems to be in my head, even in dreams. Maybe it's just exhaustion. I mean, how long am I supposed to hold it together for, really? I slump into a cross-legged pile in the cool grass and give myself permission to just go ahead and sob. Head in my hands, I am crying so much now that I don't even know if I could stop if I tried.

The last couple of months come rushing back to me in sequence. Oliver; the sort of kindness that equates to instant trust. Under any other circumstances, would I have left? Why did I leave anyway? I don't remember ever deciding to. In fact, I don't remember deciding much of anything since I left Ocean Park. Since I left Nova behind.

I mean, I really can't say that I'm regretting it. If I'd stayed there, I never would have gotten to meet Annabelle, Kate…Hank and Jerry…Evan. Nora's life was rich. She was surrounded by more love in a matter of weeks than Nova had amassed in her lifetime. If I'd never met Evan, would I have dreamt of him forever, just thinking he was a figment of imagination?

But Nora Danbert turned out to be such a coward. She ran from the people who trusted her and never looked back. Luckily, Violet was no coward. Violet Shepherd was fearless. Fiery hair and spirit. Unafraid to move forward, driven only by necessity…maybe curiosity. Sadly, Violet was fleeting…like any bright flame, she burned out too soon. Frankly, it was exhausting to be so fancy all the time!

Now Lyla. Lyla makes sense. She's building a life for herself in Connecticut. Living at the Borough house with six eccentric women, working at the antique shop, selling peculiar amounts of off-season produce in the farmer's market. And Courtney. Another friend. Someone else who trusts me. Someone else that I'll eventually let down.

Still crying, I lay down on my side, the tall grass cradling me like a sun-kissed blanket. I feel a soft pillow-like sheep brush against my back. He has plopped himself down beside me. It catches me by surprise and helps me regain control of myself. I turn on to my back so I can pet the sheep. He's watching me with what looks like empathy in his dark eyes.

"You've been here all along too, haven't you?" I say to the sheep. I sit up to look around and see that they're all still watching me. I guess I'm not really alone after all. One sheep several yards away suddenly starts to wail. She's stomping her hooves and calling out with urgency in her voice. She begins to buck wildly in between "baa" sounds. I feel like she's trying to get my attention. I stand and walk toward her.

"It's okay, girl. I'm here," I say soothingly. Instantly, she calms herself, watching me walk closer. As I approach, I see something at her feet. It's the note I wrote Evan. I can see my handwriting from here. With a swift kick of her front hoof, the little ewe flips the page over and I can see that there is now something written on the back.

I feel my heart race. "Oh thank, you!" I say to her and drop to my knees to grab the page.

Nova,

Please just tell me how to help you. There is no reason to hide. Your mom has called off the police. You're safe. Just tell me how to find you.

love, Evan

My fingers gently stroke the words on the page as if I can reach Evan through them. *Love.* I read the word over and over. "There is no reason to hide. You're safe," he'd said. *I guess I haven't been hiding for a while now. I know I'm safe.* "Your mom has called off the police." *My mom. My poor mom! What must she be thinking? And how does Evan know she's called off the police? He doesn't even know her, right? I mean, how would he?*

I haven't thought about the police at all lately. My red hair has faded almost back to my natural color now. Something of a mousy strawberry blonde is all that's left. I cut my extensions out earlier. Anyone that was looking for Nova would know me when they saw me now. So what has been keeping me from calling my mom? What has been keeping me from calling Kate and Annabelle aside from shame? I feel like I'm thinking clearly for the first time since I left home. I can't explain it.

Suddenly, I'm afraid to wake up from this place. I'm picturing my life like it's a movie, something I've been watching but not truly participating in. Have I had no control? What's been happening to me? Is it something the women of the Borough house are doing to me? I know there is something strange going on in that house. Have I been a fool to try to ignore it all?

"*Wake up, Nova,*" I hear a man's voice. It seems to be coming from the sky above me. With each word, the sun seems to flicker to blackness. "*Wake up!*" the voice booms.

I feel my grasp on this reality fading. I don't have time to write to Evan, so I kiss the bottom of the page, leaving the faint lipstick print of my kiss behind as the meadow dissolves into dark.

"*Wake up, dammit!*" the voice says, shouting now.

I'm back in my room. Just enough light from the full harvest moon is seeping in through the curtains to allow me to see clearly. I'm alone. "Who's there?" I ask in a whisper.

"*Why aren't you doing what I command?*" says the voice, more quietly now.

I know I should be frightened, but I'm not. I've been ignoring this voice for a long time now, but I'm not surprised to hear it. "What are you talking about? I am my own person, not some kind of puppet," I say. "Leave me alone!"

A wicked laugh fills my room, sending a bone-chilling shiver up my spine.

"*Oh, but you are, my little Super Nova. You are just that—my little puppet.*"

It must be the champagne. I still feel a little bit drunk. I'm having trouble distinguishing fact from fiction. From outside, I hear what sounds like chanting. I move to the window and pull back the curtain. In the orchard, I see a bonfire blazing. Six hooded figures stand in a circle. I can't make out what they're saying. It doesn't sound quite like English. Their voices move in unison from quiet to loud, arms rising and falling with the volume of their chants, hands clasped together. The brilliant silver moon hangs low over the orchard, lined up over the circle like a spectacular chandelier.

"*Crap!*" says the voice in my room. "*We're leaving right now, Nova.*"

"I'm not going anywhere," I say sternly. This is all too much weirdness for me. *Where is Eloise? Do the women know there is some kind of moon-worshiping cult in their orchard?* I pull on my jeans so I can go find the women. *We need to call the police.* I move toward my door and run head-on into an invisible barrier. I fall hard onto my tailbone.

"*I'm warning you,*" says the voice in a low hiss. "*You will obey.*"

The chanting from the orchard is suddenly louder, more urgent. I hear a hard wind whistling against my window.

"*What do you want from me?*" I have to yell to be heard above the howl of the wind.

Suddenly, my bedroom window bursts open. Glass shatters in a shower of shards. The moonlight refracts light through the slivers of glass casting rainbows across the room in shades of night. All blues, purples, and grays where reds and yellows should be. Time seems to slow as the dark light transfixes itself on the invisible shape in my doorway.

The silhouette of a man comes into focus. He's tall, over six feet. I'm lying on my back, still propped up on my elbows, afraid to move. He seems just as surprised to see himself as I am. Head down, he's watching his hands as the rays of blueish light wash away the veil of invisibility, stretching his fingers out and turning them over as if he can't believe it himself. As he lifts his head to look at me, his face starts to manifest—stubbled chin, messy dark hair, cheeks and nose come into focus, eyes like daggers. It hits me all at once. I know that face. I have always known it.

"Dad!" I breathe out, just as I feel myself begin to faint.

The Circle

Stonington, Connecticut, November 10, 5:10 a.m.

A light rain had begun to fall as Nova Daniels left the Borough house. She wore a black sweatshirt, hood pulled up over her head. Large sunglasses covered most of her face and added extra protection from the rain. Slim dark wash jeans and tall black motorcycle boots that had been sitting just inside the door of Elaina's empty bedroom completed her ensemble. No ID, no purse. Just a pocket full of cash taken from the cookie jar in the kitchen. It had been easy for Nova to leave undetected as the house was empty tonight.

The women of the circle had busied themselves with other things. Careful to take advantage of the full moon, they had begun preparations to sever the bond that the ghost of Nova's father had tethered to her soul. Just a little bit longer now, and the spell would be complete. Nova had gone to bed under the influence of alcohol. Eloise knew that would loosen the ghost's hold on his daughter. She wagered it would be enough.

Nova hurried down the long driveway and out onto the empty street. A taxi awaited her there. "New Haven. Union Station," she said to the driver in a gruff voice. He nodded and drove away in silence.

The women of the circle had heard the window break overhead in Nova's room. They knew the ghost waited while she slept. He would be aware of what they were trying to do by now. Eloise only hoped they had been able to catch him off-guard. Magic hung in the air around the circle. It was so strong when they all came together that it was palpable. The smell of snow about to fall mixed with something else, like the slow crackle of lightning during a storm.

Mary-Anne held a small vial as they released each other's hands and took one step back from the bonfire. The small cauldron on the fire had turned the flames from gold to ice blue as the full moon had come into position. Moon magic was powerful in its own right and may have been enough to banish Nova's ghost, but Mary-Anne liked to have a back-up plan in these cases. "You can never be too careful," she'd said. She'd seen some tricky spirits in her time. Something told her this one would not go quietly.

All the women were exhausted from the ritual. They had learned not to move too quickly after these types of circles. They each sat down on the damp ground, still shrouded in ceremonial robes. "Well, at least we know we'll all sleep well after this," Mae joked as she passed a bottle of the Borough wine to Suzanne who sat next to her.

Suzanne looked particularly tired. Deep circles hung under her weary eyes. Her mother's spirit energy still lingered around her. She laughed at Mae's weak joke in spite of herself, taking a long drink from the bottle and passing it to Eloise at her right. As their fingers touched, a bolt of electricity erupted between them, sucking them both into a vision of Nova. The wine bottle crashed to the ground, breaking to pieces on the rim of the fire pit.

Eloise grabbed Elaina's hand to her right as soon as she realized what was happening. Suzanne taking Mae's, Mae taking Mary-Anne's, Mary-Anne taking Carolyn's, Carolyn taking Elaina's—with their connection still alive from the ritual, it was as simple as breathing to carry them into the vision together.

Moments later, when the vision had ended, they all knew they had a part to play. The worst-case scenario was upon them. Eloise sprang to her feet and into the house. She took the stairs two at a time to her room and skidded into her desk chair. Taking a quill and dipping it into the sweet blackberry ink, she began writing:

From one Borough to a melting pot of five,
She's not safe, though she is alive.
Her body walks the streets at night,
it is but a vehicle he now drives.

The city never sleeps. Nor will she.
She cannot endure the pace he keeps.
The shepherd holds the power she needs.
Go to her. Quickly. Please!

She stuffed the poem hastily into an envelope, scribbled on the outside of it, and ran down the stairs. Mary-Anne was already waiting for her in the living room. This one couldn't wait for the postal service. Mary-Anne was chanting in a voice that sounded like a night bird's song—beautiful and delicate.

A roaring fire filled the old stone fireplace in the living room. Mary-Anne had chosen the fuel carefully to burn. Fir to see across the distance and to protect both mother and child, holly for death and rebirth, poisonous mistletoe berries to give power to love, rowan to protect against enchantment, and willow, the moon tree. Mary-Anne had carefully knotted the willow branches, whispering her wish and her gratitude to the branches as she carefully intertwined them. As she turned to face Eloise, Eloise could see that the very pupils of her eyes had transformed into yellow flames.

"It is ready," she said.

Wordlessly, Eloise handed her the envelope. Mary-Anne tossed it into the witchfire while continuing her bird song. The massive blaze swelled and then went out in a silent fragrant puff of smoke. Only cool ash remained.

Evan & Jeanette

Ocean Park, Washington, November 10

Jeanette had been awake for hours. She'd just returned from the café after baking coffee cake and oversized cinnamon rolls. She'd set them out on the cooling rack and come back home to check on Evan. His sleep had been so irregular as of late that she never had the heart to wake him. She felt a fondness toward him that surpassed explanation. The only other person in the world who loved her daughter as she did. Getting to know Evan had made Jeanette feel closer to Nova than she ever had before.

She opened Evan's door just a crack. The sun had not yet fully risen, and his room was still dark. She could hear the slow steady breath of sleep. Careful not to make a sound, she pulled the door closed behind her and went into the kitchen to start a pot of coffee. She held the glass carafe under the faucet, letting the cold tap water fill it up.

An ear-splitting sound like the blood curdling scream of a child came from Evan's room. Jeanette let the coffee pot fall and shatter into the sink, water still running. From outside Evan's door, she heard another high-pitched wail followed by a crash. She pushed the door open just as Evan jumped out of bed and onto his bare feet, broken pieces of the bed lamp now strewn across the floor. Jeanette didn't see it right away, but Evan did. She followed his gaze.

Thick smoke billowed atop the dresser against the wall, engulfing the relic of a smoke detector on the ceiling above. It screeched again, solving the mystery of where the sound had come from. Jeanette jumped. Evan and Jeanette looked from the smoke to each other and back again.

"Where's the fire?" she asked, bewildered.

"I don't know," Evan said quietly.

The smoke shimmered strangely. Images of blue flames danced in the center of the cloud as if projected on film. The flames swelled and then dissipated in a gust of cold air, sending framed pictures of Nova falling from the wall to the floor. One of her as a little girl playing on the beach, another of her mother's favorite senior picture. She knew Nova hated it, but she loved it just the same.

"There's something on the dresser!" Evan said, moving slowly toward it.

"I see it too! It looks like an envelope," Jeanette said, breathlessly. She was afraid to move an inch for fear the flames would return.

The last of the smoke seemed to disintegrate into thin air, quieting the cry of the alarm. Cool gray ashes rained down from the ceiling.

Jeanette's knees gave out and she fell to the floor.

"Are you okay?" Evan asked, hurrying to help her up.

"Yes. I think so. What…what was…" She had no words. Neither did he. He grabbed the envelope and turned it over in his hands. It was made of the same pressed parchment as the other letters Jeanette had shown him. Scribbled on the front, it simply said "Evan." He opened it quickly.

> From one Borough to a melting pot of five,
> She's not safe, though she is alive.
> Her body walks the streets at night,
> it is but a vehicle he now drives.
>
> The city never sleeps. Nor will she.
> She cannot endure the pace he keeps.
> The shepherd holds the power she needs.
> Go to her. Quickly. Please!

Evan and Jeanette moved to the kitchen table. She still looked faint, and he wanted her to sit down. He saw the remnants of the coffee pot in the sink and put the tea kettle on to boil while Jeanette read the riddled poem aloud again.

"The city that never sleeps. That has to be LA. Vegas, maybe," she mused.

"No. I think it's New York. She's on the east coast. I know it," Evan said. He had not told Jeanette about the dreams he shared with Nova. Some things were sacred. Jeanette never pushed him.

"Okay, so it's New York. Oh, wait! The Five Boroughs. Yes! It has to be," she said.

"I'm going," he said.

"I want to come with you," Jeanette said desperately.

"But if another message comes—" Evan started.

"I can't take this! Just doing nothing while my daughter is out there somewhere in danger?" She began to cry.

Evan put his arm around her shoulder. "Now is not the time to fall apart. She needs us to stay strong." He had only known Jeanette a short time but already knew just what to say to help calm her down. She was the only other person in the world that loved Nova as he did, and he loved her for that.

"You're right," she said, composing herself. "I'll stay, in case... but you'll keep me posted?"

"Every step of the way," he assured her. "I can drive it in two days if I go straight through."

"Nonsense," she said, suddenly carrying the authoritative tone of a scolding mother. "We can be at SeaTac in three hours. I'll drive. You can look up flights from your phone on the way. Go get your bag."

Without a word, Evan hurried to his room and grabbed his bag, quickly shoving what little he owned into it. He was about to leave the room when he saw something sticking out from under the covers of the bed—a piece of paper. He pulled back the blankets and gasped.

"You okay?" Jeanette called from the kitchen. She was packing him snacks for the plane. There is no switch to turn off maternal instincts. She smiled as she worked. There was hope.

"Fine. Be right out," he said absent-mindedly as he read his own handwriting. It was the letter he'd written to Nova on the back of the one she'd written to him. The paper was damp and cool as if it had been sitting on wet grass. At the bottom of the letter, where he'd written his closing, *Love,* there was a barely visible coral-pink kiss mark. He held it to his own lips briefly, folded it, and put it into his pocket. Shutting the door behind him, he called to Jeanette. "I'm ready."

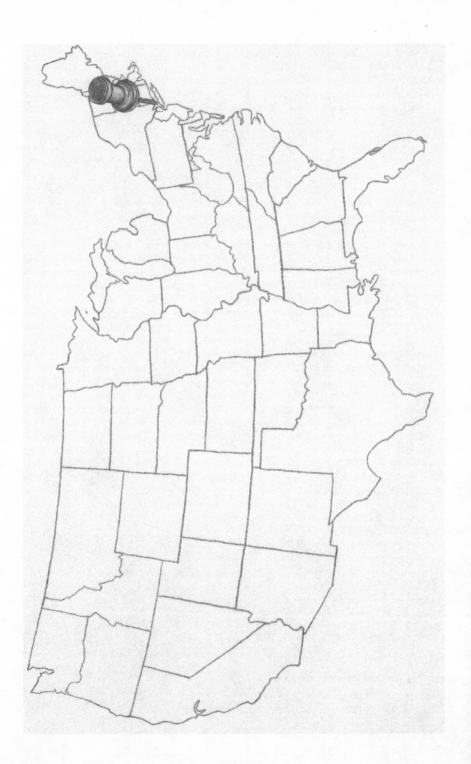

Nova

New York City, November 10

*I*t was just after 11:00 a.m. when Nova Daniels got off the Peter Pan Bus at West 42nd Street. It was just a short walk to Times Square from there. You'd be hard pressed to spot her in the crowd. It was one of those perfect fall days in New York that should be rainy and cold, but instead, the sun shone. It was definitely sweat-shirt weather, though, and Nova's was just one in a sea of hundreds of them. Even hidden behind Suzanne's oversized sunglasses, she didn't draw attention to herself.

In Times Square, Nova blended into the busyness effortlessly. She stood still in the center of the crowd, people hurrying past her in every direction. The energy—the human energy—it pulsed through her veins giving her body strength. She pulled a little bit from every passerby. Eyes closed, breathing deeply, sucking the life-force from everyone around her like gulping from the fountain of youth. On her exhale, lights burst overhead, sending a shower of sparks down over the crowded square. Tourists applauded, sure that it was a regular New York City occurrence.

Nova laughed. A guttural sound from way down deep that did not sound at all like her.

* * * * *

I don't think I fell asleep, exactly, but I ended up here just the same. It's weird, though, usually when I come to the pasture, I'm dressed in whatever I had on when I fell asleep. After a lifetime dreaming of this place, I've learned to dress modestly for bed. This time is different. I'm dressed like Evan is when he is here. Like I'm a shepherd too. I have on a long skirt that skims my bare toes. It feels like it's made of burlap and is the same nondescript brown color. My tunic is a little bit softer. A woven cotton maybe. It's relatively shapeless and drapes from a V-neck at my collar bone. My hair is in a messy bun at the nape of my neck.

It's not just the clothes, though. There is something fundamentally different about how it feels to be here. I don't have that sense of urgency mixed with a pang of desperation…the inner knowing that if I don't find Evan soon, I'll be ripped from this place. I feel peace. Belonging. It's more beautiful here than I have ever seen it.

The lines around the edges of the valley are crisp and sharp, rather than their usual blurred opacity. It's like for once, this reality isn't competing with another one, like this is all there is. Permanence. I realize that maybe that should startle me, but it doesn't. I'm tired. Tired of running. Tired of being scared. Tired of being confused. Tired of telling lies. I can't help but smile. The weight of the world is absent from my shoulders.

I sit down in the grass, warm from the afternoon sun. I point my face to the sky and close my eyes. I smell jasmine on the wind. I've never noticed that before. I lay back with my hands behind my head and let myself relax into the earth.

Evan & Jeanette

Seattle, Washington, November 11

*J*eanette hugged Evan just a little bit longer than she meant to. When she pulled away, she kept a grip on his shoulders. "You find our girl and bring her home safely, okay?" She'd never fought harder in her life to keep from crying.

"I will…and I'm going to call you every chance I get. You'd better figure out how to use that iPhone I bought you."

"Okay. I will try," she said and hugged him again. She'd been reluctant to join the "technology era" as she called it, but Evan insisted when he couldn't talk her out of hovering over him like he was an invalid.

"Insomnia is not life-threatening," he'd assured her, but she came home from the café to check on him nearly every morning. He bought her a phone and promised he'd call if he needed her, making her promise to stop worrying so much. He knew she couldn't help herself, but at least she'd started trying to be sneaky about it. The truth was, he was going to miss her more than he was willing to admit. It had been a very long time since he'd had a mother to worry about him. He let her hug him one more time before turning to get in line for airport security.

The line moved fast, but he barely made it to the gate in time to make his flight.

"Final boarding call for flight 222 to New York, JFK. All passengers, please proceed to the gate immediately."

He was barely buckled up when the plane started its taxi to the runway.

"We're next in line for takeoff," The captain's polite voice crooned over the intercom. "Sit back and relax," he suggested.

Evan thought that was asking too much.

"We should have you on the ground in about five hours and forty minutes," said the Captain.

Evan pulled the parchment envelope from his pocket and reread the letter that the strange cold fire had delivered him. *Her body walks the street…a vehicle he drives…what could that mean?* He pulled the other letter out of his pocket and unfolded it, letting his index finger trace the outline of Nova's coral pink kiss mark.

The shepherd holds the power she needs. If only he had any idea what that was or how to use it. He didn't even know how he would find her. Evan had been to New York City enough times to know his way around, but there were more than a million and a half people living in Manhattan alone, not to mention the tourist population there at any given moment. Nova could be anywhere.

He reread her letter again.

Dear Evan,

It's such a mess. I'm somewhere in Connecticut, I think. Near the water. I met a woman who has some really intense roommates. I'm scared, Evan. Nothing makes any sense. I wish you were here with me.

Also, I'm sorry. I miss you. I miss Annabelle and Kate too.

Sorry,

Nova.

What was she afraid of? Evan closed his eyes. He wanted to see her, and he saw Nova's face every time he shut his eyes longer than a blink. He knew her face as well as his own. He still couldn't believe she was real. His dream girl. His love. He had known her the instant he laid eyes on her in Sioux Falls. Different hair, a different name. Still, she was his Nova. He just never imagined she'd be real. Now that she was, he'd let her slip through his fingers. His mind raced. He tried to focus on her voice, the way she said his name.

"Evan?" he heard her say. "Evan!" Crystal clear this time. He opened his eyes and found himself sitting in his pasture. Nova was running toward him.

"Nova! It's you! Are you really here?" He wasn't sure if he was imagining it all or not until she reached him, hurling herself into his waiting arms. "Nova! I must have fallen asleep!"

"It's about time!" she said into his ear, not willing to unwrap her arms from around his neck. "Where are you?" she asked.

"I'm on a plane. I'm coming to New York to find you!" he said. He could hardly hear his own voice over the beating of his heart.

She pulled away from him then. "New York?" she asked, puzzled.

"Aren't you in New York? I got a letter..." He dug for it in his pockets but found them empty. *Wait, why am I wearing normal clothes?*

"No, I'm in the Borough house in Stonington. At least, I think I am." She sounded uncertain.

Seeing her for the first time fully, he asked "Why are you dressed like a shepherd? And...you're so...clear. In dreams, you're always a bit shimmery, like you could just fade away at any moment."

"You're kind of shimmery now!" she realized. "You're always clear here. And you're wearing jeans! I've never seen you in jeans here."

They both stood silent, contemplating each other. "What's the last thing you remember?" Evan asked her.

"I was in my room. I'm living in a house with six other women in Connecticut. I'd had too much to drink, so it's all a bit fuzzy. I think I saw—" She stopped. If she told him, that would make it real.

"You saw what?" Evan asked.

"My father," she whispered.

"But your father is dead."

"I know."

He pulled her to him, holding her tight. "I'm going to take care of you, Nova. I promise," he said into her hair. She smelled like sunshine.

"I'm fine, Evan. As long as you're here with me, I'm better than fine."

He pulled her back, just far enough to look into her big brown eyes. They looked at him with a longing...the same longing he felt. He kissed her, softly at first, then more urgently. He couldn't hold himself back. She felt solid and real, not like a dream at all. He held the sides of her face in his hands, afraid to let go even for a moment.

She struggled to find a way to get her body closer to his. They were pressed together totally, but he felt it too. The burning desire to somehow get closer still.

She buried her lips into his neck, kissing every exposed inch and finding her way back to his mouth. He couldn't breathe. Every part of his body tingled, aching for her, a lifetime of waiting to be close.

"I love you," he whispered into her ear.

She held his face in her hands now, searching his eyes.

For a brief moment, he felt his heart tighten. *How could such a beautiful thing love him back?*

"I love you completely," she said to him, touching her lips softly to his. She held his face while she kissed every part of it—gentle on his eyelids, soft along his jawline.

He heard a voice from somewhere in the distance. "Sir? Excuse me? Something to drink, sir?" He was back in his cramped window seat, 30,000 feet above the earth, and infinitely farther away from Nova.

Ruby

*I*t was just before 10:00 p.m., and a light dusting of snow covered the streets of Greenwich Village. Bleecker Street was eerily quiet tonight. Nova Daniels was crouched in the doorway under the staircase outside of The Bitter End. The Bitter End had been one of her father's favorite music venues to play when he toured the east coast. Sure, it would have been preferable to have a band in tow, but all she really needed was a guitar.

Nova looked herself up and down. *What a shame*, she thought. *Such a tight little body all covered up in jeans and a bulky sweatshirt. It's true what they say*, she thought. *Youth is truly wasted on the young.* She would have to rectify that before she got on stage.

Getting a spot on the bill at The Bitter End wasn't an easy task. Some of the greatest musicians in history had played that stage ranging from Etta James to Joni Mitchell, Bob Dylan to Miles Davis, and everyone in between. Luckily, Nova had the two most important things in her favor—a plan and nothing to lose. She saw something laying on the ground just a few feet away and reached for it—a 2 x 4. Certainly a crude weapon, but it would serve her purpose just fine. Just then, the front door of the club opened. She could hear voices.

"No, man, I didn't drop eight grand on my new axe just to get stuck using some shitty backline guitar. Tell the sound guy to plug me in or we walk."

Nova's mouth was almost watering. She could only imagine what kind of amazing guitar it was from the sound of it. She stayed stone-still as he let the door slam behind him. He had a cigarette in his lips and was trying to strike a match. *Now's my chance*, she thought. With just two side steps to her right, she was behind him. He didn't seem to notice. In fact, he didn't even turn as she swung the 2 x 4 as hard as she could into the back of his head. It made contact with a dull thud. The guitar player's eyes rolled back in his head as his knees buckled and he crumpled to the ground.

Without hesitation, she grabbed him by the back of his coat and dragged him, inch by inch, until he was just out of sight behind the stairs to the building above them. A small pool of blood had begun to form under his head.

She walked back toward the door, kicking snow around to cover the tracks she left while dragging the body. The door opened again. She froze. This time, a woman's voice called out.

"Jasper, you out here?" A blonde head poked out from the side of the door. She looked right at Nova. "Oh, sorry, I didn't know anyone else was out here. You haven't seen a guy come out this way, have you?"

Nova took one step to her left to block any view the woman may have had of Jasper's unconscious body. "Nope," said Nova as the street light burned out above them.

"Okay, thanks," said the blonde woman. She turned to go back inside. She was wearing a red sequined tank top and black pants.

She looks like a star, Nova thought. "Wait a sec!" Nova called. "Are you performing here or something?"

"If I can find Jasper anywhere," she said, annoyed. "We're on next."

Nova had moved closer to the door. She craned her neck to see if anyone else was with the blonde. Satisfied that they were alone, she quickly pulled the 2 x 4 from behind her back. The woman had turned to head back inside just in time to protect her face from the blow. Nova struck her harder than she'd hit Jasper, more sure of herself now. She fell fast.

Nova pulled her out of the door and toward the nook where Jasper lay dying. Two large trash bags were propped next to the brick wall beside them. Nova pushed them over to hide her unwitting victims from sight. The woman groaned.

"Well, it looks like I helped you find your friend after all," Nova laughed as she pulled the red tank top off over the woman's head and kicked off her boots. "So, you're welcome." Nova slipped a pair of black stilettos off the blonde woman's feet and hurried in through the door to the club.

Once inside, she saw a door to the left of the stage. She made her way through the crowd unnoticed and tucked inside. The backstage area was small and grimy. The walls were plastered with stickers. Some new, some faded beyond legibility. There were two doors. One looked like a restroom. The other was unmarked. Nova chose the unmarked room and pushed the door open. Just a small room with a long countertop on one end. A mirror lined the counter. *A dressing room. Perfect.*

Before even checking her reflection, Nova started peeling off the rest of her clothes. Once down to just bra and undies, she picked up the red tank top from the floor and pulled it on over her head. The blonde woman was quite a bit taller than Nova, so the tank came to the top of her thighs. She looked in the mirror.

"Wow. Kinda slutty," she said to her reflection. Alone, the top looked like a tight-fitting mini-dress, something Nova would have never been confident enough to wear. "Perfect." She giggled, delighted. She slipped on the shiny black stilettos. A little bit too big, but they'd work. It's not like she was going hiking. She just needed to get on stage without tipping over.

She almost fell off of her five-inch heels when the loud knock at the door startled her. "Jet and Jasper, you're on in five!" a man's voice boomed.

She opened the door a crack. He had already turned back toward the main room.

"Hey, hold on a sec. Jet and Jasper couldn't stick around. I'm filling in," she called after him.

"Damn amateurs!" he swore under his breath. "Who the hell are you?"

"Definitely *not* an amateur," she said with a wink. She looked back into the dressing room. A guitar case stood up against the back wall. It looked brand new. She couldn't contain her grin. "I just need

a vocal mic and a direct input for my guitar. I'm doing my set…
intimate," she told him.

Throwing his hands up in the air, he said, "Well, who the hell
are you?"

Pausing, she gave it a moment of thought. Looking at her dress
and then back at him, she replied "Call me Ruby. Ruby Night."

"Fine. Ruby Night, you're on in five," he said, resigned.

As he opened the club door, she heard someone from the stage
speak into the microphone.

"We've got one more song for you before we turn it over to
Jet and…oh, change of plans. I'm being told that Ruby Night is up
next."

"Ruby Night," she said aloud to herself. *Perfect.* She walked carefully over to the guitar case and opened it up. A brand new Breedlove
acoustic guitar shone in the dim light of the dressing room. It was a
work of art. Ruby couldn't help but tear up. It was all really happening. Inlaid into the neck of the guitar in gold pearl was the image of
a phoenix. "From the ashes," she whispered.

An oversized brown leather handbag was on the floor next to
the guitar case. *Jet's,* she guessed. She picked it up and brought it over
to the countertop. *Definitely Jet's.* Flyers for tonight's performance
took up most of the space. "These won't do much good in here,
idiot," Ruby said to herself. She tossed the stack over her shoulder to
the floor. A few tubes of lipstick, some black eyeliner, a few different
bottles of prescription pills—all prescribed to people not named Jet.
Vicodin for Stanley, OxyContin for someone named Michael, and
Valium for Jasper. "That's an unexpected perk." She smirked.

Hurrying, she tried her best to apply makeup. She penciled
eyeliner liberally over the tops and bottoms of her lash line. The
end result made her look a bit like a raccoon with loose morals. She
shrugged and threw the eyeliner over her shoulder, reaching for lipstick. She found a shade, bright ruby red to match her shiny little
trampy dress. Her hair was a tangled strawberry mess, which seemed
to suit the look.

A loud bang on the door startled her. "Ruby Night, showtime, babe," she could hear the stage manager muttering under his breath. "This broad had better be good…"

"It's the moment of truth," she said to her reflection. She definitely looked the part. "Just one more little thing," she said. Looking herself over one more time, she reached down and ripped the side of her short dress, creating a hip-baring slit. She grabbed the guitar and made her way to the stage.

Evan

New York, November 11

As soon as the wheels of the 747 touched down, Evan turned his phone on. He had ten new text messages, all from Jeanette. The first few were just gibberish. He couldn't help but laugh. He could just picture her trying to figure out how to send texts. The rest of them read:

> u were rite
> she's in nyc
> another letter came
> damn smoke ruined living room curtains
> call me when u land
> this is jeanette

He dialed her number and was still giggling when she picked up. "Hello?" she said.

"Hi, Jeanette. I'm on the ground. Just walking through the terminal now."

"Oh, good! That creepy blue fire about gave me a heart attack this time, I swear. Did you get my texts?"

"I did. What does the letter say?"

"Let me read it to you. It says:

> *Old habits die as hard*
> *as the bond he has with his guitar.*
> *The limelight calls him to the stage,*
> *Nova helpless in her gilded cage.*

The body count will pile up
Unless he's stopped soon enough.
Ruby's name he will defend
unless you reach the Bitter End.

"The first stanza makes sense, but not the second." Jeanette sounded grief-stricken.

"Can you take a picture with your phone and send it to me? I want to see the letter," he asked.

"I think so. I'll try now."

"Okay, I'll call you in a while," Evan said.

"Be careful, Evan. I don't like the sound of this. Whoever is writing these letters knows things. Impossible things."

"But I know Nova," he said confidently. "She won't go down without a fight."

"Be careful," she repeated.

"I promise," he said and hung up the phone.

By the time Evan got down to the cab line, Jeanette had managed to send him a photo of the letter. She was right. The first stanza made sense. The second, not at all. *The body count? What, like dead bodies? And who is Ruby?* It was his turn for a cab. He slid into the backseat.

"Where to?" the cabby asked.

Evan hadn't thought that far ahead. He was reading the letter over and over. He noticed that the last part was capitalized.

"Hey, you hard of hearing? Where you headed?" the driver asked, irritated.

"Yeah, sorry," Evan said. Taking a chance, he said, "The Bitter End. Do you know where that is?"

"Everyone knows that spot. Bleecker Street in Greenwich."

"Great. As fast as you can get me there, please." Evan smiled.

It was about a half an hour before the cab pulled up in front of The Bitter End. The meter said $60.40. Evan handed the driver a hundred-dollar bill.

"Keep it," he said and hurried out of the cab.

The driver shouted a thank you behind him before he drove off.

Money was the last thing on Evan's mind. He pulled out his phone and read the letter again.

The body count will pile up
Unless he's stopped soon enough.
Ruby's name he will defend
Unless you reach the Bitter End.

Walking up to the building, he saw a flyer taped inside the front window. "Tonight's Lineup" it said in bold lettering—The Falconers, and then below it, Jet & Jasper had been crossed out in black marker. Ruby Night was scribbled below it.

Ruby's name he will defend. Evan pulled the front door open and stepped inside. The wave of sound overwhelmed him. The crowd was on its feet in the packed space, cheering wildly. He couldn't see the stage from where he was. Evan leaned to the guy next to him.

"Who's playing tonight?" he asked the stranger.

"I don't know, man. I've never seen her here before, but this chick is wild," he said.

Evan knew it couldn't be Nova then. She was a lot of things, but wild?

"Like a spitfire cross between a junkie and goddess."

Evan didn't like his tone.

"Holy crap, you guys are a great crowd. You sure know how to make a gal feel special."

Evan still couldn't see the stage, but he'd have known that voice anywhere. *Nova.*

She continued, "Okay. This next one goes out to my daughter, Nova. I know I haven't always been the best parent, but crap, man. That girl needs to kick up her heels once in a while. I mean, hell, how did my own kid grow up to be so damn boring?"

Murmurs spread through the crowd. "Her daughter? How old is that chick?" wondered the guy next to Evan.

"Seventeen," he said, though no one was listening.

Ruby Night had started her next song. A cover of "Sweet Child of Mine" by Guns and Roses. From her first note, the crowd went silent. You could have heard a pin drop in the room. Evan quickly learned why. Not only was Ruby Night playing the guitar like a master, but her voice… Nova's voice…it was hauntingly beautiful. There was an innocence to it that was all Nova's…and a sort of sinister edge. Reckless abandon. A bit of danger, maybe, but one that Evan couldn't account for.

He pushed through a few rows of people to catch a glimpse of her. He almost couldn't believe his eyes. Without thinking, he pulled out his phone and started taking video of her performance. He knew he'd never be able to explain this to Jeanette, so he wanted to show her. It was Nova all right, but not like Evan had ever seen her.

She wore super high-heeled black shoes. Her legs were bare all the way up to what barely passed as a dress. It was so short he could see flashes of her black panties when she moved. Just a tiny piece of red sequined fabric, bright red lips to match, though the lipstick had smeared. She looked like a rock star straight out of a 1980s music video. He stopped recording and tucked his phone back in to his pocket just as he heard sirens approaching from outside. Red and blue lights flickered in through the windows, lighting up the crowd.

The front door burst open, and a stream of uniformed officers swarmed in. Evan watched them for a moment and then turned back toward the stage. Nova had vanished. Just a guitar and a pair of black stilettos remained.

Ruby

New York, November 11th

*R*uby saw the police cars pull up outside and bolted off stage. Thankfully, no one seemed to have noticed. Everyone had turned to look when the sirens started blaring. She pulled her sweatshirt and jeans on over her red dress. She'd abandoned her shoes. She grabbed Jet's big handbag and snuck back out into the crowd. With her hood up, no one gave her a second glance.

The cops were crowded around the stage area, questioning members of the audience. A couple of them had gone backstage to look for any sign of Ruby Night. She had almost made it to the door when a tall and handsome stranger grabbed her by the arm. She looked up at his deep green eyes. Something seemed familiar about him. Her arm was warm through her sweatshirt where he held it.

At that moment, an ambulance pulled up to the building and straight up onto the sidewalk. It was just enough of a distraction for Ruby to slip her arm out of his grasp and rush out the front door unnoticed. She ducked into the doorway where Jet and Jasper's bodies had been hidden. They were both gone. Jasper was being loaded onto a stretcher. He had an oxygen mask on his face.

"Vitals are weak but stable," said the EMT. A topless barefoot Jet was giving her statement to a police officer nearby. *Damn*, she thought. Neither had died. She was sure she'd hit them harder than that. *The downside of being a girl*, she thought, disappointed.

Then, just as quickly as she had arrived, Ruby slipped off into the night.

Nova

I don't think I've ever been here this long. Time doesn't feel the same here, but I know it's been too long. I'm starting to talk to the sheep, which I'm pretty sure is one of the early signs of a total mental breakdown. I'm scared. I keep going over what Evan said again and again in my head. He's going to New York to find me? What would make him think I'm there? I mean, I'm asleep in my bed in the Borough house. This is just a dream. I keep telling myself that…but then something in my gut won't let me believe it.

I'm on my way across the field to talk to another sheep who is backing away from me nervously when a scene flashes before my eyes. Just for a moment. I'm in a dark crowded room. The light is dim except for red and blue flashes. A police car maybe? Evan is there. He's holding me by the arm. He looks relieved to see me, but more than anything, he looks worried. I've never seen him look at me this way before. Something distracts him and I'm blinded by the valley sun again.

"*No!*" I yell, frustrated. My voice echoes through the hills. *What is happening to me?* Suddenly, this place feels like a prison. I squeeze my eyes shut tightly, willing my conscious mind to reconnect with my body in real life. Nothing. I scream as loud as I can. The scene in front of me blurs just a bit. More determined, I take a deep breath and scream again. This time, my scream echoes between buildings on a dark city street. Snow is falling and my feet are bare. I feel a pull at the back of my mind, like I'm on the verge of fainting.

"Not a chance!" I yell into the night. "This is my body, dammit!"

"Nova?" I hear a voice behind me and turn to find it.

"Evan! Where are we? What's happening to me?" I'm out of breath. It's taking every ounce of my will to hold onto consciousness.

"We need to get out of sight," he says, taking my hand and pulling me into an alcove.

"Why? You're scaring me, Evan. It's not like I'm some kind of criminal." His hand in mine is acting like an anchor, keeping me in the moment.

"Well, actually..." he starts.

We hear raised voices coming around the corner. Evan pushes me to the ground, throwing himself in front of me. He pulls his coat up to hide me. "Don't move a muscle!" I hear footsteps running toward us. Evan has let go of my hand. I see the light from a flashlight searching the street. Instinctively, I close my eyes like children do, believing that shutting their eyes makes them invisible.

At once, I'm in the pasture. This time, dressed in the same thing I was wearing in New York. "Crap, crap, *crap!*" I yell to the sheep next to me.

He gives a curt, "Baaaa," and goes back to his grazing.

"No! I am *not* giving up," I say out loud. I'm not sure if I'm trying to convince myself or this stupid sheep. Closing my eyes tight, I'm about to scream the only word that comes to mind... *Evan...* when I feel his lips on mine. I open my eyes in surprise. We're standing up, half a block away from the alcove we'd been hiding in.

"Nova?" he asked, cautiously.

"Of course it's me," I say.

"It wasn't you. Just a second ago, I mean...it was you, but it wasn't you."

"My father. He's found a way to hijack my body. I keep ending up in our pasture. I gotta tell ya, I used to love it there. Right now, not so much. What's the deal with all those sheep anyway?" He's kissing me again. I pull him into me until I can't get any closer. He pulls away.

"Kiss me again!" I plead.

"Those cops might circle back. We need a plan! They thought I was a homeless person asleep in the alcove back there, but who knows how convincing I was. You tried to hit me over the head with a stray beer bottle!" Evan says.

"I did? Oh, I'm so sorry!" I say as quietly as I can, reaching for his hand. "Don't let go of me."

"I won't ever let you go. Don't you know that by now?" he asks sweetly.

"No, like literally. I need to keep contact. I think it's the only thing keeping him from taking back over. You're like an anchor holding me here."

"Okay. That I can do," he says, pulling me back into his arms. "We need a plan, though."

I look down, catching a glimpse of red sequins from where my sweatshirt has come unzipped. "What the heck am I wearing?" I ask in shock, unzipping my hoodie all the way.

Evan quickly takes the zipper, pulling it back up. "Don't let anyone see Ruby's dress," he cautions.

"Who's Ruby? You'll have to tell me what all of this is about sometime soon. For now, a plan. If only I had a bottle of booze or something. Is there a bar near here?"

"There are lots of bars near here, but we can't risk you being seen right now. Why?" Evan asks.

"The only time my dad's hold on me seems to weaken is when I drink. Well, the one time I was able to drink. I guess I didn't realize how much control he had over me until I had a little break from it. It's just too bad I was too drunk to do anything about it," I add.

"Was he an alcoholic or something?"

"I'm not sure. My mom has been careful to keep a lot of their history from me. I think the issue was more drugs than alcohol, though…but an addict is an addict, right?"

"I guess so." He shrugs.

I shiver. My toes are numb. "It's freezing out here!" I notice. I reach for him, trying to tuck myself inside his coat when I hear something drop. "What's that?" I ask, looking down at a brown handbag beneath me in the snow.

"What do you mean? Isn't that your purse? You've been carrying it the whole time," he says.

I crouch down to inspect the bag, pulling it open. I see a wallet and pull it out. A New York ID is tucked in the front pocket. "Who is Jessica Farmer?" I ask Evan.

"I'm guessing it's Jet."

"Right." I toss the wallet back in the bag. Just some makeup and some bottles of..."Yes! Pills! Check these out. Valium, Vicodin, Oxy...it's like a narcotic pharmacy in here."

"Will pills work?" he asks.

"It's worth a try," I say, opening the first bottle. "I guess I'll just take one of each."

"No way, Nova! You have no idea what combining these will do to you. It's too risky."

"Okay, fine. I'll just start with a couple of OxyContin. I took them two summers ago when I broke a toe. It's not a big deal."

"Okay, that's it, though," Evan says, sounding authoritative.

I swallow two of the tiny round pills before he has a chance to protest.

"*You little fool!*" I hear a voice hiss from behind me as the bottle goes flying.

I turn on my heel. No one is there. My vision starts to fade, bright light seeping through the dark city street at the edges of my periphery.

"Evan!" I get his name out just in time. He reaches for my hand. His touch steadies me. "Evan, he's mad. He's trying to take over. We need to get back to the Borough house. I don't know how long I can fend him off. Eloise will know what to do."

"Okay, let's go. Where is it?" he asks, cradling my face in his hands.

His touch is electric. I kiss him deeply. I can't be this close and not kiss him. His kiss sends warmth through every part my body. I feel my cheeks flush and I kiss him harder, holding onto the back of his neck. I pull back a little bit so I can see his face. He's out of breath. I'm finding it nearly impossible not to tear his shirt open right here in the middle of the snow-speckled sidewalk.

"Connecticut. There's a train station in Mystic. Which way to Penn Station from here?" I ask him.

He's staring at my lips while I talk. I know I'm blushing, but I can't help it. He leans down and gently presses his lips to mine, just for a moment. Goosebumps cover my neck and chest, sending a jolt of electricity down my spine.

"There's a subway station on West 4th, just a couple of blocks from here. It's the fastest bet."

I cling to Evan as he practically carries me the two blocks and down the stairs into the subway tunnel. He stops to swipe his credit card to buy us MetroCards. I suddenly feel foggy-headed. The OxyContin is kicking in. I reach for Evan's hand to steady myself but instead fall forward into the tall sun-warmed grass of the valley floor.

Ruby

*R*uby Night waited impatiently while the sandy blonde-haired man who thought she was Nova paid for her MetroCard. He turned to hand over her card and leaned in to kiss her. She took both cards from him with her left hand. With her right, she punched him as hard as she could in the face. He cried out in pain and fell to his knees, giving her plenty of time to walk through the turnstile and take the stairs down to the platform. She'd be long gone by the time he stopped seeing stars. She giggled uncontrollably as she walked onto the train. "Like taking candy from a baby," she laughed to herself.

The subway car was packed. Standing room only. Ruby was tired of being on her bare feet. She looked around for just the right opportunity and found it. A middle aged man sat at the end of the row of seats. He was eyeing Ruby with interest. She unzipped her sweatshirt a few inches, revealing the low-cut top underneath.

As if on cue, the man stood up. "Please, miss, take my seat," he said, clumsily stumbling out of her way. She laughed at him relentlessly, sitting down before he could change his mind.

"It's good to be a woman. I could get used to this," she said, confusing the man who was watching her closely.

She crossed her legs and laid her head back on the seat behind her, suddenly feeling groggy. The grogginess pulled her in like an old friend. She felt relaxed and happy. A little numb even. "How does that feel, Dad? You like that?" said a voice from behind her. She turned too fast to see who was there and smacked her forehead into the window she had been leaning against. It should have hurt, but she didn't feel it. "*That's the OxyContin kicking in.*"

"Nova," Ruby hissed. She felt herself losing control of Nova's body. She tried to hang on, but Nova was stubborn, just like her father.

For a moment, Ruby felt a sense of pride. At least one paternal trait had passed down he could be proud of. That moment of emotional vulnerability was all Nova needed.

Nova

Penn Station, New York

*P*enn Station is just a couple of stops away. A creepy man is standing in front of my seat, steadying himself against a pole. He's not even bothering to hide his lecherous stare at my chest. I zip my sweatshirt up as far as it will go. He looks at me, blatantly disappointed.

"Do you have a phone I can use?" I ask him. I don't have much time.

He just stares at me blankly. I unzip my sweatshirt a little bit. He smiles a gross smile and hands me the phone from his pocket.

"*Attagirl,*" I hear a voice whisper in my ear.

"Oh, shut *up* already!" I shout at the voice that only I can hear. No one even looks at me, except my disgusting admirer. *Gotta love New York*, I think to myself. I don't know Evan's number, so I call the first number that springs to mind. Pearl's Diner. It's close to midnight now. I can only hope—

"Pearl's."

It's Kate. "Kay, it's me."

"Nora! Oh my gosh, you're okay! Evan has been worried sick. Oh wait, I guess your name is Nova, right?"

She suddenly sounds cold. "Kate, I am so sorry. I wish I had time to explain, but I don't. I'm in trouble and I need you to get a message to Evan. I don't have his phone number."

"Okay."

"Tell him to meet me at Penn Station. There is an Amtrak train that will take us to Mystic. I'll be waiting for him."

"Got it," Kate says.

"Thanks, Kate. I miss you," I add and hang up, handing the phone back to its ogling owner. *Note to self: find some hand sanitizer.*

Penn Station is the next stop. I stand up to make my way closer to the door. In a blink, I'm back in the pasture.

Without hesitating, I shut my eyes and will myself back into my body, just in time to squeeze through the train door before it shuts completely. As soon as my bare feet hit the platform, I start running. I'm afraid to pause at all for fear it will make me vulnerable to him. I weave my way through the crowded station to the ticket counter. I'm next in line. The board says there is a northbound train leaving in fifteen minutes. *I hope Evan can make it in time.*

"*Fat chance, babe. He's probably still seeing stars back in Greenwich Village.*" My father's unmistakable arrogance, now loud and clear.

I reach in to Jet's bag for her wallet. *I'll pay cash for my ticket, just in case.* At this point, I'm not entirely sure who I should be hiding from. These past twenty-four hours have been so disorienting. All I know for sure is that I need to keep a hold on myself until I get back to Stonington. The women of the Borough house will know what to do.

In Jet's bag, I notice the pill bottles. I decide to add one more into my system for insurance. Just a Vicodin. I am feeling out of it already and don't want to risk getting too messed up to stay focused. I pop one into my mouth as the ticket agent says, "Next!"

"A one way to Mystic please." I hand her cash and she gives me my ticket as I flash her Jessica Farmer's ID.

"Track 9," she says.

Track 9 is just across the way. I can see that the train has already arrived. Frantically, I search the faces in the crowd, looking for Evan. It's too soon to panic, I know, but I need him here. I can feel the pull, like a darkness in the back of my mind that's beginning to spread. I need Evan to hold me here.

I decide to get onboard and wait for him there. I make my way to the dining car and commandeer a booth for us. I'm watching for Evan out the window, afraid to blink, for fear I'll miss him.

"*He's not coming to save you. Face the music, babe. Daddy's gonna win this round.*"

His voice is like poison. The sound of him makes my skin crawl.

"Not if I have anything to say about it," I say, determined. I reach over the table for Jet's bag and fish out the bottle of Vicodin. One more. Not enough to hurt me, really, but hopefully enough to shut him up.

"*Don't even think about it, Nova. I'm warning you.*"

"Uh-oh, someone doesn't sound so cocky all of a sudden." I manage some sarcasm.

"*You're a little fool, just like your mother.*"

I can almost smell his sour breath as he spits insults at me. I swallow the pill dry.

"*Dammit!*" he shouts.

Still no sign of Evan. The doors will close any minute.

"*This is the last chance I'm going to give you, Nova. Get off this train right now, and I'll let you live.*"

"Idle threats from a desperate man...correction, ghost!"

The dining car has filled up and people are staring at me.

"Go to hell," I add, quieter this time.

I feel the train start to move. One last desperate glance out the window. No sign of Evan. My heart sinks into my stomach. I shut my eyes to keep the tears from falling, giving him all the opportunity he needs to regain control.

Evan

New York City

Evan must have fainted for a moment. Ruby had hit him hard. He wasn't prepared for it. He was still trying to shake the stars out of his vision when his phone vibrated in his pocket. A voicemail notification from South Dakota. *Probably Jerry checking in.* He was a better friend than Evan felt he deserved. A brother really. He'd been holding down the fort in Evan's absence with no complaints, even trading off with Kate taking Annabelle to dance class. Evan couldn't picture Jerry in a room full of little girls in pink tutus. He'd have to see it to believe it.

He'd missed a few calls from Jeanette and decided to fire off a quick text. "Found Nova in New York. Heading North. More soon."

Remembering that Ruby had grabbed the MetroCards, he walked back over to the machine and bought another. His only plan now was to search the platform for her. His phone vibrated again. It was a South Dakota area code.

"Hello?" he answered.

"Evan! Thank God."

"Kate! I thought you were Jerry calling. Is everything okay?"

"Nora…er…Nova called. She wanted me to give you a message to meet her at Penn Station. She's taking an Amtrak train to some-place called Mystic."

"Okay. Thank you, I'm on my way," he said, walking onto the subway as the door opened.

"Evan, she sounded scared." Kate sounded weary.

"I know, Kay. Don't worry. I'm going to do whatever it takes to make sure she's okay. You just take care of everything there, okay?"

"I will," she said, adding, "Be careful."

By the time Evan arrived at the station, he had just missed the northbound train. Panicked, he grabbed the arm of a transit cop walking by. "Where can I rent a car?" he asked.

Ruby

Headed North

On a northbound train, Ruby Night found herself alone and running low on options. No matter where she got off the train, cameras would capture her image. It would only be a matter of time before the cops found her. They'd return her to that damn house full of witches in Connecticut; or worse, they'd deliver her to the biggest witch of all, Jeanette. Ruby couldn't think of anything worse than going back to that boring hellhole in Ocean Park. If Evan found her first, he'd use his prince charming moves to bring Nova back for good.

No matter how she thought about it, she couldn't see a way out of this alive. She dug through Jet's oversized bag, looking for any kind of idea. Nothing but lipstick and pills. She pulled out the tube of red lipstick and applied it liberally without bothering to find a mirror. Then she walked over to the concession counter and ordered a beer.

With her Budweiser in hand, she sauntered back to the table. She'd unzipped her sweatshirt all the way and was making eye contact with every man between the counter and her seat. As she sat down, she muttered to herself, "What a waste of a great body." For a moment, she seemed sad.

Shaking it off, she pulled the three pill bottles out of Jet's bag, opening each and dumping their contents onto the table. She counted sixteen OxyContin, twenty-one Vicodin, and seven Valium. She decided to at least make it entertaining. Rather than popping a handful of pills at once, Ruby thought it would be fun to see how many she could take, one at a time, before she lost consciousness.

She sang in between swallows of pills and beer, rewriting the lyrics to "Every Breath You Take" by The Police to suit the occasion.

Every pill you take,
Every heart you break,
I'll be watching you.

* * * * *

Evan & The Circle

Mystic, Connecticut

*E*van was making good time. He got out of Manhattan faster than he'd thought possible and was speeding along I95 in his rented Mercedes. He opted for an upgrade when they tried giving him the keys to a Ford Prius. He was going to need something with some serious torque if he wanted to beat the train to Mystic. The car's navigation unit said he was just about an hour away. At this rate, he'd be at least thirty minutes ahead of Nova's train. His phone rang.

"Hello?"

"Evan! What's the word?"

"Hi, Jeanette. I'm glad you called. I meant to call you sooner… everything has been happening so fast."

Evan caught Jeanette up on the events of the night as best he could. He left out some of the details like the fact that Nova's father had completely taken possession of his daughter's body, named himself Ruby Night, dressed up like a harlot, and treated himself to a crime spree.

"She's on a train heading for Mystic as we speak. It looks like I'll beat her to the station by a safe margin," he said optimistically.

"Well, it sounds like you have things under control," Jeanette said doubtfully, but trying her best to be encouraging.

"I'll call you soon," he promised and hung up the phone. Fifty miles felt like hundreds as he sped through the night.

He pulled into the parking lot of the Mystic Depot train station nearly forty minutes ahead of the train. He'd pushed the V6 in his rented Mercedes as hard as he could. He parked in a spot at the end of the small lot. Only two other cars were there, and both looked abandoned.

He decided to get out and walk around for a few minutes. After a long day of travel and no sleep, he needed to get his blood flowing. He stepped out and shut the door, leaning on the car for support while he stretched out like a cat. He stood up and stretched his fingers up as high as he could. What he saw when he turned around made him freeze in position, arms still in mid-stretch above him. Three women stood in front of him quietly as if just waiting to be noticed, though Evan could swear no one was there a moment ago. Suddenly aware of himself, he dropped his arms to his sides, blushing.

The women looked like the most unlikely friends he'd ever seen. An older woman with olive skin beneath a wavy mess of golden hair all piled atop her round face stood to the right of the other two. She wore a floor-length dress that looked like something out of a turn of the century museum display—all petticoats and ruffles.

In the middle was a much younger woman in workout clothes—yoga pants and sneakers. Her long brown hair was pulled into a severe ponytail at the back of her head. On the left, the third woman towered over the other two. She had to be over six feet, skin the color of dark chocolate, with silvery hair that seemed iridescent in the moonlight.

"Is this your shepherd?" the tall woman asked the little round one.

"It's him!" she chittered, clapping her hands in excitement.

The woman in the middle looked skeptical. "I imagined him taller or something, I guess," she said, sizing him up.

"Nonsense!" snorted the cheerful woman. "He's perfection." She offered a hand to Evan. "Hello, Evan! I'm Eloise."

He shook her hand, not sure what to make of the situation.

"Allow me to introduce my friends, Elaina and Suzanne."

They each offered him a handshake in turn.

"Nova has been staying with us this season," she explained.

"Uh, nice to meet you. How do you know my name?" Evan tried to be polite but was only partly successful.

"There's no time for that," Suzanne said coolly. "We have a plan, and that's all you need know. Elaina, are you ready?" Suzanne asked her.

"Yep. Go ahead."

Evan watched speechlessly as Suzanne, hand outstretched, somehow transformed Elaina from a sporty thirty-something to a spindly little old woman dressed in rags. The color had left Evan's face. He stood statue-still, jaw agape.

"Oh Lord, boy! It's just a glamour. These young ones today are so easily shaken. I mean, honestly!" Suzanne threw her hands in the air to illustrate her exasperation. "C'mon, Elaina. Let's find a spot for you." Suzanne took Elaina's now frail arm and led her toward the train platform.

Eloise waited for Evan to stop staring before she spoke. "Nova is in trouble," she started slowly.

"How do you know? How do you know me?" he asked, though a large part of him didn't want to know the answer. This was one of those pivotal moments in life that would change everything. The border between fantasy and fiction had gotten blurry for Evan ever since Nova had showed up in real life. This was taking it to a whole other level.

"I'm a sibyl. Do you know what that is?" She waited patiently for his answer as if they had all the time in the world.

"No," he whispered.

"I'm a seer. I come from a long line of them, a gift passed to me by my mother. Isn't that wonderful?" She grinned at him. When he didn't return her enthusiasm, she continued undiminished. "I have visions of things to come. Things like Nova coming to stay with us or Lyla as she calls herself. Or like Nova going to New York." She spoke slowly, trying to read his reactions, careful not to say too much. Eloise found that it was easier for others to come to these sorts of realizations on their own.

"You sent the letters," he said, looking her in the eyes for the first time.

"Yes," she said, grinning at him again.

"The cold fire?"

"Witchfire! Yes, isn't it marvelous? Well, that was Mary-Anne's influence, but time was of the essence, you understand."

"Makes sense," he said, though he wasn't sure if anything made sense all of a sudden.

"We need to act quickly now, Evan. I know this is a lot to take in, but I need your focus. Nova needs your focus."

Evan shook his head a little, not to say no, but just to shake off the impossibility of all of this.

"Okay. What do I need to do?"

"Well, I'm afraid I can no longer see Nova."

"No longer see her? What does that mean?" he asked, worry lines appearing on his brow.

"I saw her searching for you at the station. I saw her board the train. Now, nothing. We fear the worst," she said gravely.

"What do you mean the worst?"

"The last vision I had, I saw her lying in a hospital bed. The doctors won't know how to help her. Conventional medicine will fail them. That's where you come in. Ah, wonderful! It looks like you have a fast car!" she said, peeking behind him. Eloise quickly explained the plan to Evan. Somewhere in the explanation, his emotions took a backseat to his adrenaline. He had always been good in a crisis.

Part 3: **Beckoning**

Mystic, Connecticut, November 12

A frail old woman slept alone in the eerie early morning fog on a bench outside the Mystic train depot. To a passerby, she would have gone unnoticed. The sound of sirens nearing the station startled her into an upright position. An ambulance screeched into the small parking lot at a nearly reckless speed. It turned around in the narrow lot, barely missing the black Mercedes with New York plates.

The driver backed the ambulance up as close as he could to the platform. He hadn't even completely stopped when two EMTs burst out through the backdoor, rolling a stretcher with them. A police car had entered the lot behind them and parked right in the center at a slant, blocking any other cars from entering…like police cars do.

A train whistle blew long and loud in the distance. "Get the oxygen!" one of the EMTs shouted to the other. "They've got her on a manual respirator, but her vitals aren't registering!" The train whistle blew again, this time closer. Within seconds, the train was visible. As it slowed to a stop at the station, the doors opened at the dining car. The EMTs ran as fast as they could with the rolling stretcher between them, an oxygen tank dragging behind wheels squeaking in protest. Two men in Amtrak uniforms pushed through the door, cradling Nova Daniels in a sitting position between them. They laid her gently down onto the stretcher while the men shouted questions back and forth.

"How long has she been unconscious?"

"We found her twenty minutes ago. I don't know how long. We think she swallowed a bunch of pills. There were empty bottles with her things."

"I'm going to need to see those bottles. Get me an ET tube, stat! We're going to have to pump her stomach on the scene," he yelled to the ambulance driver. He brought the equipment over quickly and started the procedure while the other two men worked on Nova, one checking vitals while the other started her on an IV of fluids.

The ambulance was unattended just long enough for Evan to slip in and swipe a manual respirator and a few other supplies.

The old woman watched quietly from her bench as the scene unfolded before her, waiting until the first responders gave some indication that they had stabilized their patient. Evan walked slowly and unseen to his rented Mercedes at the end of the lot. Almost silently, he put the medical supplies into the backseat, reclining the passenger seat back as far as it would go. The steady sound of the train pulling away camouflaged the sound of the car door closing.

"Her blood pressure is dangerously low. Heart rate is stable," one EMT said.

"I think we have her stomach cleaned out. Quite a deadly cocktail you swallowed there," he said to Nova's unresponsive body. "Any ID?"

"Nope, there was a wallet in the bag she had with her. ID, but it's not her. We've got a Jane Doe."

"Let's get her loaded," said the EMT that had driven the ambulance.

For the first time since they arrived on scene, everyone noticed the little old woman who had been watching from the bench. She stood up, let out a bloodcurdling scream, and collapsed to the ground. All eyes were on her. The police officer was speaking frantically into the radio at his shoulder. All three EMTs rushed to the old woman's side, driven by instinct. Only a couple of minutes had passed before the old woman could speak to them.

"Ma'am, let's get you on down to the hospital for a closer look," said the police officer authoritatively.

"Don't be silly! It was just a dizzy spell," she said, standing again.

One EMT turned back toward the stretcher to tend to Nova. "What the?" he started, looking between the empty stretcher and the train platform, clearly baffled. "Where's Jane Doe?"

The other first responders turned in disbelief, scanning the parking lot and train depot for any sign of their patient.

"Oh, the girl on the stretcher? I just saw her walk away," said the old woman.

"What? That's impossible!" said the policeman.

"Just a moment ago. Did you not see her? She walked off that direction," she lied, pointing away from the parking lot. All of the men took off running. By the time they circled back to the train platform, all they found was an empty stretcher near an empty bench.

Stonington, Connecticut, November 12

*E*van's black Mercedes made its way slowly up the long gravel drive to the Borough house. He was too preoccupied to have noticed the oddity of the gardens ripe with an abundance of summer fruits and vegetables in mid-November.

Nova's limp body lay next to him in the reclined passenger seat. Suzanne and Elaina had been taking turns manually respirating Nova and holding her IV liquids up high enough to let gravity do its job. Eloise had been silent for some time, trying to force herself to have a vision that might help. She opened her eyes as the car came to a stop.

"I can't see it," she said, defeated.

"It's okay, El. C'mon." Elaina squeezed her hand reassuringly.

Eloise did not feel reassured.

Suzanne had gotten out of the car and was carefully pulling Nova out of the passenger seat when Evan came up behind her. "Let me take her," he said, gathering Nova into his arms like a child.

Suzanne carefully pulled her IV out and let it fall to the ground.

"The respirator!" Elaina shouted as she barreled out of the backseat.

"Wait!" Suzanne held her arm out to stop Elaina's advance. They watched in awe as Nova started breathing on her own. She curled herself into Evan's chest and settled there.

"It's Evan," Eloise said reverently. "He's her anchor."

No one spoke as they followed Eloise into the house. Mary-Anne sat cross-legged on the hearth in front of the fireplace. A huge fire burned and crackled within it, taking up all the space so that no stone could be seen behind it. She sat so near the fire that it created the appearance that she herself was ablaze. Her eyes were steadied on them as they came in, though her focus was somewhere else entirely. Bright flames flickered in her eyes where pupils should be.

"Lay her on the hearth," Mary-Anne said in a monotone voice. She stepped out of the way.

Evan hesitantly did as she instructed. The oversized stone hearth was certainly wide enough for Nova's small frame, but Evan worried about her being so close to the fire. As he moved toward it, though, he realized that there was no heat coming from it at all. In fact, it felt cool. It glowed ice-blue just like the flames he had seen at Jeanette's house.

"Witchfire," Eloise said with a cheerful smile.

"He's here," Mae said. She'd been watching Nova closely since they came in. "That nasty demon has tucked himself underneath her now that he can't connect to her body."

"He's here? What about her?" Eloise asked anxiously.

"I'm sorry," Mae said, shaking her head.

"What's she saying?" Evan asked Eloise. He crouched down next to Nova, taking her hand.

"Wait a minute," said Mae, coming toward them. "She's not here, but she's not exactly gone now either, is she? Fascinating…" Mae had cocked her head to the side and was fixed on Evan and Nova's intertwined fingers.

A low growl came from Nova's body, causing Evan to drop her hand and fall backward.

"*Show yourself, coward!*" Mae's voice boomed.

"She's not breathing!" Suzanne cried. "Elaina! The respirator!"

"Wait a moment," said Mae, calmly. "Evan, please take her hand again."

Evan quickly did as Mae instructed. Instantly, Nova took in a deep breath and exhaled, her breath visible against the coolness of the witchfire.

"Don't let go, no matter what happens," Mae told him.

"Never," he said, only to Nova.

"Show yourself, you filth!" demanded Mae.

Silently, the six women of the house formed a circle before the fireplace. One by one, they joined hands. A guttural roar seemed to come from Nova's head, though she lay gravely still.

"We'll bring him out and then banish him to the spirit plane. From there, the fates can take care of him," Suzanne said. "There is no escaping judgement." Suzanne knew that once Nova's father passed on, he would not return. Only souls of the light had the ability to transition back to the mortal world when called upon. Souls of the dark would be exiled to the netherworld.

Mary-Anne began to chant an incantation.

"Wait!" cried Eloise, pulling her hands from Mae's and Carolyn's grasps and breaking the circle. "I've had a vision!" She was clearly shaken. "Nova dies!" Tears streamed down Eloise's face. "Banishing her father...it kills her."

The women were silent. Evan held Nova's hand tightly.

"Ah, it's clear to me now," said Mae. "His soul is tied to hers. He's like a leech drinking of her life-force. We banish him, we banish her."

"Well, then, how is that you can feel her spirit now?" Elaina asked.

"It's him." Mae pointed a weathered finger at Evan.

"The anchor," said Eloise.

"Her soul is paired with his. It has always been. That's how she's been able to dream walk to him in this life. His touch is the only thing keeping her soul in this body now," Mae explained.

"Soul mates," Eloise said, a look of wonder on her face. "It's beautiful, isn't it?"

"Star-crossed, I'm afraid." Mae was overcome with sadness for them. To have finally found each other in this life, only to be separated again. "Maybe they'll have better luck in their next incarnation."

"Wait, dream walk?" Evan was trying to keep up.

"She comes to you in your dreamscape. She always has, am I right?" Eloise asked slowly, though she knew all too well that she was right.

"Well, we have our dream place. I mean, this place we always go together. It's a pasture in a valley. I'm a shepherd. She's...well, I don't know exactly how she fits in to the whole sheep thing." His brow furrowed.

"That's because she doesn't, my dear. It's your dream. Your soul's purpose in this life is to lead others. The shepherd is you. It has always been you, the constant. That is how she has known to find you there." Eloise paused, letting him process it all.

He stared at Nova in awe.

"Nova has more power than she yet knows," Eloise added.

"So she's been coming to me. Actually really there. I thought she was a figment of my imagination," he whispered.

"You cannot love what isn't real, dear." Eloise smiled a sad sort of smile.

"It's a cruel twist of fate…the only way to banish this ghost…" Eloise started, and then could not say the words.

"…is to let her die with him," Suzanne surmised.

"No!" Evan shouted, standing up.

"The overdose. Her body is too far gone. Too weak now," Elaina said as if just realizing it herself. "There is no other way. She'd never survive the ritual."

He dropped her hand for just a moment and heard a weak breath escape her body. He fell to his knees and took both of Nova's hands in his, laying his head on her chest. "But she's breathing! I mean, as long as I stay with her, she can breathe," Evan argued, fighting back tears.

"Her body is not strong enough to host her soul. Your touch anchors her to this world, but it is not a means to an end," Mae said.

"You're witches or something, right?" Evan asked. "Can't you use your magic or whatever to heal her?"

"It's not that simple." Carolyn had come back into the room, her apron splattered with what looked like yellow cake batter. "I am working on an antidote to help her detox from the drugs. It may give her body strength, but the spirit of her father waits in the wings to move in. His life force is stronger now."

Evan kissed Nova's closed eyelids. "I'm sorry," he whispered.

A moment of silence passed before anyone spoke, each of them coming to terms with the inevitable tragedy unfolding before them.

"There may be another way," Mary-Anne said in an unearthly voice, her eyes consumed with an ice blue fire now.

"It's too risky," Suzanne said sternly.

"Maybe not. It would take all of our energy, but I think together, we can do it." Mary-Anne sounded like herself again. "Are you up for it?" she asked Suzanne.

Suzanne sighed audibly, seeming to give in to the idea.

Eloise clasped both chubby hands over her mouth as if to keep from crying out.

"Do what?" Carolyn asked. She knew intuitively what they were talking about, but they couldn't possibly be considering it.

"We have to kill Evan," Mary-Anne and Mae said in unison.

Evan had been giving it a lot of thought. He'd tried everything he could think of, even trying to just will Nova awake. He was coming to terms with the absence of hope. Now that he knew her—really knew her—how could he even consider letting go? Life without her would be simply unbearable.

Six sets of eyes were fixed on him.

"I'm ready," is all he said.

Stonington Borough, November 12

*T*he women of the Borough house made their preparations hurriedly. Carolyn was bringing small dishes out of the kitchen to lay along the hearth next to Nova's body—something that looked like chilled butter, an oval tasting dish with jam and mint leaves, a small canning jar of preserved lemons.

Evan didn't ask questions. He was trying to focus on what Suzanne had told him.

"Picture your pasture, shepherd. Don't let the picture go. If there is any hope of this working, you need to be there when she passes over. Just don't stay there."

He sat on his knees, holding Nova's now cold fingers, trying his best to hold the image of the valley in his mind. She sucked in shallow labored breaths. He felt no warmth when he touched her. Nothing.

Mae's voice repeated in his head. "She's not here, but she's not exactly gone now either, is she?"

He wondered if she'd still say that Nova wasn't exactly gone now. She was slipping away—all the way away—and Evan could feel it. She was literally slipping through his fingers despite how tightly he held on.

Mary-Anne had added elements to the witchfire. A few different types of normal looking wood, but some other things too; things that definitely did not look flammable, an abalone shell. "For healing," she'd whispered to him when she'd seen his nervous curiosity reach a boiling point. A handful of stones. "Aqua for connection to spirit, citrine lending power to the light, epidote for opening closed doors, hematite for protection, and a little jade for luck."

Suzanne sat cross-legged on the floor, clasping the medallion she wore around her neck. She was talking to someone that Evan couldn't see. A white light seemed to shine around her, though, originating from her chest. The irises of her eyes flickered like a candle in a breeze.

Evan found it funny that none of this disturbed him. Though he'd never really thought of such things, he had always had an open mind about the supernatural. It made sense to him on some level that witches would live in a place like this. He was just glad that Nova had happened upon them.

"Close your eyes, Evan," Mae ordered. She'd been watching the situation closely. Nova was fading for sure. Mae could only see traces of her spirit around the place where Evan's hands touched hers. Nova's father, on the other hand, seemed to be growing stronger. It was as if this time of preparation in the house had given him just the rest he needed.

Mae was worried. The timing would have to be perfect. He had bound his soul to Nova's, yet seeing her barely alive only seemed to be a nuisance to him. A minor setback. He couldn't bring himself into her body nor could he make himself seen by the others...but Mae sensed a growing confidence. Almost a smugness. She addressed him.

"What kind of a monster revels in the death of his own child?" she hissed toward his presence.

Eloise and Elaina both watched closely, cautiously moving to sit on either side of Mae.

"What, nothing to say now?" Mae asked, taunting him. "No smart aleck remarks?"

Though he made no sound, Mae could feel his energy level rise, just as she'd hoped. If she could make him angry enough to manipulate a physical object, it might weaken him. "Coward," Mae growled. No reaction. She thought for a moment. Obviously petty insults weren't going to do the trick. "So I heard you were a musician. It must have been nice living the life of a rock star, right?" She tried on a sticky sweet voice. "I bet you got all the girls. Am I right?"

A wicked laugh seemed to come from Nova's feet. Mae could feel a sickening pride welling up in him. It was thick in the air. "Well," she said, slow and sultry, "lucky for the rest of us you killed yourself. Your music was garbage."

His laugh turned into a hiss.

"People are saying that your performance in New York was total crap. What did the poster say? You're just a kidnapper, singing off key." Mae's voice had turned to ice.

Evan had chills. He shut his eyes tightly, trying to picture his dreamscape.

She continued, "I'm going to find every terrible record you ever made, put them in a pile, and burn them. The world will thank me!" She was laughing now.

At that, a wind picked up in the room. Nova's body suddenly flew from the hearth to the floor, toppling Evan. He didn't let go. He just flung his arms around her stiff waist and embraced her, covering her as best he could with his body.

Mae felt the exertion come from the ghost. It had taken a lot out of him. She had to strain now to find his essence in the room.

"Now!" she yelled to Mary-Anne.

Mary-Anne dropped to her knees in front of the fireplace, casting her fiery gaze down on Evan and Nova. The women now formed a circle around them. A suede drawstring pouch hung from a cord around Mary-Anne's neck. She reached into it, retrieving a small vial. "I had a feeling this would come in handy," she said. "Moon magic," she told Evan.

He looked at her expectantly. She merely nodded as if that explained everything. In a strange faraway voice, she instructed, "Open her mouth and tilt her toward me."

Skillfully, Mary-Anne poured a few drops into Nova's slightly open mouth. "Swallow," she whispered with the wave of a hand. Nova's body obeyed.

"Drink," she said, turning to Evan. He tilted his head back, letting her pour the rest of the contents of the vial into his own mouth. "Remember, shepherd. Don't stay there," she warned him. With a swallow, a final breath escaped both Evan and Nova's lungs at the same moment.

"So romantic. It's very Romeo and Juliette, don't you think?" Eloise swooned before joining hands with the women next to her.

"They're gone," Mae said, looking blankly at Evan and Nova's still forms. "Now it's your turn." She turned to face the ghost of Nova's father. Energy surged through him like the last over-animated breath of a dying man. Mary-Anne reached into the fire next to her, taking a handful of the flame and throwing it in his direction. He was suddenly visible to all six women. He was hissing and spitting like a snake. No words; just the sound of pure evil.

"Back to the darkness from whence you came, you filth!" shouted Suzanne.

The low rattle of thunder, distant at first but moving closer, filled the room. The women of the circle began to chant in unison. One by one, the lights in the Borough house flared and burst, sending tiny fragments of bulb glass to the ground like a delicate rain. Soon, the only light came from the waning moon outside and the eerie blue tint of the witchfire. The now faint outline of Nova's father withered with the coming of the thunder.

In Dreams, November 13

*I*t makes sense that the light would seem bright. I mean, it feels like I've been in a dreamless sleep forever. It's like I can remember it all, though; like time kept moving at the same excruciating pace while I stared ahead into blackness. I'm waiting to open my eyes until they adjust but am starting to wonder if that will ever happen when I feel a warm kiss on my forehead.

"Evan!" I open my eyes, blinking away the light. I'm lying on my side in the tall grass, wrapped tightly in Evan's arms.

"Where have you been?" I ask, sitting up.

"I've been with you," he says simply, brushing a lock of hair away from my eyes. "Even when you weren't you," he adds.

"My father." I feel like crying, but no tears come. *Is it possible to just run out of tears?* "Where is he now?" I ask, a little bit afraid to hear the answer.

"Dying, I guess," Evan says with an apologetic shrug.

"Dying," I repeat. I'm not even sure what that means anymore.

Evan pulls me into his arms. "Listen, I'm not sure how much time we have here. I just need you to know that I love you, okay?" he says.

I look up at him. "Okay," I say, "I love you too."

"Okay," he says. He holds my face in his hands, just looking into my eyes for a moment before he kisses me. Electricity moves from my lips through every inch of me all at once. I wrap my arms around his neck and draw him in, afraid to let him go for even a moment. He pulls me up with him until we're standing.

"Don't let me go," I say in protest.

"Don't you get it? I won't ever let go," he says seriously.

I have a sinking feeling in my heart.

"Evan? Why are we here right now? Are we asleep?"

He takes my hand silently and starts walking toward the hills.

"Where are we going?" I ask.

"I don't know. I just know we can't stay here."

We walk for what feels like an hour, both dressed as sheep herders, up to the top of the highest hill and toward the other side. On the south side, the green grass of the hilltop seems to fade into a dense fog bank. In a few yards, we will be below it.

"Wait." I jerk his hand back so he'll turn to face me. "Do you know what's down there?" I ask.

He leans down to kiss me and then turns to keep walking, holding my hand tightly as he goes.

As we step into the fog, the slope of the hill seems to flatten out beneath us. We're in blackness. Well, not true blackness. More like nothingness. A charcoal gray backdrop devoid of angles. No walls or corners; a shapeless infinity.

"Super Nova." I hear an all too familiar voice come from behind me. I take a deep breath and turn to face him.

"Dad."

He's standing before me as I always remembered him, like he's thirty years old. He's wearing a black Ramones t-shirt with a flannel shirt unbuttoned over the top and dark jeans, tousled hair, and a five o'clock shadow.

Evan moves protectively behind me. His hand is on my lower back as if to let me know he's here if I need him.

"You've got a good one here, babe," my father says, motioning to Evan. "Seriously. It seems like he'd really take a bullet for you. That is all a father could ask for, I guess, right?" he says with a smile.

"Really? You're giving your blessing on my choice of boyfriend right now? Are you kidding me? You tried to kill me, Dad!"

"Actually, he did kill you," Evan says in my ear.

"What?" I say looking back at him. "You killed me?"

"Listen, it's nothing personal. It was you or me, babe. You were wasting your life walking in circles in that crap-hole of a town with your fool mother. I did you a favor. You should really be thanking me," he says smugly.

"For what? Kidnapping me? For turning me into some kind of pathological liar and criminal? For isolating me? For killing me? Thank you? Are you *actually* saying that to me right now?" I'm yelling. I can feel myself shaking…the rage rising up in my chest.

Evan takes a hold of my shoulders as if he's expecting me to lunge at my father. I don't know what to think.

"And my mother is not a fool. She's actually sort of amazing. I can see now that everything she did was to protect me from you!"

"Oh, like that makes any sense. I'm your father, for God's sake," he scoffs.

"Really? You want to play that card right now?"

"Well, maybe I won't win any awards for father of the year. Still, you would have had way more fun with me in LA than stuck in BFE with Jeanette."

I wiggle out of Evan's grip and slap my father hard across the mouth.

"Don't you ever talk about my mom again," I growl.

"Ah, you've got a bit of your dear old dad in ya after all," he says proudly, rubbing his jaw gingerly.

I let some time pass before speaking. In this grayness, time seems unsteady. "What you did what reprehensible—"

"Oh, so it's reprehensible to want to spend time with your own daughter?"

"Let me finish," I say. "And no, it isn't. Haunting your daughter, demonic possession, and playing mind control games throughout my formative years, though, does not count as 'spending time' together. What I was saying is that what you did is unforgivable... and insane. I am willing to take some of the blame, though. It took me a very long time to realize that I can control my own destiny. I think I spent so much time just feeling sorry for myself and waiting for life to start that I completely missed the point. If you hadn't ripped me away from everything that I knew, I might still be stuck in that same pitiful state."

He is looking at me curiously. No remorse on his face. Not even a little bit.

"I forgive you, Dad," I add.

With that, he moves toward me, arms outstretched. I'm so taken off-guard that I don't have time to move away. In his embrace, I see my childhood flashing before my eyes like a grainy home movie. Memories of him trying to manipulate me. Guilt trips and ultimatums. Memories of him threatening my mother with violence. It's like a door of repressed memories has been unlocked in my subconscious. Memories of whispers on the ocean wind when I was young, telling me I would never have any friends. That I would live and die in the café. His voice…the one that I had mistaken as my own sub-conscious all my life, telling me I was afraid of people. That I didn't need love.

I push him away hard, steadying myself with one hand on his shoulder to keep myself from retching. I look up at him. "Go to hell," I say, breathless.

All at once, a blackness seeps in from behind him. I smell sulfur and death. A look of panic crosses his face. He opens his mouth to scream but is gone before the sound escapes his lips. It's like the blackness reached out and took him.

I turn and bury my head into Evan's chest. I scream into his shirt. The scream my father meant to scream. A scream of horror from what I just witnessed. Like hell itself answered my beck and call and came for him. A scream because I am free and I just need to scream to remind myself that I'm alive. Or…wait.

"Evan am I…are we…are we dead?" I start.

"Nova, I am fading. I can feel it. Hold me tight!" he says, fear in his voice.

"I will never let go!" I promise him.

Stonington Borough, November 13

Six women sat hand in hand in a circle on the living room floor. All eyes on the lifeless bluish bodies of Evan and Nova. Mary-Anne was soaked with sweat. This was the kind of magic she'd been preparing for her whole life. Visitors had come before who had needed their help, but not like this.

"He has passed into darkness," Mae said.

"Go and get them!" Eloise said, excited as always.

Mary-Anne stood stoically. She smoothed down the front of her damp wrinkled shirt, cleared her throat, and stepped up onto the hearth in front of the enormous stone fireplace, a giant fire filling the entire space of it. Now a lilac tint, the flames emitted a cool gentle breeze. She closed her eyes and walked into the blaze.

The women were silent. Mere seconds had passed, but in times like these, seconds can feel like hours. No one dared to breathe.

Mary-Anne reemerged from the fire with a hopeful look. She quickly stepped down from the hearth and rejoined the circle. They all looked at Evan and Nova expectantly. Seconds again passed agonizingly.

"The moon magic should have brought Nova back, right?" Elaina asked.

"No. I can't bring Nova back. Not without bringing her father back with her."

"What?" Elaina sounded horrified.

"Carolyn healed her body, but her father was bound to her. I can't do anything to directly call her back. Even if he has passed on, there is still a chance the bond would be strong enough to tether him."

Elaina clasped her hands over her mouth as if willing herself not to scream.

Eloise was crying.

Just then, Evan coughed, color returning to his face. His eyes opened. He glanced around, smiling at Mary-Anne before turning to face Nova, his arms still tightly wrapped around her.

"Oh, Evan... I'm so sorry," Eloise began.

Evan looked to Eloise, confusion in his eyes.

In a heartbeat, Nova coughed as she took a sharp breath into vacant lungs.

"Nova!" Eloise looked at Mary-Anne.

"I couldn't bring Nova back...but I *could* bring Evan back." Mary-Anne smiled like a sly cat.

Eloise threw a balled up tissue at her. "And Evan brought her back with him! Soul mates! Isn't it just so romantic?" Eloise clapped her hands excitedly.

Nova reached up for Evan's cool face. She kissed him long and deep like no one was watching.

Epilogue

The cool eerie fire scared Jeanette out of a deep sleep. She heard the smoke detector screeching from the front hall and fell out of bed trying to get to it before it woke the neighborhood. She had fallen asleep after her early morning baking at the café. She hadn't slept the last couple of nights, and something about a walk home in the crisp autumn breeze helped sleep come more easily. Evan hadn't responded to any of her messages, and she was starting to fear the worst.

The smoke filled Jeanette's entryway. She waited nervously for it to dissipate so she could retrieve whatever message it carried. It just hung in the air, thick and stubborn. A bright blue flame rose and, in a blinding flash, vanished in a plume of fragrant smoke. She walked through the falling ash it left behind and yanked the front door open. Nova stood on the doorstep, beaming at her mother.

"Nova!" she cried. Before she could utter another sound, Nova had thrown her arms around her in the tightest hug she'd ever gotten from her daughter.

"Hi, Mom! I'm home!" she said into her mother's hair.

"Oh, thank God!" Jeanette held Nova at arm's length to get a good look at her. "Are you okay?"

"I'm okay," she said to her mother.

"Where's Evan?" Jeanette asked.

"He's in South Dakota. Well, on his way there at least."

"But his car…"

"How do you feel about spending Christmas in South Dakota?" Nova winked at her mother. "C'mon, Mom. We could use a road trip, and you know your staff can run the café without you for a few weeks."

"When are we leaving?" Jeanette asked.

"As soon as you can get packed!" Nova said excitedly. "Can we stop at Kiss of Mist for lattes, though? I haven't had a decent latte since I left the peninsula."

They shared a laugh.

Both women hurried through the house, collecting Jeanette's things, chatting excitedly. Nova promised her mother she'd have more than enough time to fill her in on all the details of the past months on their trip. She wanted to know all about the time her mom had spent with Evan.

They swapped stories while they finished packing, then walked over to the café to say goodbye and get Evan's car which was still parked beside the building. Jeanette couldn't help but grin. She had hoped beyond all reason that Nova would come back to her, but even in her wildest dreams, she hadn't imagined this. Nova so full of life, sharing things with her, finding love. Her heart was bursting.

Before they got into the car, Nova stopped, grabbing her mother by the shoulders. "I need to tell you how sorry I am," she said.

"No, baby," said Jeanette, "no need to be sorry."

The two women were barely off of the Peninsula when Jeanette had started snoring softly. Nova smiled. Soon they would be with Evan, Kate, Annabelle, and the others in South Dakota.

Eloise and the other women of the Borough house were planning to join them for the solstice. Oliver had promised to come for the week. They'd celebrate the holidays together as one big strange family. She reached down to turn on the radio. "Ah, how appropriate," she giggled aloud as "On the Road Again" by Willie Nelson came pouring through the speakers.

"*It's not too late to turn back. Ocean Park is where you should be right now,*" a voice at the back of her mind tugged.

It makes sense, she thought to herself, *to be a little bit homesick after spending so much time away and then just passing through for an hour.*

"*No, really. You should turn around.*"

"Old habits die hard, I guess," Nova said aloud. Biting on her bottom lip to keep herself from yelling, she turned the radio down and waited. Sure, everyone had a subconscious voice. A sort of inner monologue constantly running and helping to work through every-day choices. There was just one little problem. Usually, your inner monologue didn't sound like an English woman with a thick accent.

"*Please, turn back,*" said the voice again.

"Well, crap," said Nova to no one in particular.

Acknowledgements

Writing this book was an incredible journey for me. One of self-discovery, learning more about myself while Nova's story revealed itself. I absolutely could not have gotten to this point alone.

Thank you, Eric. My rock. Thank you for letting me chase my dreams, however lofty they may be. Your belief in me made me believe in myself. To my sons for listening and seeming interested while I used bedtime story time to work through a late draft.

Thank you, Nicole. My Swan. For traveling from one coast to the other with me. For taking sketchy train rides to find Nova's path. For too much champagne and matching tattoos. For letting me bounce ideas without fear of judgement.

Thank you, Mom. For cheering me on through the editing process. For watching my babies when I needed time to work. For being awesome.

Thank you, Grandma. You were the first one to finish my clunky first draft – and in one 5 ½ hour sitting to be precise. Your approval was and is the wind in my sails.

Thank you, Marcie. My medical expert. In the time it took me to write, edit, and publish this book, you finished med-school and launched your career. I could not have navigated the whole Nova-on-the-brink stage without you.

Thank you, Carolyn. My Airbnb host in Stonington, Borough. I couldn't afford to stay there, but I had my heart set on the location. You took a chance on a stranger. Your space and your antique shop became a part of this story. You became a part of this story.

Thank you, Haley Dean, Heather Kristian Strang, and Chelsea Pitcher. Three authors I admire who were willing to share their insider knowledge with a new and eager novelist.

Thank you, Ariel and Melissa for dreaming up book launch ideas with me. Thank you to Elaina DiDimenico for being my character inspiration, completing The Circle.

Thank you, Super Readers. The early adopters. I'm sure it felt out of the blue when I posted on social media announcing I had a novel in draft and needed readers to provide feedback. Your notes were so helpful. The positive reinforcement got me through the next two drafts.

Robyn Schultze, Gloria McGrath, Meghan Schultze, Renée Schultze, Jack Longbine, Nicole Amend, Nicole Lane, Nicole Schultze, Jennifer Caliman, Aimée Amend, Susan Fairchild Verekar, Kathy Hale Hoblitt, Kristen Wike, Sarah Stewart, Melissa Moran Madsen, Amanda Price, Stephanie Willing, Heidi Gray, Lesley Marshall, Shawn Currin, Yolanda Reed, HelenKate Peterson, Tricia Caldwell, Alyssa Guillot, Melanie Storer, Jessica Klein, Katie Lovell, Jasmine Whitney, Catherine Duran, Casey Kelson, Emily Gilmore, and Diana Kimmerle.

Thank you to Joy Gregory who got me unstuck and taught me the art of font selection. A special thank you to my online community. It has been such a treat to share the publishing journey with each of you. I can't wait for you to read this book!

To my Dad who was a real rock star in my eyes. To my Grandpa for fanning the little witchfire flames in my imagination. I hope you guys are seeing this from the great beyond. I love you.

Last, but certainly not least, this novel was inspired by a song of the same name…which went on to win the John Lennon Songwriting Contest's grand prize. I'd been trying to write the song for years — but it took collaborating with a musical genius to inspire it to completion. Michael Herrman is that genius. Thank you Michael for being my songwriting partner and friend. This song, in a lot of ways, gave me the confidence to try my hand at writing this novel. To all my bandmates in The Heritage, Will Amend, Ben Landsverk, Scott Stevens, Ross Seligman, and Eric Longbine: thank you for being the soundtrack to my life. www.theheritage.com

About the Author

*J*enn studied at Oxford and Cornell Universities along the path to discovering her passion for storytelling. A fourth generation musician, creativity is in her DNA. An award winning songwriter in her own right, she's drawn inspiration from loved ones, travel, and motherhood.

Jenn lives with her beloved husband Eric and their three children in the Pacific Northwest.